MAKE IT last

JESSIE HARPER

Cover Design: Y'all That Graphic

Editing: Librum Artis and Austin Ryan

Ebook ISBN: 978-1-955326–00-1

Print Book ISBN: 978-1-955326-01-8

✱ Created with Vellum

ALSO BY JESSIE HARPER

The Mint Springs Series

Make It Shine

Make It Burn

The Finally Falling Series

Fight For It

Forget About It

Fix It

1

Jenna

"Ready for another?"

I swirl the remnants of my martini around in my glass and then raise it to my lips to finish it. "Sure. You only live once, right?" I don't even bother making that sound any less trite.

The bartender nods his agreement but doesn't stick around to wax poetic about my unnecessary use of cliché. He goes right to work, pouring the vodka into the shaker and adding enough olive brine to make it exceptionally dirty. His arms flex as he shakes the drink, and I consider for a split-second what he might look like with that crisp white shirt crumpled on the floor of my hotel room instead of covering his chest. The thought doesn't hold my attention for long. Picking up the bartender would most certainly not fall under the category of smart choices. Things may be spiraling a bit out of control for me, but I'm not that desperate.

Not yet.

He drops the drink off with a smile. "How's that pasta?"

Uninspired. "It's fine, thank you." It's unfortunate the restaurant here couldn't have been worthy of my last meal in civilization, but I hadn't had much hope as I'd perused the menu. It was all standard fare—nothing to even make me sit up a bit. I could have gone out, could have sought out one of Atlanta's great restaurants, but I opted to stay in tonight and really drown my sorrows. Bland pasta at the hotel bar sounds just about right for that.

I scan the room. Glitzy, but in that generic sort of way—sparkling chandeliers and mirrored walls, those sunken booths that are actually terrible to sit in. Other travelers sit at the various little tables scattered throughout the room, most of them obviously having a better time than I am. Or maybe I'm projecting. Maybe they're all as miserable as me, headed to business meetings or family reunions they would rather slit their wrists than attend.

I blow out a big breath.

"Whoa, that's a big noise—"

"For such a little girl? Don't you dare." I give a death glare to the man who has appeared next to me. I am not a little girl—not in age or in size. I like to eat, and that means I've got a little extra here and there. Being a chef means enjoying good food, and I love that part of my job. *Loved.* I keep forgetting about that. Losing my restaurant on my fortieth birthday was definitely a blow. Having my business partner—and recent ex-husband—be the reason for it only put salt in the wound.

The stranger raises his hands in defeat. "Yes, ma'am."

"And cool it with the 'ma'am' stuff. Jesus." I take a gulp of my martini, letting the cold vodka take some of the fire out of what I'm going to say next. "Do you need something?"

"Saw a beautiful woman sitting alone and thought she

might like some company." The cheek on this one. And the accent. Give me a break.

"She does not." I turn as much as my bar stool will allow, giving him nothing but my back.

"Oh, come on, now. At least let me buy you a drink."

"I have a drink." I shoot him a look over my shoulder and catch a glimpse of the dimple in his chin. He's tall and blond and way too young. He has no idea what he's getting himself into.

"You're not eating that pasta, are you?" He leans over my shoulder a bit to look at the sad plate of my dinner.

"Not if I can help it. Why? Do you want it?" It would make sense for this overly friendly boy to take my leftovers.

"God, no. I never eat anything here."

I turn to face him, and he shudders.

"Not that there's anything inherently wrong with the food here," he clarifies. "There are just so many other interesting choices a few blocks away."

This has my attention. "Do you have a recommendation?" I raise an eyebrow, and he gives me a cocky grin.

"What're you in the mood for?"

I'm in the mood for something to make me forget all about this day—hell, this entire year. I want something to make me feel an emotion other than complete and utter defeat. "Surprise me."

Good food invariably makes me want other good things. It's a weakness for sure, but one I don't necessarily always try to control. And after the barbeque I've eaten, there is only one thing I want.

Sex. The good kind.

And, after taking me to find the most amazing fusion of American and Korean barbeque I've ever tasted, I intend to reward what's-his-name. *What is his name?* I'd had the good sense to ask him before we got in his car, had the even more brilliant idea to text a photo of his smiling face to my friend Addison in case anything weird happened.

Nice! she'd texted back. She knows I could use a little pick-me-up after all the bad mojo I've had.

But nice does not cover the things he fed me. The spicy Korean pulled pork? To die for. The brisket? Melt in your mouth. That's not even thinking about the sides or the sauces. I was disappointed when we pulled up to the restaurant, although that's a strong word for the building that ended up in the headlights. It was more of a trailer, really. Good barbeque in the South often comes from places like that so I wasn't being snobbish—I was more let down about the idea itself. I've had great barbeque and wouldn't turn up my nose at that, but I'd been hoping for something a little different. A little special, maybe. And then blondie here had supplied it. Delicious and unexpected. No wonder I'm pushing my new friend up against his hotel room door with enough force to rattle the hinges.

He runs his fingers through my hair and tries to take control of the kiss. *Absolutely not.* I like a little feisty, but tonight I need to be the one in charge.

"You always this aggressive?" he asks when we come up for air. I'm already unbuttoning his shirt as he fumbles around for the room key.

"Just get the door open." I run my hands along the section of chest I've exposed. He's muscular. Fit. I have no reason to back down now. This night can end on an even better note than exquisite smoked meats if he'll stop talking. He was a constant stream of upbeat words while we were having dinner. The place didn't have much in the way of seating, so we'd gotten takeout and eaten in the car. As I'd moaned and groaned my way through the food, he'd been trying to subtly flirt. I'm sure he thought there was no way he'd be getting lucky tonight. Turns out he's hit the lonely lady jackpot.

We tumble into the room as soon as he pushes the handle. His room is identical to mine—king bed made with pristine white sheets, desk against the far wall. Neither of us seem to have much of a view. His room's still neat and tidy though, while mine looks like I've been camped out there for weeks.

"Do you want a drink? I've got whiskey from—"

"No." I'm quick to cut him off. "All I want right now is your cock in my mouth."

This shuts him up. He swallows and blinks a few times. I've frightened him, maybe, but the bulge in his pants seems one hundred percent on board with my plan.

"Excuse me?" His voice is an octave higher than it was two minutes ago.

"You heard me." I put my hands on my hips, cock my head to the side. *You in or out?*

"You don't mess around." He seems less terrified and more interested, standing there with his shirt askew and an obvious hard-on.

"No, I do not, so either get your pants off or move out of the way so I can leave."

He locks his eyes on mine, letting his hand move to his waistband. "You sure about this?"

"Positive. But every second of my time you waste is one you won't be getting back. Understand?" He doesn't, but he will in a minute. He's going to enjoy himself, but it's going to be on my terms. My way. There is no other option.

"And this is what you want?" He drawls, sliding a hand down over the front of his pants and palming his erection.

"I think you heard me the first time. That's more time off the clock, Country. Come on, don't be shy."

He says nothing about the new nickname I've given him, clearly a little thrown by my resistance to giving him the reins. I have no intention of doing that, and he's going to need to give in or this won't work. His eyes glitter as we stare each other down.

"Fine, then." He slowly unbuckles his belt and moves to the button. "We'll do this your way."

That's exactly what I was hoping.

2

Charlie

Holy shit.

What in the hell have I gotten myself into? When I'd seen her sitting alone at the bar, I'd had no idea I was signing up for anything more than the possibility of a little harmless flirting. I hadn't been counting on anything else, but blowing off a little steam after a week of boring meetings? Heck yeah, I'd be down for that. And she'd looked like she'd know how to have a good time. I couldn't resist all that wavy dark hair beckoning me from across the room, so I'd let it pull me from my corner of the hotel bar over to her.

Her initial dismissal of me only made me more determined. I am hardwired to accept any and all challenges—it's a weakness I've had since birth—and this one had curves in all the right places. Her tight leggings and form-fitting T-shirt didn't hide any of that, and I was more than happy to look my fill once I got closer to her. The knee-high black boots didn't hurt either. She was a little dangerous, maybe, and definitely didn't take any shit. But that was me making her who I want her to be. That's fine for a one-night stand;

she didn't need to tell me her life story. She barely told me her name. *Jen. Just Jen.* Easy enough.

For her to really love food made it easy for me to get to know her a little. Her eyes had lit up when she'd realized I hadn't taken her to some regular old barbeque joint. That's my kind of girl right there. Life is too short to waste eating the crap they serve at this hotel. It's convenient to the airport and priced right, but it isn't known for delicious meals. She'd seemed in complete agreement. Watching her lick her fingers as she sat in the passenger seat of my car, devouring every last bite of the brisket I'd bought her, I had started to entertain some pretty serious fantasies about what we could get up to later.

But this right now is defying anything my imagination could dream up.

She's standing in front of me, hands on her hips, all but daring me to pull my cock out. And it is the hottest thing I've ever had the pleasure of experiencing. Jen wants to be the boss? I'm down for that, especially when she drops to her knees in front of me. I reach my hands out, ready to thread my fingers through all that silky hair and give it a tug.

Jen's head snaps back. "No touching. Put those wandering hands behind your head." It's not a request, and her dark eyes stare up at me in a way I might normally have considered menacing. It's not the look I want on a woman's face right before my dick comes into contact with the possibility of her teeth.

"Yes, ma'am." I put my hands behind my head and thread my fingers together. I'm not about to ruin what is looking to be a fabulous Saturday night. Jen slides my zipper down and reaches inside my boxer shorts. Her grip is firm and I hiss as she takes me into her hand.

"The rules are *I* make the rules." She pumps me once. "Is that clear?"

I'd agree to pretty much anything right about now. I groan as she removes her hand.

"I asked you a question."

I fumble with the words, desperate to get her back to touching me again. "Y-yes. Crystal clear. Could you—"

Jen tilts her head, pulling even farther away from me. "Could I what?"

I bite my tongue and shake my head. Every word that comes out of my mouth makes it worse. *Time to shut your trap, Charlie.* "Nothing," I manage to squeak out.

"Great. Let me know if you want to waste more time, Country." Jen rolls her lips between her teeth and I could swear she's fighting a smile, but in an instant that look's gone and she's all business. She frees me from my boxers and regards my dick like it's a used car she's thinking of taking on a test drive. Finally, she smiles. "Impressive. This'll do just fine." And then she takes me so deep into her mouth I nearly come right then and there.

"Ohhhh, God." It shoots out of my mouth before I can stop it, and I silently pray that isn't the sort of talking that will make Jen stop the things she's doing with her tongue. It's not the kind of subject one should really send prayers up about, but my rational brain is no longer speaking to my body. I'll probably have to pray a bit about that later, too, but right now I'm willing to wait to settle that issue with Jesus.

Jen works me with her hand in tandem with her mouth, making a slippery mess of me. I want to move my hips, but when I do, her free hand shoots out to still me. It is the best kind of torture to be made to stay still, and just when I think I'm going to need to warn her about my impending orgasm, Jen slows down to a pace so agonizingly slow I have to suck air in through my teeth to keep from cursing. She hums a little at my discomfort, and I can feel her smile against my skin. *Damn, she knows what she's doing.* And she's killing me.

She lets me go with a *pop* and I groan in frustration.

"What? Did you think this was going to be all about you?" The way she says it is one hundred percent tease, and I know I'm going to enjoy whatever else she's got planned. I have no complaints about how tonight is working out. None at all.

Jen stands and takes two steps back, pulling her shirt over her head and giving all that hair a toss. I can feel my pulse drumming in my ears as she reaches for the zipper on one boot and then the other. She steadies herself on the edge of the bed and loses about four inches of height once she has them off. I start to move toward her, but she stops me before I get too close.

"Nope. Right now you're only watching." Her steely glare tells me she's not kidding, and since following directions has worked out well for me so far, I do as I'm told. "Good," she purrs and reaches for the top of her leggings. She eases them down her hips and ends up standing across from me in nothing but a lacy black bra and panties.

Jen's tits are impressive, but I had assumed that even when she'd been fully clothed. They rise and fall with each breath she takes as we stare each other down. I break eye contact to run my eyes all over her, and I take my time doing it, especially since I've been told there's no touching. I don't think I've ever used the word luscious in reference to a woman, but that's what she is. Jen's curves were barely hidden earlier and now, nearly naked, they're impossible to ignore. She's brazen in the way she taunts me with her body, and I'm loving every second of it.

She runs a hand through her hair and then lets her

fingers trail down the front of her. I imagine the way her skin must feel—silky and soft—and my own fingers flex as she slides that hand over her breasts and down her stomach. When she reaches the top of her panties, she pauses, raising an eyebrow at me. Her mouth quirks up on one side, and I'm sure she's reacting to the way my jaw's hanging open as my eyes track her movements. Her fingers dip lower, moving to where I can't see them, but from the way Jen's eyes roll back, I'm nearly certain of where they are. She sucks in a breath, and I'm desperate to be able to pull her to me and let my hand take the place of hers.

"What you thinking about over there, Country?" Jen's hand still moves underneath the lace of her panties.

"You laid out on that bed. My mouth on you." I'm barely speaking in full sentences. Imagining what her fingers are up to is making me stupid.

"Your mouth where?" Her eyes are at half-mast.

"Everywhere. I want to taste all of you, Jen."

She shivers a bit at that admission, still working those fingers. "I think I'm going to let you. But first, I want you out of those clothes." Her eyes rake over me. "You have a farmer's tan under there?"

I'm still basically dressed. Sure, my dick's out, but I'm still wearing everything I started out in earlier. And I don't have much of a tan at all, despite spending a chunk of time on farm chores. Trips like these have eaten into my time at home. Not that I'm complaining, especially now. I manage to shuck off every stitch of clothing in five seconds flat. Probably a world record.

Jen laughs, tilting her head back. "Eager. I like it. Now get over here."

3

Charlie

I crack one eye open. The light coming in from the window is making it impossible to sleep in. Normally I'd have made sure to close the blackout shades so I could sleep as long as possible, but that seemed like a minor concern last night when I had Jen pressed against the window, my cock buried deep inside her. After last night I should be exhausted, but instead I'm strangely refreshed—actually considering getting out of bed before noon even though I'm not expected back at the farm until tonight.

I'm alone, but I guess that was to be expected. Jen—if that was even her real name—didn't seem the type to stick around for breakfast. I doubt I'll see her in the lobby or ever again for that matter. She made it clear she didn't need personal details and wouldn't be giving any to me either. I'd asked about her—where she was from, what she was doing in Atlanta—but she'd basically told me to mind my own business. Fine by me, I guess. She wasn't interested in more than a one-night thing, and, even though I was interested in knowing more about her, she made it clear she had no interest in knowing more about me. *Country, how about you focus on putting your mouth on my pussy instead of telling me your life story?* Hard to argue with that. And if the number of times she used that nickname is any indication, Jen didn't even bother committing my name to memory. She certainly wouldn't have wanted to know all about my family business or my week in Atlanta, no matter how successful it had been.

And it's been successful. Good enough to have me singing in the shower and then humming to myself all the way down to the lobby to check out. The great sex helps too, of course. Can't forget to give credit where credit is due. But last night was only the icing on the cake. I've had a week of securing suppliers and wooing potential employees that went so much better than expected, I can't wait to make it back home to brag about it to my brothers.

They'll put up with the bragging, because any good thing for me is a good thing for them too. We're getting ready to open the restaurant on our family farm, and, after spending the last year making sure everything is absolutely perfect, all the pieces are finally falling into place. I take the back roads to give myself a little more time to savor my recent victories, and, if I'm being honest, to replay my night with Jen a few more times before I need to wipe this ridiculous smile off my face. It was the perfect way to end a perfect week.

I pull into the entrance of the farm and wave to the guys working out front. It's a Sunday, but that's not stopping progress around here. The guys from Sullivan's Nursery are unloading all the new plants for the landscaping we've got going in tomorrow. Right now the turn off the country road toward my grandfather's old farmhouse doesn't look any different from all the other farms out here, but tomorrow it'll be impossible to miss the entrance to the Allen family farm, our distillery and restaurant, and the prettiest place to get married in all of North Georgia. At least it will be, once all the flowers come in.

I slow down and roll down my window. "Hey!" I call out to Matt Sullivan, giving him a low wave. "Thanks for bringing all this by on a Sunday."

"Can't have you boys being the only ones working seven days a week." Matt shades his eyes with one hand. "This'll all be here ready and waiting tomorrow for y'all once the sign's installed. I watered all of them really deep before we loaded the truck so they should be fine even if you can't get them in the ground tomorrow."

"Oh, they're getting planted tomorrow," I assure him. Nothing's going to stand in the way of progress if I've got anything to say about it.

"If you say so," Matt laughs, the barrel of his chest shaking a bit. "I'm just saying if something goes wrong—"

"Ah, ah! Do not jinx things." I'm joking, but I'm also well aware I shouldn't let anyone tempt the universe.

"Fine." Matt wipes his brow with the back of his hand. "Lily knows how she wants everything arranged. Don't let anybody place the plants any old way."

"I wouldn't dream of it." If my sister-in-law has a plan, I know better than to mess with it. "I'm sure I'll see you in the next couple of days." I wave my goodbyes and let Matt get back to supervising his crew. He's been back and forth for the past few weeks, helping to decide what will grow best in the Georgia heat. This place has to look fabulous year round, and although we don't usually have hard winters, we can have brutal summers. He and Lily have had their hands full making sure the landscaping's beautiful for four seasons.

I pull up in front of my aunts' house with a few minutes to spare before supper. Today really is my lucky day. I haven't even missed grace. I put the car in park and walk up the front porch steps just as my older brother calls out behind me.

"We weren't expecting you back so early." Chance is holding his wife's hand as they walk over from their house. Well, it's their house now, but not that long ago it belonged to my grandpa. After spending the majority of our childhood summers here, it's the place I tend to think of as home more than any other. Once our grandfather passed, Chance came to the farm to help fix it up to sell, or at least that was the plan. Instead, he fell in love with Lily and decided to buy the place. Now we're all here in Mint Springs, Georgia, opening a family business with a capital F. The money Chance made from selling his tech business is getting us started out, but eventually we'll need to turn a profit, and I intend to have that be sooner rather than later.

"When you're as good as me, you get things done ahead of schedule," I brag. "Seriously, you will not believe the major scores I made this trip."

"I've got a little something to brag about myself." Chance pretends to dust his knuckles off on his chest.

Lily rolls her eyes. "Y'all can argue over which one of you has the biggest"—she gives me an eyebrow waggle —"accomplishments at dinner. You're making us late." She tugs Chance's hand. "I don't want to be denied dessert because you two were lollygagging out here."

That is the kind of thing my great-aunts would do—

make us miss dessert because we kept everyone else waiting. They've done it before. Granted, we were much, much younger, but I can remember plenty of times when a few of us were being punished and that meant watching everyone else eat peach cobbler. I'm not about to do that tonight. I hustle inside.

I'm greeted by the undeniable din of my family. When people find out I'm one of four boys, they always say my mother must be a saint. She's far from it, and my father's significantly worse, which is part of the reason my brothers and I have ended up here—eating supper together almost every night in the house my great-aunts share. Sadie and Mae took care of us when we'd come for summers at the farm like we were their own and, in a way, I guess we always were. Now Chance, Cooper, Cade, and I are all here full time, making sure we take care of our aunts as much as they take care of us.

"There he is!" Aunt Sadie shouts and comes over to wrap her arms around me. I accept the hug, careful not to squeeze her too hard. She and Mae look sturdy, but they're not invincible.

"I stopped by that little place you love." I hand Sadie the wrapped box and she beams up at me.

"Charlie, always so thoughtful. Although you know you shouldn't have."

They always say that, but I know they don't really mean it. Mae says the same thing when I hand over her gift. "You don't have to get us presents every time you leave town." That might be what she's saying, but it isn't what her face tells me. Her smile's at least three sizes bigger than when I walked in the room.

"Where are the bribes for the rest of us?" Cooper demands from his seat at the dinner table.

"I didn't bother with anything for you knuckleheads." I fake a scowl for my oldest brother. "But I did bring back something for Lily and something for Hadley that she might be nice enough to share." I hand over the gifts and watch as they open them.

Hadley pulls the bottle of whiskey I've bought her from the gift bag and looks over at Cooper. It was hard to find exactly what I wanted, but Atlanta's got a much bigger selection of specialty liquor than a small town ever could. I know Cooper and Hadley will appreciate the effort and enjoy tasting the hooch. They've been working hard on getting our distillery up and running, and they always love to sample other people's product. It's the best way to check out the competition. Hadley's usually a squealer when I get a gift just right, so I'm confused by her subdued response. All eyes stay pinned on her as my brother clears his throat.

"I know Chance and Charlie have announcements tonight, but I may have to steal their thunder for a second here." He looks at Hadley with that mix of love and admiration that always gives me a little pang in my chest. My two oldest brothers have found what look like perfect matches. They love their wives in a way I never would have thought possible.

"Hadley and I just found out we're having a baby."

The decibel level in the room increases exponentially. Everyone is hooting and hollering, and Lily jumps out of her chair in a rush to hug Hadley. Sadie and Mae are both tearing up, and Cooper's getting a good dose of back slapping as we all congratulate him.

"It wasn't planned, obviously, but we're both really happy." Hadley looks at Cooper like there's no one else in the world.

"I asked her to marry me and she said yes, so we're going

to need a little help to pull off the shotgun wedding of the year." Cooper's smile's a mile wide even as Hadley gives him a playful punch in the arm.

Yeah, my announcements are big, but not as big as this. They can wait until Monday.

4

Jenna

"Seriously?" I pull my car over to the side of the road. I'm officially in the middle of nowhere—at least that's what my GPS says. It's currently telling me the road I'm on doesn't exist. "Look, I can see why you think this stretch of dirt doesn't count as a road, but I'm driving on it. Can't you help me out a little here?" I've officially gone insane. I'm talking to the navigation system.

I take a deep breath and put my head on the steering wheel. I'm going to be late to my absolute last chance. Probably get fired before I even have an opportunity to really give them a reason. That sounds about right, actually. That would be the way this would all work out. It would make sense I would get stuck out here in the boonies and never find my way out. What do I have to go back to anyway?

At least there's a tiny bit of cell service. It's flickering between one and two bars, but I don't use that lifeline to call my would-be employer to explain myself. Nope, I go right ahead and waste that opportunity. Instead, I pull up Addison's contact information and call my best friend to commiserate. Never let it be said Jenna Bard didn't dig the hole deeper before she buried herself in it.

"Hey there, farm girl, I didn't think I'd be hearing from you so soon." Addison's cheery voice does nothing to make me feel better.

"Farm girl? Please. Don't even joke." I do manage to crack a smile, though.

"Isn't that what you're going to turn into? Fall in love with a farmer and raise some goats or something?" Addison chuckles to herself. "I can actually see the farmer thing happening."

"Well, don't get your hopes up, Addy. This adventure looks to be ending before it even begins. I'm hopelessly lost out here and my GPS isn't helping."

"What? Aren't there friendly neighbors out there you can ask for directions?" Addison apparently thinks I've moved to Mayberry.

"No. There's literally not a house in sight, and I haven't seen a road sign in *forever*. Maybe this is an omen." I sigh more dramatically than I intended.

"An omen? Where is Jenna and what have you done with her? I thought we made our own luck. Since when do you believe in omens?"

Since everything went to shit and I let it happen despite the warning signs. Since busting my ass somehow ended up with me sitting on the side of a dirt road in a rental car in the middle of who-knows-where Georgia. "I don't know. Things seem to keep falling apart."

"Excuse me, didn't you just have a no-strings-attached evening with a handsome Southern boy? That has to count for something." The note of teasing in Addison's voice should make me angrier than it does. "There's one positive."

"I hardly think one night of sex trumps the rest of my

life grinding to a halt. Or ending up dying on the side of this road." I scan the horizon. "This is the kind of road they put in horror movies."

"Oh, come on. That's supposed to be a beautiful part of the country. Tell me what you see. All I've got to look at here is dirty, melting snow."

"I don't think this is much better. I've got trees and dirt, that's about it. There were cows earlier. I'll take a picture for you if I ever figure out how to get back to the main road." In truth I had been starting to enjoy the drive. Early spring in Georgia was growing on me. I'd liked the green and the start of what looked like flowers along the side of the road, but an hour of hopelessly lost had taken all the fun out of that.

"No strapping farm boy to help you find your way?" Addison drawls, or tries to at least.

"Sadly, no. And I have no time for farm boys. If I don't figure this out soon, I'm likely to be back on a plane to crash on your couch before the sun even sets." The familiar pinprick of tears threatens to make this conversation into a sob fest.

"You're always welcome, you know that, but I don't think you're going to need my couch. I predict the triumphant return of Jenna Bard starting now."

I'm about to disagree when I see a cloud of dust in the distance. Do mirages exist out on country dirt roads? I can't make out exactly what's coming toward me, but at least it's a sign of some kind of civilization. "Addison, I have to let you go. I think I may have an honest to God tractor coming this way."

"Ohhhh, your farm boy! See? You basically manifested one by thinking about him. Call me back if you need more psychic energy." And she hangs up.

Once the tractor gets close enough for me to flag it

down, the strapping farm boy turns out to be a wizened man with enough lines on his face to be his own road map. Which is probably lucky since I hadn't even considered the safety issue of being alone with a stranger out here. In the city, I'd be on red alert, but I'd gone ahead and assumed a random tractor held very little threat.

He's quick to point me in the right direction, and once I'm back in the car and a little farther down the road, my GPS suddenly wakes up and directs me the rest of the way. By the time I pull up to the entrance of the farm—where they're setting up a sign big enough for even me not to miss —I start to think the day's looking up.

Another little jaunt down a gravel road and I'm in front of what must be the distillery building. No sign here yet, but I'd been given a description of the place. It's rustic in a way that doesn't make me want to gag, so I give the establishment two points and park my car. I can clearly see things are still under construction, but from the looks of things it won't be long until it can be open for business. Still, I start to get the familiar feeling that's caused me so much trouble in the past. This restaurant's going to be in the middle of nowhere. No matter how great the food is or how beautiful the building, it's still going to be a monumental step down from where I've been. But I try not to let my pride get the better of me. Right now, I don't have another choice. It's the Beverly Hillbillies or nothing, and I cannot afford to choose nothing. I square my shoulders and pull the front door open.

I have to blink a few times once I'm inside to be sure I'm not seeing things. While the outside might still make you think you're stepping up to a barn, the inside tells a different story. It's warm wood and shiny copper, with a casual feel you can easily dress up with a few changes. I love it immediately and am so busy looking around, imagining what the lighting in here must do to the wood and the metal, I completely miss the man standing behind the long copper bar.

"Hello?" he calls out, coming around to greet me. He's tall, with dark blond hair and hazel eyes that certainly don't look like he was expecting me. "We aren't quite open to the public yet."

"Hello." I extend a hand, which he takes with some trepidation. "I'm Jenna. I'm looking for Chance Allen."

He relaxes a little as he gives my hand a firm shake. "That would be my brother. I'm Cooper. Is he expecting you?"

"I hope so," I start. "I'm the new—"

"Jenna?" Another tall blond comes through the front door, already extending his hand. "Sorry I'm late. I hope I didn't keep you waiting long."

"Actually, I was afraid *I* was late," I confess. "I got lost on the way out here."

"Then it worked out perfectly. You meet Cooper?" He tilts his head toward his brother.

"We just met." Cooper crosses his arms over his chest and raises an eyebrow. "Hadn't gotten past the first name information, though."

"I'd rather explain it once Charlie's here. He's gonna lose his mind." Chance grins. "He's always a little late."

"You haven't told them—"

"Okay, okay, what's so goddamned important it couldn't wait until after lunch?"

I lock eyes with the man who has burst through the front door. Also blond, tall, with hazel eyes. He freezes, his hand still resting on the door handle. "Jen?"

Chance looks between us, the smile falling a bit from his

face. "Jen-na. Jenna Bard. The new chef for your new restaurant."

Remember when I said today was looking up? Yeah, scratch that. My no-strings hook up has turned out to be anything but.

He's my new boss.

5

Charlie

"You hired a chef without consulting with me first?" I pace in front of the bar.

"I had to act fast. I thought you'd be thrilled I was able to get her. You've eaten at her restaurant. You couldn't stop talking about it. I thought you'd be happy." Chance furrows his brow. "Why aren't you happy?"

"Because *I'm* supposed to be managing the restaurant. We agreed on that. You can't hire people without consulting me." I'm fuming, but for all the wrong reasons. Hiring Jenna Bard for the restaurant is a major score—one I never would have thought we'd be able to pull off. Normally, I'd be celebrating with my brother, congratulating him on pulling off the surprise of the year, but that was before Jenna turned out to be Jen. And before I'd had my hands all over her.

"I would have told you last night, but all the baby stuff kind of took precedence. And I thought you'd be patting me on the back. Jenna Bard, Charlie. And we've got her early enough to have her put the menu together and finalize the kitchen. We need her. She's a pro."

Oh, she's a pro all right. I try to get the image of Jen— Jenna—wearing nothing but her panties out of my head. Jesus, this is a mess. How am I going to be able to look her in the eye, much less work with her?

"No, you're right. You caught me off guard, that's all. She wasn't on our list." I make a show of leaning against the bar.

"She wasn't, but that's because I just found out she was looking. There's some kind of a situation with her and the co-owner of her restaurant. Everyone's talking about it. I made a call before she had a chance to look at other options." Chance's face is smug, pleased with the coup he's managed, but I'm more concerned with what's happened to make Jenna leave her restaurant.

"What kind of situation?"

"The kind that results in divorce and her getting screwed in the division of assets, I think. He basically tossed her out on her ass." Chance shrugs. "I'm guessing she won't be sticking around Mint Springs for long, so make good use of the time we've got her."

I swallow. Jenna's got a lot on her plate right now. Adding the other night to all of that isn't going to help. I can be a professional, and Chance is right, she's not going to stay in this small town forever. Hell, she'll probably be gone in a month. And we need her. I can keep it together until she moves on.

"I'll take her over to the restaurant once Cooper brings her back." My oldest brother was kind enough to take Jenna on a tour of the property so Chance and I could battle it out. I'm sure that made her feel right at home. Nothing like a family fight to start off her tenure here.

"Great idea. And, hey, I'm sorry I didn't tell you about her sooner. I really thought you'd be excited to work with her." Chance's mouth turns down into a frown.

"I *am* excited to work with her." It isn't a lie, although I'm going to need to temper my excitement about the other things I'd like to do with her. "And Cooper's news kind of stole the show last night. It isn't like you weren't telling me on purpose."

Chance shakes his head. "Can you imagine those two with a baby?"

"Actually, I can. He's gonna be a great dad." And I'm going to be the best fun uncle in the tri-state area, if not the country. Maybe the world.

"Yeah, he is." Chance smiles. "Now go dazzle our new chef with the fabulous kitchen we've been building."

When Cooper brings Jenna back down to the distillery, I'm sitting on one of the worn wooden stools, trying to sip a cup of coffee. In reality, the stools are new—they're just meant to look old. Most of the things in the distillery are like that. They all look like they've been here forever even though you know that isn't the case. Even this building's technically new. When we realized we couldn't use the existing barn structure, we'd used the original wood to build something new in the old footprint. The floors in here are one hundred percent old barn wood, and we used the rest in other parts of the construction. You'd never guess it isn't all wood from 1947, though. Chance and his crew did a great job making the place look seamless. The distillery is Cooper's baby, and his stamp's all over this place too, from the copper still to the choice of the light fixtures. He knew exactly how he wanted the place to feel and look, and now that it's all come together, we're all excited to open it up to the public.

Cooper's talking excitedly as they come through the

front door, saying something that's got Jenna laughing, tilting her head back and revealing the long, tan expanse of her throat. It's been less than forty-eight hours since I ran my tongue up the length of her neck and less than five minutes since I thought about it. Getting through the rest of this day is going to be torture.

Jenna stops laughing when she sees me, her mouth snapping shut and transforming into a tight smile.

"You ready to show Miss Jenna here your pride and joy?" Cooper's clearly elated, and why shouldn't he be? He hasn't slept with the woman who can now make or break a significant part of our family's plan. "Charlie'll take good care of you."

I notice the way Jenna's mouth twitches and the tiny little shake she gives her head. *I already did that, brother.*

"*Charlie.*" She says it like it's the first time she's heard it. "The restaurant's your pride and joy?" She narrows her eyes.

"Yep." I stand, giving up on the coffee that's only making my stomach more irritated anyway. "We can walk from here or we can…" I take a look at her feet. Stiletto boots cover her feet and I have a flash of those boots in the hotel room.

"You should probably drive," Cooper offers. "Those are not farm shoes."

I close my eyes for a second and try to get my equilibrium back. To Cooper it must look like irritation, because he shoots me a look that should have me playing nice or expect retribution. At the very least it's a question of manners and at the worst it's an issue of how we treat employees. Jenna, if she doesn't go screaming out the door in the next two seconds, is part of the staff. Part of *my* staff. I'm technically the boss, and I know better than I should how much she likes to be in charge. And those boots are killing me a little bit.

"We can take my car." I turn to walk to the door. "Unless you want to drive." It's not an offer I'd usually make, and Cooper raises an eyebrow.

"I'm fine for you to drive." Jenna's tone is the kind you'd use at the doctor's office. Not an ounce of familiarity. I nod, and she lets me lead her out to the tiny gravel parking lot, missing the warning look I get from my brother when her back is turned.

Once we're in the car, Jenna rounds on me. "Did you tell him?"

"Tell who what?" I keep my eyes on the road ahead of us. We'll be at the restaurant in less than two minutes, and I'm determined not to fuck this up any more than I already have.

"Your brother. About the hotel." She turns back toward the road. "I assume you're only taking me over here as a pretense. We both know you won't want me working here after what happened the other night."

I pull over on the side of the road and put the car in park. Jenna startles a bit and her hand comes out to rest on the door handle. It's a far cry from the easiness she'd had when she was in my car the last time, barbecue sauce all over her fingers.

"I did not tell my brother. I won't be telling Chance or Cooper or Cade, for that matter. I won't be telling anyone anything about what happened at the hotel, and it won't be happening again." It comes out harder than I intend and Jenna flinches. "If I'd known who you were—if I'd had any idea about any of this—" I wave my hand in the general direction of just about everything. "I never would have started anything."

Jenna's mouth pulls itself into a hard, thin line. "Don't want anyone to know we slept together?" She lets out a little huff. "Typical. Didn't want everyone to know you were slumming it." She gives me a withering look.

"That I was what?"

"Look, I need this job, Countr—Charlie."

"And I need you to take it." I close my eyes and take a deep breath. Count to five. Wait for the need to pummel the steering wheel to pass. "Let's get a few things straight. First of all, I would hardly call sleeping with you 'slumming it.' In fact, that's the opposite of what I would call it, just so you know." I make the mistake of letting my eyes travel over her. *No, Charlie. Not allowed.* "And the reason I'm being emphatic about it never happening again is not because I wouldn't like it to—far from it—but because if you're working here I need things to be as professional as possible. I need this restaurant to be the best it can be, and you can help me get there. I've eaten at your restaurant. I know what you can do. I can run the front of the house with the best of them, but I'm no chef."

"You've eaten at my restaurant? In Boston?" Her face tells me she finds this hard to believe.

"Of course."

"You went to *Boston*?" Jenna says this like I've claimed to have gone to the moon.

"Yes, I went to Boston. I've been there plenty of times. Why is that surprising?" I raise my hands in frustration.

"It's a little far from here." Again, Jenna's face clouds.

"Jen—*Jenna*, I have traveled much farther than Boston. Yes, I live out here in the middle of nowhere, but that doesn't mean I haven't been other places." I pause and look her full in the face. "I think we can both see who thought they were slumming the other night." I try to swallow my pride and push forward. Jenna thinks I'm some kind of a country bumpkin? Fine then.

"You've eaten at Ana's?"

"I just told you I have."

"Tell me about it." Jenna's face softens, and I feel the angry lump in my throat loosen a bit.

"It was crowded, so we had to sit at the bar. But sometimes I prefer that." I try to remember the details. "We had a dozen oysters to start, mainly because when I'm someplace with local oysters, I have oysters."

Jenna nods. "And?"

"And what?"

"How were they?" She leans toward me.

"Perfect. Juicy. A little sweet." I nearly close my eyes thinking about them. Unfortunately, it makes me think of other things I've recently tasted that fit that same description.

"What else?" Jenna asks me, breathless.

"I was with someone who wasn't very...adventurous." That's the nicest way of saying Ashley Clinton doesn't eat anything but white bread and likes her spicy foods to be on the level of turkey lunchmeat. I had eaten the entire dozen oysters by myself after she'd turned up her nose. That was the last time I took Ashley Clinton anywhere. I don't need people ruining delicious meals, especially not ones I've had to travel to eat.

"Let me guess, she had a salad and not even one of the good ones." Jenna folds her arms across her chest.

"Yes, and no dressing or on the side, something ridiculous like that." I shudder. It had been a waste of an opportunity to taste something different, something special, and she'd thrown it away. Ana's had all the things you could find at other restaurants, but that's not why I had wanted to eat there. "I had the pernil. Mofongo. Finished with your rice pudding."

"*Arroz con dulce*?" Jenna nearly whispers it.

"Yes. All delicious. Obviously I have a soft spot for pork. I went to Ana's specifically to try yours. I wasn't disappointed."

Jenna's chest rises and falls as she stares at me over the center console. "More."

"More?"

"Describe it. How it tasted. What you liked." Jenna's lips part and her tongue darts out enough to distract me.

It's a test and I know it. But it's also borderline seduction sitting this close, talking about food. It is for me, anyway, and if Jenna's body language is any indication, it's having the same effect on her.

"It was falling off the bone. Perfect that way. But the skin…the way it stayed crispy. The meat was delicious—all the citrus and garlic—but the skin was the star. Worth the trip for that alone."

Jenna's cheeks are flushed. "But I couldn't make that here. Not at your restaurant."

"Why not? People would love it." I make myself face forward instead of focusing on Jenna's mouth. "At least come and have a look. Don't turn down the opportunity because of one mistake." I don't necessarily consider my night with Jenna a mistake, but it's obvious she does. It's an inconvenience I can get over if I can convince her to do the same. And if I can stop looking at her tits.

Jenna lets out a breath. "Fine. Show me this diamond in the rough."

I put the car in drive before she has a chance to change her mind.

6

Jenna

There isn't actually anything rough about Charlie's restaurant. The drive to the building is a little bumpy, but once we pull in front of the place, I can already see potential. The restaurant's meant to fit in with the other buildings —there's a farm feeling and more of that rustic stuff I can take or leave—but it's also got its own vibe. It isn't the glitz and glam of Ana's, but it doesn't make me shudder either. And I'd never really loved the interior of my restaurant. I'd let my husband take the lead on that and regretted it more than I'd like to admit. Frank seemed to think we were opening a nightclub and couldn't see how the mismatch between the food I'd wanted to cook and the way he wanted to decorate might hurt the experience for our customers. I had wanted to do upscale versions of the food I'd grown up with—the kinds of things my grandmother had been teaching me to cook since I'd been old enough to handle a wooden spoon. But he thought all that "ethnic" stuff was going to hold us back. Sure, he'd been a third-generation

Italian immigrant with a *nonna* making sauce every Sunday, but he thought incorporating my Puerto Rican dishes was a step too far. Who was going to eat that?

It turned out, plenty of people wanted to eat what I was serving. As confusing as that was to my thick-headed husband, it made perfect sense to me. Who didn't want something delicious, especially when it was comforting? They might not have been raised on my *abuelita*'s *carne guisada*, but they could recognize the essence of what that dish meant even when it was surrounded on the menu by nondescript burgers and salads. Talking to Charlie had just proved my point, and as bittersweet as that was, having already lost the restaurant I called my own, it gave me hope that I might be able to get some of that back in the future. Not here, obviously, but somewhere. Eventually.

"The kitchen's basic," Charlie warns me. "So don't judge the place by that alone. I've left it open for the chef's interpretation. We can add or subtract however you like if you decide to take the job." He's nervous, and I try to keep my inner bitch from coming out. I'm already sure this job isn't anything but a stepping stone for me—if I can even take it now. I was momentarily blinded by Charlie's appreciation for my food, but that can only go so far. It takes a lot to dazzle me when it comes to kitchens, and I'm sure whatever Charlie's created inside this would-be barn isn't going to go very far toward convincing me this is my dream job.

But I'm proven wrong the second we step inside. Charlie pulls open one of the giant front doors and I'm transported to a place so serene I can't believe it's sitting out here in nowhere Georgia.

The front of the building belies its actual size. The restaurant goes on forever once you're inside, but it still manages a cozy feel. The way Charlie's laid the place out with several different seating areas makes the large space feel intimate in the ways that count. I can see people having large group events here, but a couple could just as easily have a romantic dinner for two. The entire back wall is floor to ceiling windows, and the view of the mountains in the distance is only topped by the quaint little pond out back. I can see the beginnings of a dock, and crews are already hard at work this morning planting things I can't begin to name around its edges. It screams sweetness and has me imagining weddings and proposals out there even before anything's finished.

Inside is sweet as well, but not overly so. There are long tables for family-style dining running down the middle of the space and smaller tables arranged around the edges. Chandeliers hang from the high ceilings, and even in the middle of the day I can imagine the soft light they'd cast. It's rustic but high end, homey but sophisticated.

It's beautiful.

"Things are still in flux, obviously," Charlie tells me as he steers me deeper into the restaurant. "All of these tables can be moved around so we don't always have to have it arranged like this. I'm envisioning being able to have some of the receptions and parties in here—the smaller ones. The larger ones would be in the actual event space. Did Cooper take you by there?"

I nod, still taking in all the small touches I can see now. The chairs look comfortable, welcoming. I can almost hear the clink of silverware against plates. The rough-hewn beams above me hide some of the building's duct work. The construction's solid and thoughtful. This place looks like it's been built to last. Like the Allens intend for this all to be here forever. I love it, and I haven't even laid eyes on the kitchen.

"I'll show you inside over there once we're done here, if you want. It's similar, but since we need even more flexibility over there, it's more of a shell right now. There's a kitchen there too, but more for catering. I'd like this to be the main kitchen, but I'd welcome your suggestions. You'd know better than I would the kind of gymnastics it would take to run the restaurant and the catering out of the same space."

Charlie's hand comes to the small of my back. It's not a touch I would normally allow, and my back stiffens a bit. His hand drops back by his side, a sheepish look on his face. I step back a fraction, well aware that he's touched much more than my back.

"Where is this kitchen, then?" I can already see part of it from where we're standing; shiny stainless steel glints from the back of the room.

"Over here. We went with sort of an open plan, but I'm hoping you find it provides enough privacy. Not everyone loves having their work area on constant display." Charlie moves in front of me, careful not to get too close. This right here is a prime reason to turn down this job and get as far away from Mint Springs as possible. There's no way Charlie and I can work together if things are awkward. And constantly picturing your boss naked tends to make things more than a little uncomfortable.

But I could rein it in, right? I wouldn't always be thinking about the way Charlie looked as he licked his way down my body. It would fade in time. Although my inability to keep my eyes off his ass as he walks is not a good sign. But where else will I go if I don't try here? Charlie's broad back in front of me is leading me toward something that could be my nightmare or could be a dream come true. Even if the kitchen is a mess, I'll probably be telling myself I'll make the best of it. What choice do I have? But now, with this extra complication, I'll need to make some serious decisions.

"Well? What do you think?" Charlie's smile is no match for my own. I have never seen a kitchen like this one.

I am in so much trouble.

7

Charlie

"Are you sure inviting her for supper was the best idea?"

"Of course, who better to show Jenna what I mean by family dinner than my own family?"

My great aunt Sadie's expression tells me she disagrees.

Her sister Mae seems to be in violent agreement. "We don't normally cook for *chefs*, Charlie. We're home cooks. Good ones, but not on the level of whipping up a dinner for a famous chef at a moment's notice."

"Who told you Jenna was famous?" I try not to laugh at the way my aunts are running around the kitchen.

"Your brother! Chance hasn't stopped crowing since he convinced her to come out here." Sadie flies over to the stove to give something a stir.

"Well, she's hardly famous. People who know food might know her, but she's not Giada or anything."

"Be that as it may, she cooks for a living. People pay her for it and we—" Sadie's hands fly to her hair. "Oh, Good Lord. This is a mess, isn't it? Maybe Hadley can come a little early and try to work her magic?"

"And the house," Mae exclaims. "It is nowhere near ready for company."

My aunts are two of the most unflappable people I've ever had the pleasure of meeting, but this afternoon that isn't an adjective I'd use to describe either one of them. They are running around like chickens with their heads cut off, all because I invited Jenna Bard to break bread with us.

"You've never cared before when I showed up with an extra friend." When my brothers and I spent summers here at the farm, it was always the more the merrier for dinner. Sadie and Mae loved having a full house and would never have trouble finding a spare chair to pull up to the dining room table.

"This isn't a *friend*." Mae wipes her hands on the edges of her apron. "This is someone who cooks for a living. On top of that, she's still feeling things out. What if our cornbread is the thing that convinces her to leave?"

"I doubt that'll happen." Sadie and Mae make exceptional cornbread. "If anything, that'll convince her to stick around. Maybe try to steal your recipe."

"We'd gladly give it if it meant having a world-class chef working in that restaurant," Sadie volunteers.

"Well," Mae hedges. "We'd at least consider it." My aunts are known for keeping recipes close to the vest. "But you haven't given us enough advance notice. Had we known, we would have made something really special."

"I'm sure whatever you're making will be fantastic. She doesn't need anything fancy; I want her to meet the family and get a feel for how things work down here. She's going to love whatever you serve. I promise."

"What time did you tell her to come over?" Sadie asks, looking at the clock on the ancient stovetop.

"Six." I look at my watch. "We always eat at six."

"Six?" Mae gives Sadie a panicked look. "We won't have time to make a cake. Charlie, you'd better make yourself useful and at least run the vacuum cleaner through the living room. I do not want anyone saying Sadie and I have dust bunnies."

By the time everyone else arrives, I've been tasked with dusting every stick of furniture in the living room, sweeping the front porch, and setting the table with every fancy thing my aunts have ever even thought about bringing into the house.

"Whoa." Chance picks up one of the candlesticks I've been told to put on the table. "What's the occasion?"

"Casual family dinner," I deadpan. "Thanks for making them freak out about Jenna." I promised her something low-key, and this is going to be anything but.

"I didn't realize it would mean *this*." Chance waves his arm around.

"We're ready for the Queen, if she decides to swan through here," I grumble. "And they've changed their minds about what to cook so many times I'm not even sure what we're having."

"Where are they?" Chance peers toward the kitchen.

"Upstairs. They made Cooper bring Hadley to set up a remote location of Hot House Flowers. I fully expect to have Hadley seeing clients up there for hair emergencies starting tomorrow. Fingers crossed they're presentable by the time Jenna gets here."

Cooper's been out on the screened-in porch, trying his best not to get sucked into any housecleaning or hair-dressing.

Right on cue, the doorbell rings and my youngest brother, Cade, goes to let in our guest, leaving the rest of us standing around uncomfortably.

"So I'm guessing you're the brains of the operation, then, with an MBA and all that." Jenna's smiling at Cade, and I get the slightest twinge of something in my chest. Come on, there's no way I'm feeling jealous about the way she's looking at my brother. I stand there, still holding the feather duster, as I try to convince myself that the sight of Jenna paying attention to someone else can't be making me feel so unsettled.

Jenna's wearing a black dress that makes her look like a 1950s pinup. It's tight through the waist but flowy and short enough to show off her legs. She catches me looking at them, of course, and I make a show of moving my sister-in-law Lily over to her. Jenna's still giving me the stink eye as they shake hands.

"You're Cooper's wife?" Jenna asks, obviously overwhelmed by the gaggle of new faces.

"No, I'm Chance's wife. Cooper and Hadley aren't married yet. She's upstairs helping Sadie and Mae get ready. She should be down any minute." Lily reaches for the bottle of wine Jenna's still holding. "Do you want me to take that?"

"Sure. It isn't much, but I didn't know what else to bring. I'm not even sure where to go to get anything else and I almost got lost again finding my way to the liquor store." Jenna shrugs her shoulders. "I guess I really am a city girl."

"You'll figure things out in no time," Lily assures her. "I can take you into town. Show you all the hot spots, if you like. Not that there really are any hot spots."

"I'd appreciate that." Jenna hands over the bottle, and I make a mental note to be sure to take her into town myself. That's just what a good boss would do, right? I should help Jenna feel comfortable. That's what I tell myself, anyway, as I continue to sneak glances at the way her ass looks in that dress. Ready to bite. Like a summer peach.

"Oh, she's already here!" Aunt Mae coming down the stairs saves me from my overactive imagination. "Sadie, Hadley, hurry up!" She's rushing, and every single one of us moves toward the stairs, ready to catch her if she stumbles.

"Take your time, Mae," Cooper cautions, offering her his hand. "A trip to the emergency room will mean Jenna doesn't get to enjoy supper."

"I know, I know," Mae mumbles as she finally hits flat ground. She's quick to get herself over to Jenna, releasing Cooper's hand the second she's off the stairs. "You must be Jenna. We're delighted you could come tonight and even more delighted you're going to be working at the restaurant." It is impossible to resist my aunts when they turn on the charm, and Jenna seems particularly susceptible. Already Mae's hugging her and pulling her toward the kitchen. "Sadie'll be down in a minute and we can talk food." She holds Jenna's hand as they walk.

"I'm not sure if that's going to save us or send her running." Chance tilts his head in the direction of the new best friends.

"One of us should probably make sure Jenna's got a drink at least." Cade's headed to the kitchen before I can volunteer, nearly running to catch up with them. Cooper raises an eyebrow, and I try to pretend I think it's funny, shrugging my shoulders and rolling my eyes. But I already know the feelings I'm having are not at all humorous.

And I'm going to need to get that under control before I ruin everything.

8

Jenna

Charlie's family has to be the sweetest thing I've ever seen. They're like biting into a chocolate covered cherry—there's so much sugar in there you can barely fit your mouth around it. Charlie and his brothers joke and tease, and his sisters-in-law are the best of friends. Don't even get me started on his elderly aunts. From the moment I walked into their farmhouse, I've been welcomed like a long-lost daughter. Sadie and Mae remind me of my grandmother, the way they dote on all the Allen siblings. It makes me miss her even more than usual. I could use one of her *empanadas* right about now. Instead, I'm tucking into Sadie's pecan pie.

"Do I taste a hint of bourbon in here, Sadie?" I hold a forkful up to the light and admire the gorgeous amber color.

"You might," she teases. "If you stick around, I might let you take a peek at the recipe." She gives me a little wink.

"I'll keep that in mind. It really is delicious. This crust is to die for." I put a bite in my mouth and appreciate the way the pastry holds its own until the very last second, finally crumbling. Not too dry, but not too chewy. Perfect.

"Sadie and Mae have set the standard for good food around here. They've been feeding us since we were tiny." Cooper motions with his hand down to the end of the table. "Slide the rest of that pie back down here."

"You grew up here?" I've gotten some of the details of how everyone came to be living here full time, but I've still got some gaps.

"Naw. We grew up in Nashville. Only got to come here for the summers." Cade uses the side of his fork to cut another bite of pie from his slice. "We weren't lucky enough to eat this good all year long."

"Your mother wasn't a good cook?" I ask innocently, but all four brothers burst into laughter. "What?"

"Our mother was hardly what you'd call domestic," Chance says. "I can't even remember her making much more than toast."

Mae and Sadie shake their heads, but the guys don't seem too bothered by it. I guess things weren't always sugary sweet.

"I remember her *burning* toast—oh, and that birthday cake she tried to make that time. Was that for Cade?" Cooper looks to his brothers for confirmation. It's obvious they're related. Four sandy blond heads all nod in agreement.

"How was I supposed to know the icing went on after you baked it?" Charlie asks, in what I think must be an imitation of their mother's Southern drawl. "It's funny now, but she managed to smoke us all out of the house, remember?"

"She felt guilty enough to buy me pretty much everything I asked for that year. Turned out to be a pretty good birthday after all." Cade shrugs. "She's better at other things. Cooking's not her strong suit. Not like Mae and Sadie." He turns his gaze toward the two older ladies, and they beam back at him.

"Everything was delicious." I wipe the crumbs from the corners of my mouth. "That cornbread was everything Charlie built it up to be." It really was a thing of beauty, and I'm considering how rude it would be to ask for a few pieces to take back with me to the hotel.

"We're so glad you enjoyed it. It isn't every day we get compliments from a chef. Charlie raved about your food when he came back from Boston this last time." Mae's eyes shine as she looks toward Charlie.

"He did, did he?" I can't help making eye contact with him across the table. Big mistake. I've been doing my best to avoid his gaze through dinner. That's been difficult with him directly in front of me, but I've persevered. Now, however, his eyes lock with mine and I'm not thinking about food, unless you count Charlie and the things I'm thinking about doing with my mouth. *Cool it, Jenna. This is a family event.*

"I did. I told you how much of an impression your cooking made on me." His eyes stay focused on mine. It's not a throwaway compliment, and for a second he and I are the only two people in the room.

"Definitely the way to an Allen man's heart," Sadie informs us. "Slaves to their stomachs."

I startle and look away from Charlie's amused face. "I don't think Charlie's heart's in this."

"Of course it is! That restaurant's his one true love. Right, Charlie? It's the most committed he's ever been. He needs someone special to really make it shine." Mae gives me a wink.

"Yes, ma'am. I am in love with the restaurant. That's for sure." Charlie nods his head.

"When are we going to have a name for this fancy restaurant?" Copper asks.

"It doesn't have a name?" I'm incredulous but really shouldn't be, considering it never even occurred to me to ask despite spending the entire day here.

"I need a little more inspiration." Charlie puts more pie in his mouth and chews.

"We've all given you great suggestions." Hadley looks a little peeved. "We need it to be on brand with the rest of the place, inspiration or no inspiration."

"I'm working on it," Charlie says through another bite of pie.

"What was your restaurant named, Jenna?" It's an easy enough question, and I'm sure Sadie doesn't mean anything by asking it, but it puts a knife in my heart all the same.

"Ana's. I named it after my grandmother. And it still exists, it just isn't mine anymore." I try to act like it's no big deal, like the idea of Frank and his side piece trying to cook my grandmother's signature dishes doesn't make me sick to my stomach, but I'm a terrible actress. All of the faces at the table fall a little bit.

"Well, I'm sure your grandmother loved the sentiment," Mae volunteers, trying to smooth things over.

"She did." And loved seeing all my dreams finally coming true. I am thankful she didn't get to see them all snatched away.

"You didn't see us having an issue coming up with a name." Cooper points his fork at Charlie. "Better get on the stick. We need to be finishing the signage, and if you don't come up with something brilliant, we're going to do it for you."

"I've got ideas," Charlie says. "And Stolen Barn Spirits

was easy. Your distillery lives on the spot where the barn used to be."

"But why 'stolen'?" I've been dying to ask.

"That's a long story." Sadie stands. "Might need coffee for that. Any takers?"

Several hands shoot up. It looks like no one's really ready to go home quite yet.

"If y'all play nice, Hadley and I might give you a taste of our apple brandy." Cooper looks at me. "Can't call it Calvados, really, and it's still young, but it's one of the first things we've had in production. The whiskey's aging, though. Would be great if we could get a little synergy between the distillery and your kitchen."

I nod. Synergy sounds doable with this group.

"Let me help you with that coffee," I call after Sadie, the wheels in my head already turning.

"Wait, so someone took an entire wall of the barn? How do you steal part of a barn?" I'm pretty sure Charlie and his family are pulling my leg. This story sounds too crazy to be true.

"Well, it was only Sadie and Mae living out here at the time," Cade calls from the kitchen, where he's up to his elbows in dirty dishes. Lily's in there helping as well, but I've been told guests don't need to worry about cleaning up—at least not on the first visit.

"We didn't notice, I'm sad to say." Mae's lips thin. "But now that we've got everyone back out here it'd be hard to do much sneaking around with a flatbed truck."

"Yes, and I think most people know now that coming on our property wouldn't be so easy without an invitation."

Chance's arm rests on the back of Lily's empty chair. "I'm going to make sure Cade's doing his share."

"We all know you can't go more than four minutes without your wife," Charlie teases.

"Guilty." Chance throws it over his shoulder as he saunters into the kitchen. "You should get one of your own."

Charlie rolls his eyes and I try not to look at him. His brothers are all pairing up; it wouldn't be unusual for him to think about doing the same.

"And you never figured out who did it?" Again, that seems implausible. I wait for someone to finally tell me this is all some elaborate joke.

"Nope. We've all got our suspects, though." Cooper rubs Hadley's neck. "We're going to have to get going."

Hadley looks sheepish but exhausted. "Sorry, y'all. This baby is taking all my energy."

"Baby?" I blurt it out without thinking. No wonder Hadley passed on the brandy.

"Yeah, I'm not that far along. Hopefully I'm not this worn out through the whole pregnancy." Hadley looks at Cooper. "I'm not much fun lately."

"You're plenty fun." Cooper kisses her on the forehead. "Let's get you home."

The party starts breaking up, and I'm given multiple invitations. It seems everyone wants to be sure I'm given the red-carpet treatment. Mint Springs might not be much, but everyone thinks I need to see all of it. As we all scatter from the front porch, I'm a little sad to be going back to my empty hotel room.

"Hey," Charlie calls out, catching up to me as I walk to my car. "That wasn't so bad, was it?"

"They're lovely. And the food was delicious, as promised." I hold up my bag full of leftovers. You can bet I'll be having another piece of cornbread before I go to bed tonight. I'll probably help myself to some more brandy or a taste of 'Sadie's Bathtub Gin.' Cooper was generous enough to give me a bottle of the other liquor they've got in production. Sadie pretended not to love having it share her name, but you could tell she was pleased.

"I was hoping you'd say that." Charlie shoves his hands in his front pockets and rocks on his heels a bit. "So, will I see you tomorrow to get started?"

Maybe I should say no, go back to the hotel and pack up to be on the first flight out, but I hesitate. That's trouble, of course, because as soon as Charlie sees me pause, a huge smile lights up his face. He starts backing up before I can change my mind.

"Get here early. We've got a lot of decisions to make." He trots off to his car, turning to look at me with that hopeful face that's going to be the death of me. "You won't be sorry; I promise."

I unlock my rental and slide inside. If only that was a promise I was sure Charlie could keep.

9

Charlie

"You're here early. Thought I was going to have to leave these on the porch."

I jump. "Jesus, Faith. You could give a little warning. I didn't even hear you come in."

"You should probably start locking the front door if you don't want surprise visitors. At least until you get more staff in here." Faith trots in carrying a crate nearly as big as she is.

"Hand that to me." I come around from behind the bar and take the box. It's loaded to the top with early spring vegetables.

"I brought you what I had. It's mostly lettuce, but there are a few carrots and some of the stuff from the greenhouse. If we were thinking about having enough of everything you want to actually feed a restaurant full of people, we'll need to get planning. Make a decision about how much you want to grow here and how much you want me to budget for you at Happy Trails." Faith follows along behind me, just a hair too close and bouncing like a bunny.

"I need to talk to my chef about that."

Faith stops mid-bounce, her blonde ponytail still swinging. "Chef? Ooh la la."

"Don't give me that. You knew we were planning on hiring the best we could find. Jenna's the best." I try to keep my attention on the vegetables in case my face gives something away. Faith has known me forever and can always tell when I'm hiding something. "Man, look at these leeks."

"Jenna, is it? Hmmm." The way she lets Jenna's name hang in the air tells me Faith has already caught on. No amount of fawning over her homegrown vegetables is going to distract her if she thinks there's something to explore there.

"That's her name."

"A little informal, don't you think? For a new hire?" Faith raises one eyebrow. "Do I need to rustle up a cup of coffee and sit here while you tell me all about this Jenna person?" She gives me one of her toothy grins, the kind that makes her look twelve years old, and leans a hip against the bar.

"No. In fact, it would probably be best if you went ahead and got moving. She's going to be here in a minute, and I don't need any distractions." And I don't need the girl who's as close to me as a sister perched at the bar to spill any teenage secrets or tell incriminating stories.

Faith makes herself at home, coming around to the back of the bar and helping herself to a cup of the coffee I specifically brewed for Jenna. It's a special blend I'd like to serve at the restaurant, and I had wanted her to try it. Faith takes one sniff and gives me a knowing look. "What is this? Not the usual muddy water you've been serving the construction crew."

"I'm considering it for the restaurant. I needed to try it out." I shrug.

"You made special coffee. And you've ironed that shirt."

She considers this for a moment. "What does this Jenna look like?"

"Like herself. I don't know." A billion other adjectives run through my head. *Beautiful. Voluptuous. Flawless.* "She's an employee."

"Just teasing you. Gosh, calm down." Faith adds cream and sugar and gives her coffee a stir.

"I'm trying hard to be professional, Faith."

"I'll be good. Promise. If you let me stay, I can tell her all about the farm. Pick her brain for next year's planting." She gives me her wide-eyed little girl face. "Satisfy my curiosity before I have to head back for a long, arduous day of farm work."

"You love farm work." I try to frown, but it's hard to when Faith's turning on the cute.

"Come on. I can help you with your sales pitch about the farm-to-table stuff." Faith comes over next to me and slides her shoulder against mine, looking up and batting her eyelashes at me. It's a ridiculous display that only serves to make me laugh and I'm about to tell her to knock it off when someone behind us clears their throat.

Both Faith and I jump, bumping into each other. I turn to see Jenna standing behind us, her mouth in an angry twist.

"See? You should lock that front door," Faith tells me, giving me an elbow to the ribs.

"I didn't mean to interrupt. We did say eight." Jenna's eyes move between me and the pixie beside me. "I didn't realize you'd be busy."

"Busy? I'm not... Jenna, this is Faith. Faith, this is Jenna, the new chef." I make the introductions, ignoring the way Faith's mouth stays in that sly little half-smile.

"Faith Baker." Faith sticks out her hand. "Which is kind

of funny, because I'm a farmer, not a baker." It's one of her little jokes, but Jenna doesn't crack a smile.

"Faith's family has a farm up the road. They supply eggs and vegetables to several of the restaurants around here. Atlanta, too."

Jenna shakes Faith's hand but doesn't do anything else to appear friendly.

"I brought over some of the things we have going in the greenhouse. Too early for much else, but it'll give you a taste. In a few months I'll have some really wonderful stuff." Faith keeps smiling even though Jenna's staying stone-faced.

"Faith grows all kinds of crazy stuff. We can talk about a wish list, if you want. I've been talking with her about having some garden plots over here. I'm getting ahead of myself, but know that come summertime we'll be knee deep in the prettiest tomatoes you've ever seen." I grin at Faith, who gives me a little bow.

"Peppers, too. And this year I've got tomatillos, don't forget those." Faith looks like she's about to start spouting off a list of endless possibilities when she notices Jenna's lack of enthusiasm. "I should get going. I'm taking this coffee with me, by the way." She gives me another elbow to the ribs. "Nice to meet you, Jenna. Good luck working with this knucklehead."

"You'd better bring back that mug," I call after her.

Faith waves dismissively over her shoulder. "You know where I live."

I'm still grinning as Faith walks out the door. Jenna clears her throat again.

"What?" I move toward the coffee. Luckily there's still plenty in the pot.

"You that cozy with all the distributors? Maybe you should warn me when we're going to get a liquor delivery.

Wouldn't want to walk in on you humping that guy's leg."
Jenna crosses her arms over her chest.

"First of all, I would never hump Gary's leg. He's not my
type." I accidentally give Jenna's body the once-over. She's
casual today—jeans and a T-shirt—but she still looks good
enough to eat. Most certainly my type. "And Faith's an old
friend. I've known her since elementary school."

"A *friend*." Jenna obviously doesn't believe this. "I don't
want this job to be any more complicated than it already is.
If she's your girlfriend—even if it's casual—I'm not getting
swept up in some stupid love triangle, got it? I don't need
that drama."

"She's not my girlfriend. I wouldn't have done..." I
concentrate on pouring her a cup of coffee so she can't see
how hard it is not to think about *exactly* what she and I have
done. "I wouldn't have done what we did if I was in a relationship. I'm single. One hundred percent. And I meant
what I said before. I need you here too much to jeopardize
things. I'm not trying to drag you into any drama. And I'm
not the kind of guy who'd take advantage of a trip out of
town to cheat. That's not my style."

Jenna narrows her eyes at me.

"Here, try this. Cream and sugar's over there if you need
it." I direct her toward the counter, hoping coffee will put
her in a better mood.

Jenna takes the cup and reluctantly sips. I know I've got
her when her eyebrows shoot up a bit toward her hairline.

"Good, right? Locally roasted. I was thinking it might be
good to be kind of our signature blend. Or we could ask
them to make us something special. I think they'd go for
that if it meant a steady income stream. And if you could be
a little less prickly when we meet with them." I give Jenna a
sideways glance. "If you can manage that."

"They don't all need to be our friends, Country."

"Around here they do. And it's Charlie. I doubt you want to be explaining why you've given me a pet name two days into this."

Jenna frowns. "Okay, *Charlie*, what are we going to do with all this produce?"

"Cook, obviously." And then I turn my back on her to get things started in the kitchen.

10

Jenna

"I'm glad you find it so funny."

"*Funny*? Oh, no, honey. Toilet paper on the bottom of your shoe when you made your grand entrance at your fortieth birthday party? That was funny. In a sad way, but still funny. This is *hilarious*. And, I might add, the kind of blow I didn't expect the universe to give you. It's really kicking you while you're down."

"Thank you, Addison, for not only reminding me why I shouldn't tell you everything, but for also reminding me about the toilet paper." I shut my eyes and pinch the bridge of my nose. "I have to quit, don't I?"

"I'm surprised you didn't quit the second you realized the new boss was that little beefcake from the hotel." Addison makes an enthusiastic noise like a lion roaring, and I'm pretty sure she's doing some approximation of claws in the air. Thankfully I can't see any of her antics through the phone, but I've spent enough time with Addison to be able to imagine them. She's one of the few women I met in culinary school who's stayed in my life. Through ups and downs, there's always Addison.

"Can we not make that sound, please? And can we never, ever, ever use the word *beefcake* again?" I wince. Charlie's hardly a beefcake. He's handsome, all right, but in that boyish kind of way. Probably because he's legitimately a boy. Can he even be thirty years old?

"What are we going to call him, then? I need a code name, especially for when I visit." I can hear Addison's smile through the static on that one.

"Addison, you are sworn to secrecy. There are no code names. And there are probably no visits." I don't imagine I'll be here long, despite Charlie's assurances that we can get along fine. I put the phone on speaker and set it down on the bathroom counter.

"No visits? Don't hold out on me, Jenna. Handsome men, homemade cornbread, and local whiskey? You know I'm getting on a plane. What are you getting up to today in Mayberry?"

I scowl, even though it's wasted on Addison and this phone conversation. "Meeting up with Charlie to talk about staffing and then getting a tour of the farm his girlfriend owns." I lean toward the mirror over the sink and wing my eyeliner.

"Whoa. Girlfriend?"

"He denied it, but I walked in on them all cozy yesterday." I try to sound nonplussed even though just thinking about Charlie and that tiny little blonde thing all snuggled up at the bar activates some pretty strong feelings. The ugly kind.

"You sound a little..." The hesitation in Addison's voice only irritates me more.

"What?" I snap, accidentally pushing hard enough on the brush to smear the liner on my left eye.

"Jealous."

"I'm not jealous. I'm annoyed. This whole situation is ridiculous." I wipe the mussed eyeliner from my face and start over.

"Next level. That's why I'm glad we're friends, Jenna. Better you than me." I know Addison's kidding, but it stings a little just the same. I'm the one who never lets anything keep her down for long. I thought I was headed for the culinary stratosphere. I took big risks and had an even bigger fall. Addison kept it slow and steady and now her life's... predictable. Something I thought I'd hate but now sounds like heaven. "Does he cook?"

My mind automatically rewinds to yesterday when Charlie and I worked our way through the box of produce Faith left us. He'd been adept in the kitchen, even giving a few great suggestions here and there, but he'd let me be the boss. He'd "Yes, chef"ed me into a hot mess. Between the deference and the sight of his forearms as he'd chopped every onion in the bottomless box, my time in the kitchen had been full of temptation. And the food we'd made had been delicious.

"He is proficient."

"Ah, a good little sous chef for you."

"Addison..." I warn. "We're strictly business."

"Of course, of course. Do you even have any shoes you can wear to a farm? A real farm?"

"I'm wearing boots." I look down at the most sensible pair of shoes I own and realize they are nowhere near appropriate for mucking around.

"Please tell me they have at least a two-inch heel..." Addison snort laughs when I don't answer her. "Take tons of pictures, please. Love you, Jen Jen." I can hear her cackling as she hangs up on me.

"You are really giving Hadley a run for her money with the shoes." Charlie takes his focus off the road to get a better look at my boots. "We need to get you some reasonable footwear for farm life."

"I wear sensible shoes in the kitchen," I protest. I cannot believe I'm getting a lecture from a man who showed up at my hotel looking like he milks cows for a living. Not that I can complain about the way he's filling out those beat-up jeans. *No, Jenna, keep it professional.*

"We don't have to do the farm today. We could wait until you're really dressed for it." Charlie gives me the once-over, his eyes snagging for a second too long on my chest. When his eyes meet mine he has the good sense to look sheepish and make a show of watching the gravel road in front of us.

"What's wrong with this outfit?"

"Nothing if we were planning on going clubbing." Charlie fights a grin. "I don't think those pants are really for digging around in the dirt."

"They are very comfortable." I try to glare at him.

"I believe you; I just think maybe we'll head back to the restaurant. Faith'll understand."

I roll my eyes. Actually roll them. I'm turning into an adolescent. "I'm sure she will."

Charlie ignores me. "Change of plans." He hits the brakes and gravel goes flying, his sharp U-turn plastering me against the passenger side door for a second.

"What the hell?" I scramble to find something to hold onto.

"I'm taking you to the best breakfast place in town." Charlie pulls the baseball cap from his head and runs his fingers through his hair. He gives himself a quick glance in the rearview mirror and fixes a few errant strands.

"The *best* breakfast place? What? In a competition of two?" I try to recall passing much more than a fast food place on my drive out to the farm.

"You'd be surprised." Charlie gives me one of those grins that reminds me not to smile back at him. It's too dangerous to let my guard down when presented with all those straight teeth.

I am not at all surprised when we pull up in front of what looks like the greasiest spoon in the history of greasy spoons. "A diner? Is that what this is?" I read the sign as Charlie parks the car in one of the only available spaces. "Ham & Eggs? Am I about to be amazed or am I about to get food poisoning?"

"Maybe not amazed, but perhaps pleasantly surprised. Come on, we'll be lucky to get a table." Charlie darts from the car and rushes around to open the door for me. I bite back the urge to tell him I'm more than capable of getting myself out of a motor vehicle without assistance. I'm guessing I won't be opening the restaurant door, either. Sure enough, he rushes in front of me before I can put my hand out to grab the handle.

Inside is as crowded as Charlie predicted, with the constant clamor of forks hitting plates and frequent shouting when an order's ready. It's the kind of busy restaurant noise I miss, even if it's a far cry from fine dining. It gets noticeably quieter when Charlie's hand hits the small of my back and eases me into the room. Several conversations seem to stop outright as he waves down a waitress and tries to find us a place to sit.

"Well, well. Charlie Allen here with... Is this the new chef we've heard so much about?" The woman gives me the slow perusal only an older Southern lady can, cocking her head to the side and ignoring the other customers.

"Debbie, this is Jenna Bard. And, yes, hopefully she's going to stick around and help make the restaurant fabulous." Charlie's hand stays behind me, his fingers grazing my back.

"Hmmm." Debbie considers this. "I'll be sure to tell Henry who he's cooking for." She looks back toward the stainless steel opening to the kitchen.

"Oh, please don't." Already I'm self-conscious. How does everyone in town already know so much about me? My food is good, but you'd think I was Julia Child the way they're all looking over at us.

"Don't worry," Charlie assures me. "It won't change a damn thing Henry does back there."

Debbie laughs—a good, long laugh that has more patrons turning to see what all the fuss is about. "I'll be sure to tell him you said so, Charlie. You two want a table? I've got one more. Other than that, it's the counter."

Charlie defers to me, giving me the opportunity to make the decision. "Table? Or counter?"

"Counter's fine." I don't want to spend too much time having to look away from Charlie's face and sitting at a cozy two-top will be nothing but that. The counter will be easier. Safer. And look less like we're a couple who just rolled out of bed and drove down to the local diner for a little post sex bacon and eggs.

Debbie hands Charlie two menus and leaves us to it, weaving back through the busy tables while we make our way to the counter. From here I've got a great view of the kitchen and the burly man flipping various things on the grill. I assume this must be Henry, and Charlie confirms it as soon as we sit down by calling out to the man. He gives us a nod, but barely looks up from his work.

"If I had my way, we'd poach that one right there." Charlie hands me a menu. The stools here are closer than I bargained for and our arms keep bumping as we get settled. "But he'd never leave here, and they'd never forgive me if I convinced him to."

"I'm sure we can bring enough talent in." I let my eyes slide over the breakfast selection, trying to ignore Charlie's knee nearly on top of mine.

Charlie shakes his head. "I want to look local first. For everything. Local if we can get it. We're doing it with the distillery, and even if it might be tough, I'd like to do what we can to make it worthwhile for the community to have us here." His leg bounces against mine.

"If that's what you want, that's what we'll do." I don't have a ton of faith in Mint Springs as a place full of great kitchen staff, but I'm willing to try.

"See? We're a great team already." Charlie reaches over and impulsively gives my hand a squeeze. He holds it a second too long, long enough for me to consider pulling back or flexing my fingers, long enough for Debbie to notice it when she comes over to fill our coffee cups.

"I'm assuming you two need coffee." She raises an eyebrow at our hands, still touching on the countertop.

"Yes, please." I pull my hand into my lap and notice the slight hitch of Charlie's lips. Debbie gives him a wink and I go back to facing forward for the rest of breakfast.

11

Charlie

Do not look at Jenna. Do not look at Jenna. My eyes refuse to listen to the mantra I've been chanting for the last week. If Jenna's in close proximity, I'm going to be sneaking glances, and Jenna and I spend hours and hours together. Which means I'm looking at her. A lot. I'm watching her test menu items for the restaurant, her hair fastened back and her chef's coat on. I'm watching her shop for linens and flatware, testing out the way all of it feels in her hands. And I'm watching her reduce a teenager to tears in what's supposed to be an interview for staff.

"Why don't we take a break for a second?" I have to look at Jenna to ask this question. Her eyes narrow at me, more than ready to cut this conversation short and get on to making the next candidate squirm. "I'll get Brian a Coke, and you and I can have a little chat. Just take a second." I try to coax Jenna away from her spot at the center table like I would a cat out of a tree.

"Sixty seconds, Charlie. We have a lot of people to get through today." Jenna stands and gives Brian Copeland a nod. He might be fearless on the high school football field, but I swear he flinches.

"Come over here, Atilla," I whisper once we're closer to the bar. "You don't have to come into these interviews guns blazing. He's just a kid."

"A kid who wants to work at this restaurant. If he can't take the pressure of talking to me, he can't be expected to work for me." Jenna grabs a glass and fills it with water.

"He's a little nervous, that's all. He hasn't had this kind of job before. And technically, he'd be working for me. He'd be front of the house, not reporting to the kitchen." I put a scoop of ice in the glass I'm planning to bring to Brian and reach for the soda gun. "He's a good kid, and we can easily train him to bus tables. We're going to have to spend some time getting people up to speed, but it'll be worth it in the end."

"You said you wanted us to be up and running this summer, Charlie. We can't waste time with a completely green staff if you want a soft opening in the next month or two." Jenna runs an exasperated hand through her hair.

"Look, I want you to participate in these interviews, but you can't scare off everyone who dares to try to work here. You make sure your kitchen is solid, and I'll make sure the front of the house runs well. Deal?" I put out my hand but Jenna scoffs.

"You're going to hire him, aren't you?"

"Right after I give him this soda." I wink and offer her my hand again. She takes it reluctantly in the weakest handshake I've ever been subjected to.

"You'd better know what you're doing."

"Always."

"You sure you know what you're doing?" Cade's shaking his head.

"Not one hundred percent, no, but I've got a good feeling about it." I lift my glass of whiskey to my lips and take a swallow. "Cooper's getting good at this."

"You've basically hired the entire offensive line." Cade stares me down. "To work in what's supposed to be a fine dining establishment. You really think you can get those boys organized enough and serious enough? They're high schoolers."

"I think they'll rise to the occasion." I take another sip.

"Jenna's okay with all of this? That's like ten bulls in her china shop."

"She has some reservations, but I think I've convinced her." I'm not as sure about that as I pretend to be. No need to let my little brother worry for nothing. Jenna and I are getting along and progress is being made. So what if we've had a few disagreements here and there? And so what if I'm distracted by everything about her? I've got all of that under control.

"Have you decided on anything menu-wise?" Cade looks off past me, staring out at the pasture in front of Sadie and Mae's house.

"I'm still trying to keep ingredients as local as possible, and Jenna's experimenting with that. We need more of a cohesive idea, though. She's got a ton of Puerto Rican and Latin American dishes, but not all of that's going to translate well if we're working on something here that's more down home in a traditional way. She's been getting a little frustrated. She'll come up with something great, though."

"A name might help that," Cade volunteers and then hides his smirk with the rim of his rocks glass.

"Fine. It probably would, but I want it to be perfect, you

know? It might be my one and only chance to get to name a restaurant." The fear I usually tamp down rises a bit in my chest. I don't want this to be my one and only chance, but even if it is, I want it to be phenomenal.

"You working with Faith?" My brother still doesn't make eye contact.

"Yep. Hoping to have some garden plots going out here, too. Faith is going to help manage those."

Cade's head snaps up. "You didn't tell me that."

"I'm sure I did. That's been in the plan all along. An herb garden this summer for sure, but hopefully more than that if Faith can get away from Happy Trails for a bit every day." Why does Cade even care about this? "Paying Faith actually helps lower our food costs."

"Every day seems extreme." Cade takes a gulp of his whiskey.

"I'm sure she won't be here *every* day, but plants need tending." I look at my brother's stoic side profile. "I promise it won't break the bank. Why is this such a big deal all of a sudden?"

"It isn't." Cade drains his glass. "We should go in. Supper'll be ready soon." He stands so fast I'm surprised he doesn't fall over. He's marching to the door before I have a chance to say anything.

"Nice talking to you," I mumble after him. Of all of us, Cade's the one who knows the most about the business side of things. I can't fault him for trying to keep the rest of us from running through the money before we even get started. Still, I don't like him questioning my ideas—especially ones like having Faith help me out. Whatever bug's up his butt, I can't let it interfere with having my best friend do what she does best. I shake Cade's doubts off and finish my drink.

Nothing a little family dinner can't fix. I go inside to see what my great-aunts have whipped up tonight, still thinking about the things Jenna was testing in the kitchen this afternoon. That's when inspiration strikes.

"Mae? Sadie? What are y'all doing tomorrow afternoon?"

12

Charlie

"Are you sure this is a good idea? We can't necessarily compete with a chef. Not a trained one. Jenna went to cooking school, right?" Mae looks terrified.

"It's not a competition, Mae. I just wanted to see what the three of you could come up with. You and Sadie are excellent cooks. School isn't the only way to learn things. Look at Cooper." My brother was always a horrible student, but that doesn't mean he can't make fantastic liquor and run his business as well as the next guy. Now that he knows that, there's been a definite change in his life.

"Yes, but Cooper had a good reason for his school difficulties. That's not the same as putting Sadie and me in a professional kitchen." Mae wrings her hands. I'm lucky the restaurant is technically walking distance from my aunts' house. I'm hoping the exercise will take some of this nervousness out of them. The morning's still cool enough to be a little chilly; in a few months we'll all be sweating if we try to trek over here.

"A kitchen's a kitchen. You two will do fine. And once

Jenna sees what Sadie's packed in these bags... Well, let's just say I doubt she'll turn us away." I'm regretting not giving Jenna a heads-up, but I'm not lying about the bags. Once Jenna sees the fresh eggs and herbs, she's going to be very interested in having them stay. That's not even counting on the jams and pickles to tempt her. I'm hoping her manners kick in as well, but if she's already started cooking, all bets are off. Jenna can be a beast when interrupted. But she wouldn't yell at nice old ladies, would she?

Our entrance to the restaurant kitchen tells me she most certainly would. Jenna fights it like a champ, though she saves her most menacing stares for me and bites her tongue about unexpected guests.

"I had a brilliant idea last night," I announce as I shepherd Sadie and Mae toward the cavernous kitchen in the back of the restaurant. "Thought maybe you'd like some company out here, so I brought you a couple of experienced kitchen hands."

Both Sadie and Mae bristle at this, but I know I can smooth those ruffled feathers much more easily than I'll be able to contain the dragon that is Jenna in the kitchen. I know she likes to be in charge, and not just in front of the stove. Bringing my aunts with me today is a gamble. One I'm hoping lights some culinary sparks but doesn't burn the whole place down.

"Always lovely to see you, Mae and Sadie. Charlie." My name doesn't get the warm treatment she gives my aunts. "Can I speak to you for a second?" Jenna's eyes tell me she isn't excited by my appearance here this morning.

"Of course, you two get settled a bit. Why don't I get you some coffee? Or sweet tea? We've got some in the fridge." I've been mainlining the stuff since I started working with Jenna. I'm probably rotting my teeth, but it's the only sweet thing I'm allowed to put in my mouth at work. And definitely not the sweet thing I'm constantly craving.

Sadie and Mae nod, but still stand stiffly in front of the bar. They know invading someone else's kitchen isn't something you do lightly. I'm bound to get a talking-to as soon as they have me on my own. Sweat prickles my neck a bit just thinking about it. But I've got to deal with Jenna first.

Jenna leads me into the room that will eventually be our office. It's a mess right now. There's a table piled high with papers and no place to sit. I make a mental note to get this space in order this week.

"What the hell do you think you're doing?" Jenna snarls at me, fisted hands propped on her hips.

"Have you had coffee today? I can make a fresh pot. I think you might need a little caffeine." I try to make that sound inviting, but Jenna only closes her eyes.

"We're on a deadline here, Charlie. I can't spend the morning screwing around. I cannot entertain Sadie and Mae when I'm supposed to be testing recipes." Frustration rolls off her, and her dark eyes flash in a way that makes me glad we didn't try to have this conversation closer to the kitchen knives.

"I was thinking about that. I know this feels like a lot of pressure, but maybe having Mae and Sadie help in the kitchen will be beneficial. You'd have someone other than me to bounce ideas off of, and they're both phenomenal cooks. They've got recipes we could incorporate into our menu—"

"Charlie. I need to be in charge of this kitchen." Jenna's frown is the only thing I can see.

"You are in charge of this kitchen, but I have a vested interest in what comes out of it. I was thinking, your other restaurant had two really separate influences. It was either

Italian or Puerto Rican. I like both of those things, but they aren't always complimentary. The food you grew up making and the food my aunts make is influenced by some of the same things. There's a common ground there. I'd like you to explore it. That's all." I reach out to touch her, my hand landing on her upper arm. Even through her chef's coat I can feel the heat of her skin. "Indulge me. It might be fun."

Jenna's brow furrows. "Not everything is supposed to be fun, Charlie. Some things are just work."

"Not cooking. Not for you." I let my eyes stay locked with hers, hoping she'll see that this is supposed to help, not hinder her progress. "If you hate it, I'll take them home."

"Fine." Jenna tilts her head up toward the ceiling and lets out a long, tortured breath. "But you'd better not be setting me up to become the most hated woman in Mint Springs. You know I can snap a bit when I'm cooking."

I feign disbelief. "What? You? I'm sure we won't have a problem." I give her arm a squeeze even though I know I probably shouldn't. "I'll get the coffee going." Then I hustle out of there before she has a chance to change her mind.

13

Jenna

"Not so heavy handed."

"More like this?" I try to mimic Sadie's hand motions.

"Better. Definitely better." Sadie gives me one of her sage little nods. "You'll be making better biscuits than us in no time."

I scoff. "I doubt that."

"Be gentle and they'll come out tender. Once you get a feel for it, you'll know if the dough's right." She takes a sip of her tea. "I do like the mint in this, Charlie."

Charlie barely raises his head from his laptop screen.

"I've never really been great with breads. I can make empanadas, but I get impatient making the dough. I delegate that to my pastry chef." I give the dough another turn on the floured surface of the board. "What do you think?"

"I think we still need to hire a pastry chef," Charlie calls out from the bar. "We need someone to make wedding cakes eventually. It's on the list."

"I was talking about this." I gesture down to where my flour-covered hands still rest on top of a mound of white biscuit dough. "But you're right. That'll be hard to find around here maybe."

"I think you're ready to roll it out." Mae gives me a pat on the back and hands me the rolling pin. "And you might be surprised. Patty's got a few girls who've been working with her for a while now. They won't have much formal training, but Patty teaches them everything she knows."

"Patty?" All morning I've been playing catch-up with the local residents of Mint Springs. I know no one, and Sadie and Mae know absolutely everyone and what they ate for breakfast.

"She owns a bakery—Patty Cakes—I'll take you over there later. We'll see if you think it's as good as everyone around here does." Charlie doesn't look up enough for me to decide if he's being serious or sarcastic.

"It's not just locals who think Patty makes excellent pastry, Charlie." Sadie gives him an eye roll he doesn't see. "And I know four little boys who used to love pressing their noses up against the glass case at Patty's to see what she'd made that day."

Charlie smiles. "I guess that's true. Jenna, you want to try any of the things you made at Ana's? What's the etiquette there?" His face is serious over the edge of his computer.

"They're still open, so I probably need to be careful. But I wouldn't be using any of Frank's family recipes, and I would hope he'd be reasonable and let me still use some of mine." I hadn't thought that through when we were making plans for Ana's, and I'd been blindsided enough by Frank's betrayal I hadn't been specific in the divorce decree.

"Frank?" Mae asks. I guess I'm pretty good at introducing characters no one knows anything about, too.

"My business partner. Ex-partner. And ex-husband. He owns Ana's now."

This has everyone's full attention.

"Your ex-husband took the restaurant you named after your grandmother?" Sadie's face is only less shocked than Mae's. "I've never heard of anything so horrible." Her hand comes dramatically to her chest.

"He was the majority stakeholder, and I couldn't figure out a way to buy him out." I shrug and keep rolling out the biscuit dough.

"We don't need his tiramisu, anyway." Charlie's voice is hard. "We've got plenty of our own ideas right here. But you're doing a version of your rice pudding. He'd have to challenge me to a duel over that."

I smile a bit in spite of myself. "Frank's hardly the kind to duel."

"Then we shouldn't have a problem. Not that I'd mind fighting for the honor of your rice pudding." He gives me another little nod before he lowers his eyes back to whatever spreadsheet he's working on.

I get the slightest little rush. I don't mind firm Charlie one bit.

"Not so much pressure!" Mae nearly yanks the rolling pin from my hands. "Good Lord. Don't put that aggression in the biscuits."

Little does she know. That wasn't so much aggression as lust.

"Y'all are going to have to roll me out of here." Mae pats her stomach.

"We can do that exercise walking back to our house," Sadie suggests, pumping her arms wildly. They both burst into laughter.

Charlie looks at me across the table. We've worked our way through another box of Faith's produce, and I managed to not want to strangle every single cute vegetable we pulled out of it. I think he's really on to something with the food fusion here. At the very least, I've had a more relaxing time in the kitchen than I've had in years, probably. And I've learned how to make cornbread and buttermilk biscuits using the family recipes. That has to be worth something.

"Where's my invitation to this party?" Cooper comes into the dining room with more than a little swagger, kissing both Sadie and Mae on the cheek in turn. "Y'all made lunch and didn't think to tell anybody else?"

"We're testing menu items," Sadie offers.

"And teaching Jenna how to cook Southern." Mae winks at me. "She's a quick study."

"Well, I was just coming over here to see if y'all might be available to cater a wedding in two weeks." Cooper shoves his hands in his front pockets. A giant grin takes over his entire face.

I nearly spit my tea out all over the table. I'm not about to start drinking the pre-sweetened kind, but I'm easing in. "Two weeks?" I look at Charlie. Surely he's going to set his brother straight. There's no way we can be *any* part of a wedding in two weeks.

"Hadley doesn't want to look like a beach ball when she walks down the aisle—those are her words not mine, by the way. I think she looks beautiful no matter what." The look on his face almost has me chucking my cynicism aside and believing him.

"We can't be ready to do anything in two weeks." I look to Charlie to back me up. "We've got no staff, no menu— they're still putting all the fixtures in the bathrooms."

Charlie wipes his face with his napkin and then puts it

back in his lap. "I don't know... I think we could pull something together."

My mouth hangs open as his brother slaps him on the back. "I told Hadley we could make it happen. I'll go tell her to fast track the rest of it." He basically runs for the door. "And don't worry, Jenna. We'll probably have it up at the distillery anyway, so the bathroom issue won't be a problem." He gives us all a little salute and lets himself out.

"Charlie." I'm trying to keep the irritation out of my voice. "You know there's no way we can do justice to a wedding in two weeks."

"Sure we can. We just need a basic menu for one event. Dinner for fifty or so." He says it like I can pull all of that out of my ass at a moment's notice.

I gape at him, wishing his family wasn't still here so I could literally slap some sense into him. "Charlie, that's no easy feat."

"We can use some Allen family recipes and tweak them. Take some of yours and do the same. Come on, it's a challenge, but I know we can pull it off. It's a family wedding, Jenna, not the coronation."

What Charlie fails to recognize here is that I'd give equal weight to both those occasions. I would never think I could just phone it in. And this will be the first taste most of these people are getting of my food—of me. I need things to be flawless. Even if Hadley was a beach ball in a white muumuu, I'd be working my ass off to give her perfection.

I rub my temples. "It isn't as easy as you're making it sound, Charlie."

"Well, I think it isn't as complicated as you're making it out to be."

Out of the corner of my eye I see Sadie and Mae quietly packing up their things and trying to make their getaway.

"We'll leave you two to it," Sadie whispers, and they're out the door almost as fast as Cooper.

"Charlie." My voice wavers. "You can't rush something like this. We don't even have a name. If it's terrible it'll set us back, and we're not even open yet."

"Then we'll have to make sure it isn't terrible. They want to get married here. They want to do it in two weeks. What are we going to do, Jenna? Hire someone else to cater it? Tell them we can't?" Charlie's not kidding around with the guilt.

"Should we set them up for disappointment?" I pose it as a question, but Charlie takes it as more of a challenge.

"I don't plan on doing that. Do you?"

We stare each other down. I break eye contact first, not able to keep looking at Charlie's determined face.

"Let's get to work then."

I have never hated looking at his backside more as he walks back to the dishwashing station with a handful of dirty lunch plates. I still sneak a peek, though. I've got to take my perks where I can get them.

14

Charlie

"And then you set it down, like this." I slide the plate in front of an imaginary guest and wait for some kind of acknowledgement. Instead I get eight blank stares. "Do you guys have questions?"

Every face looks like it should have at least one question. I'm worried, though, that some of those questions might involve what day of the week it is or if I think underwear is optional. The first day of training for my bussers and food runners isn't going as well as I'd hoped. Finally, one hand tentatively raises over their stupefied heads.

"Mr. Allen?" The voice sounds strangely timid coming out of the giant body of one of Mint Springs High School's largest defensive ends.

"Charlie. You can call me Charlie." Jenna is going to kill me for letting this group of kids call me by my first name at work, but Mr. Allen is my jerk of a father. No way am I going to let people insult me like that all day. Besides, I want the staff to be friendly, which to me means surnames are out.

"Charlie," he starts again and clears his throat. "Can we

talk more about why you can't just stack the plates all at once? I'm sure I can carry ten or twelve plates at least and then I've only got to make one trip."

The rest of the heads nod in agreement with the exception of the one lone female in the room. Annabel Miller really shouldn't have to be subjected to all this. I can feel her IQ lowering with every passing second.

"He told us, Jonah. He's told us like fifteen times." Annabel lets out the kind of exasperated breath only a sixteen-year-old girl is capable of. "It isn't great for the plates, and it makes it more likely you'll drop something, possibly *on* someone. And customers—guests, sorry, Mr. Allen—guests don't like the way it looks. All the food piled up like that is gross." She wrinkles her freckled nose.

"But we aren't supposed to leave one person eating alone, so how do we..." Jonah shrugs.

"Some of that you can leave to the servers. You're picking up little things as people finish. We don't want guests to sit for a long time looking at an empty plate, either. It's like a dance; you'll get the hang of it." I look at the adolescent faces in front of me, pretty sure ninety percent of them have two left feet. I try again. "It's like football. You practice. That's what we're doing now. Training camp." I probably should have tried to get more kids from the debate team than the football team, but too late now.

I notice Jenna coming from the back of the restaurant, my great-aunts close behind her. I can't tell if they're having a great time back there in the kitchen or if all hell's about to break loose. Either way, I need to be prepared to deal with it.

"Why don't we take a break for a few minutes? Y'all can go outside and stretch your legs." I try to make leaving the restaurant sound as appealing as possible. There's nothing much to do out here but mill around, and more than once

I've caught the boys rough housing during the five or so minutes I've left them alone. Now I'm not sure if I'm going to need to break up a fight outside or inside.

Jenna goes straight to the coffee, turning her head from side to side like she's trying to twist it off. I come up behind her and clear my throat. "How's it going?"

Jenna barely glances at me. "I had no idea people could be so militant about pimento cheese."

I laugh, but Jenna isn't cracking a smile. "Do you want me to tell them this isn't helping?" Sadie and Mae might get upset about that, but technically I've hired Jenna to run the kitchen.

"I didn't say it wasn't helping." Jenna takes a swallow of coffee. "They're helping me get a better handle on a possible concept. There's a lot riding on this event. I know you keep saying it'll be only family—and I'm not sure I believe you— but even if it was just your brothers I'd want to impress them. And it's their *wedding*, Charlie. I want it to be perfect."

I smile in spite of myself. Determined Jenna is hard for me to resist. The way her face gets so serious and her cheeks flush the tiniest bit... I silently count to ten so I don't blurt all that out.

"We're headed back to the house," Mae calls out once she and Sadie are within shouting distance. "We can come back later, if you need us."

Jenna waves her away. "No need. I'm interviewing for kitchen positions this afternoon. Why don't you two take the afternoon off? I know you'd probably like a break from putting me through my paces." I'm relieved that Jenna's teasing is obvious. She must be getting along better than I'd hoped with Sadie and Mae.

Mae shakes her head. "I think it's you who's been the taskmaster today. After watching you whip that meringue!

Whew!" She pretends to wipe sweat from her brow. "We'll stay out of your hair but we'll be back bright and early tomorrow morning unless you tell us otherwise."

Before they walk out the door I get an arm pat from Sadie. "Can you bring that pie in the fridge over to our house for supper?" She leans in closer to whisper in my ear, "That one's a keeper." She shoots a look at Jenna, still preoccupied with her coffee, and then gives me a wink.

"Yes, ma'am." I give myself permission to enjoy the two seconds of pride I feel about how well things are going. Jenna's fitting in with my family, and we've got an event on the horizon. Most importantly, I've not only been able to keep my hands to myself but I have managed to keep my carnal knowledge of Jenna a secret.

Jenna sits at the bar, her right hand coming up to rub her neck. She lets out a little groan.

"Is your neck bothering you?"

"It's stiff, that's all. Those hotel pillows aren't firm enough." Jenna winces.

"You really should look for a place of your own. You can't stay in that hotel forever." Jenna ignores that suggestion. "Here, let me..." My hands are on her before I can think things through. Her skin is warm under my palms and silky when my fingers slide over it. I use one hand to move her dark ponytail to one side, and the other to tentatively explore. There's an obvious knot and I try to work it out, kneading my knuckles against the back of Jenna's neck.

She groans and lets her head fall forward. The sound goes straight to my groin.

"Yeah, like that." Jenna's voice is husky and low. She leans into my touch and I press forward, wanting my body to touch as much of hers as possible.

"Mr. Allen? Charlie?" Annabel's voice has me pulling

away from Jenna, removing my hands from her body so fast she's probably got whiplash now instead of just a sore neck. "Should we come back in now? Brian and Jonah are getting pretty rowdy." She seems to know she's interrupting but she's not sure exactly what's going on.

"Sure. Tell the boys to come on back in and we'll finish up for the day." I give Jenna's neck one last lingering squeeze, but I don't say anything to her.

"You training servers this afternoon?" Jenna's question gets asked in that same low voice, and it feels like we're still in that hotel room bubble from before only now she's not so much of a stranger. She's still a mystery, but one whose contours I can easily see.

"Yeah. We'll see what we get." I keep my voice low too, using that as an excuse to stand a little too close. But the spell is broken by the herd of buffalo I've hired tumbling through the front door. At least one boy's got a new rip in his shirt, and they've all got grass-stained knees. So much for staying under control. Jenna shakes her head, and I give her a shrug before moving to corral the high schoolers.

But I make a mental note to go into town tonight. My chef needs new pillows.

15

Jenna

"And that's Bootlegger. It's technically the only bar in town so you can see why people have been excited about the distillery."

I follow Lily's pointing finger and see the gravel parking lot and squat brown building in the distance. It's the kind of place I can already tell isn't meant for anything fancy. It's a hole in the wall kind of place, but maybe that's the kind of thing people around here go for. I'm not exactly sure how many of Mint Springs' citizens will be coming to Charlie's still nameless restaurant with any frequency. We drive along with Lily narrating the entire time until we get to town—or at least what can be considered "town." I'm not sure any of my Boston friends would agree.

"And over there's Southern Comforts. Do you mind if I stop in real quick to see if we're low on paint? It'll only take a minute." Lily's already parking the car before I can protest. She's been driving me around all afternoon, showing me the sights. So far, I've seen the high school, the hair salon Hadley's family owns, and every single spring flower. Either

Lily really loves flowers or there isn't much else to see around here. Now it seems I'm going to be treated to a tour of Lily's family's shop. I'm still unclear on what exactly they sell there, but I haven't exactly been out of the kitchen long enough to find out much of anything about anyone but Sadie and Mae.

And Charlie.

I keep trying not to find out anything more about Charlie because every new thing I discover makes it harder and harder to keep my distance. He's sweet to his elderly aunts; he's patient with the exceptionally amateur staff we've hired. He's fine to let me be the boss and takes orders like a champ. That's the main reason I finally agreed to Lily's tour. As much as I need to be in the kitchen working on the wedding menu, I need a break from my constant kitchen companion and his helpful, eager presence. Not to mention his handsome face and his shirtsleeves he seems to always need to roll up his forearms.

The inside of Southern Comforts surprises me a little. Lily and Hadley kept calling it a "junk shop" when they were explaining Lily's family's business, but there's nothing junky about this place. It's a cavernous warehouse, but it looks a lot like the kind of quaint shops I see on those antiquing shows I mindlessly scroll through on my hotel TV. Those things are always on at two a.m., and I'm grateful for them. They keep me from thinking too much about how lonely that bed is and how nicely Charlie would fit in it for a couple of hours.

"This is it," Lily announces. "Make yourself at home. I'll only be a minute. This is my grandma. Bunny, this is the new chef at the restaurant I was telling you about." She leaves me by the front counter with a wizened old woman who immediately gets to work looking me up and down.

"Hmmm. Prettier than I thought you'd be." She doesn't get up from the stool she's sitting on and doesn't make a move to offer me one. She's got a stack of those grocery store tabloids in front of her, several of them already dog-eared.

"Thank you?" I'm not sure her comment was a compliment.

"Should have expected that maybe. Can't imagine Charlie hiring someone he didn't like looking at, especially if you have to do it all day." She cocks her gray head to the side. "Can't imagine you're complaining about the view either."

Jesus. I crane my head, hoping to catch a glimpse of Lily's bouncy walk headed this way to save me. No dice.

"He's..." I stumble. *A good boss? Easy to work with?* What am I supposed to tell this woman? "Very nice."

"I bet." She smirks. "What kind of food you cookin'? Please tell me it ain't all fancy. Don't get me wrong, fancy can be nice, but not if you overdo it."

I cannot even begin to imagine what this woman classifies as "fancy," but I can talk about food all day. So that's what I do, explaining how Sadie and Mae are helping me to better understand local flavors and ingredients, and I'm trying to blend that with the things I grew up eating. I expect Lily's grandmother to cut me off. Most people do not want to hear a twenty-minute soliloquy about how close the influences are in Southern cooking and Puerto Rican cuisine, but she keeps bobbing her head and making encouraging noises, so I keep right on talking until we're interrupted by Lily and a woman who looks so much like her I nearly do a double take.

"Is this your..."

"Mama? Yes." Lily smiles at the woman next to her. "Mama, this is Jenna."

I stick out my hand like I'm there for a job interview. "Very nice to meet you..."

"June. June Gentry. And so nice to meet you." The older version of Lily looks at the younger one. "Is she coming tonight?"

"Tonight?" Please tell me this tour doesn't last until dinner.

"We're having Hadley's bachelorette party tonight, although I'm not sure how much of a party it'll be. She can hardly go for an hour without puking her guts out. A pregnant bride complicates a good time, bless her heart." Lily gives a little head shake. "You're welcome to come, of course."

I'm about to give them all my most heartfelt excuse. I have plenty of reasons not to insert myself into Allen family events. I'm already spending my days with Mae and Sadie, and I've only got a while longer to tweak the recipes we've chosen for the wedding. I should be getting a good night's sleep so I can be up to be in the kitchen bright and early. Add to that the meeting I have with the possible pastry chef Charlie's lined up and I don't even need to invent any fanciful stories. My schedule is legitimately packed. But then I think about another night in front of the TV in my lonely hotel room.

"I'd love to come, if you don't think Hadley will mind."

"Are you kidding? Hadley will be thrilled. She's all about the more the merrier when it comes to things like this." Lily's smile is a mile wide. "We're starting at the distillery at seven."

"We'll need a few drinks to make this any fun at all," Lily's grandmother says as she thumbs through one of her magazines.

"You're coming?" The surprise in my voice has her cackling.

"Afraid you can't keep up?"

I actually am.

~

It turns out not only are Lily's mother and grandmother coming to this shindig, but so are Hadley's. I'm marveling at how young all these ladies look and having a hard time not asking them to give me all their secrets. We're sipping on cocktails specially made with Stolen Barn spirits—along with signature mocktails for the bride-to-be—when Sadie and Mae come strolling in. This really is not at all the kind of party I was expecting.

I'm about to ask Lily if we should be giving all these ladies such extremely strong drinks when Charlie comes sauntering in. I haven't seen him all day and the way his hungry eyes rake over me lets me know he missed me. I try not to make my interest in him so obvious, but when I turn on my bar stool, Hadley's staring at me. One of her perfectly manicured eyebrows shoots up, but she doesn't say anything. I guess I'm not as discreet as I'd imagined.

"Are you trying to crash this party?" I ask, already a little bold from the drink I've inhaled. My hands itch to smooth themselves down the front of Charlie's freshly pressed shirt. He still looks like a country boy to me, but one who has the style to look presentable off the farm too. I take another giant gulp of my cocktail, letting the gin keep me from talking.

"Crash it?" Charlie nods to the other ladies. "I think you all know I *make* this a party." Several women cluck in response to this.

"No roosters at this hen party," Lily's grandmother complains. "Some of us have had just about all the cocks we can stand."

"Bunny!" Lily looks mortified. "Jenna hasn't known us long enough for you to be yourself around her like that." She gives me an apologetic look, but I couldn't be more amused. These older ladies seem like my kind of people.

"Don't worry, Miss Maggie, I'll try to keep my distance, but that might be hard now that we've combined these parties."

Lily's grandmother scowls, and I learn two very important things: her first name isn't actually Bunny, and I've made a big mistake. A night out with a few local ladies is one thing, an evening trying not to look lustfully at Charlie is another. But it's too late now. As the rest of the brothers tumble in, along with a few new faces, it's impossible to make a reasonable excuse to leave. And when Faith breezes in after I've downed my third Hanky Panky there's no way I'm leaving.

She slides up to Charlie and hugs him with her entire body. His hand lingers on the small of her back as he leans over the bar to order her a drink. She gets more hugs of welcome from Charlie's family, and I'm annoyed to find myself wishing I was the one on the receiving end of all that happy attention.

"Well, if looks could kill I know one little girl who'd be going up in a puff of smoke right now." Lily's grandmother sidles up next to me at the bar, pushing her walker to the side as she tries to climb onto one of the high bar stools. I help her up and she gives me a sly little grin. "You should probably have another. Looks like this party's going to be more entertaining than I thought."

I flag down the bartender and get us set up with another

round, determined to prove Maggie Gentry wrong. She might be a little old lady with plenty of life experience, but she doesn't know the first thing about me. I can keep my emotions in check, especially ridiculous ones like the ones I'm feeling now.

I'm always cool, calm, and collected. She'll see.

16

Charlie

True to form, it doesn't take long for the party to get out of hand. As a family we have a reputation for taking things a bit too far sometimes, especially if we're celebrating. And tonight we're all celebrating. Since we don't have our kitchen up and running, we order pizza and spread the boxes out on the bar top. Jenna keeps a sour look on her face, probably offended by the cheap delivery option we're serving. It isn't the best pizza I've ever eaten, but it's hot and fresh and comes from right down the street. Everyone else grabs slices and digs in without complaint.

Jenna isn't much happier when we move the party to Bootlegger, where everyone in town slaps Cooper on the back and buys him drinks. Hadley's really missing out on this opportunity, although she looks green enough without adding alcohol. Lily keeps her stocked in water with lots of ice and makes sure there's a straight path to the ladies' room. Hadley's all-day morning sickness is no joke at this point, and that tiara the girls made her wear isn't helping at all. We lost most of the older members of our party early on and I'm thankful for that when a fist fight breaks out in the back of the bar and we all have to pour out into the parking lot to avoid being swept up in it. Cade goes back inside to pay our tab, but we all agree we should take what's left of the group back to the farm.

"Back home?" Cooper slurs as we load him into the passenger side of Chance's truck. "But it's early."

"It's late enough," I tell him before I shut the door. He immediately rolls down the window, pouting. "If you make it all the way home without passing out, we can keep things going." This cheers Cooper up considerably, even though we all know he won't be able to last the whole ride.

A reluctant Jenna comes up next to me as we divide up into the remaining vehicles. "Can you give me a ride back to the distillery?" Somehow this doesn't sound as much like a request as an order.

"Sure, come on." I motion for her to follow me, and the gravel crunches under her feet as she trudges along behind. I think if I had to gauge Jenna's overall mood tonight, it would be one small step above a trip to the principal's office. Ever since I walked into the distillery, her face has looked like she would rather be anywhere other than hanging out with all of us.

"Can I go with you?" Faith calls out as she runs up behind us. She's got that tiny bit of flush to her cheeks that tells me I shouldn't let her figure out her own way home, even if it means I won't get any time alone with Jenna.

"Of course." I slow down enough to end up with a girl on either side. Faith bumps up against me playfully, occasionally jamming her fingers into my ribs. When I move to escape her roving fingers, I jostle Jenna. After the third time Jenna lets out an angry huff and tries to move farther away from us.

"Maybe I should try to go with someone else." Jenna scans the parking lot, but we're the only ones left, all the other trucks' taillights already fading in the distance.

"Hey, wait up!" Cade jogging up behind us at least breaks the tension a little. "Were y'all really going to just leave me here? After I settled up for everyone?" His shocked face is illuminated by the street lights Bootlegger has had to put out here after one too many drunken brawls was stopped inside only to continue out between the parked cars. He looks from me to Jenna. "What's wrong?"

"Nothing," we both answer in unison, and although normally I might find that funny, neither of us even cracks a smile.

"Seems like it." Cade shakes his head.

"Sorry. I didn't realize you hadn't come back out yet." At least I can turn my attention to my brother instead of the fire-breathing dragon that is Jenna. If she didn't want to come tonight, she could have stayed home. No one forced her to stare daggers at me all night, and no one's making her stand here right now with that glare on her face. "Let's just get home."

Cade wanders off in front and Faith falls into step beside him. That leaves me and angry Jenna facing each other down. Her chest rises and falls in the most dramatic and distracting way. Eventually she breaks eye contact and stomps off. I'm not sure what's got her in such a mood, but I'm sure this car ride is about to be a treat.

Jenna ends up in the front seat, after Cade and Faith circus clown their way into the back. Jenna's mouth makes its way into a surprised "o" as they fumble around. Faith's coordination is never great, and after a few drinks she's basically the equivalent of one of those inflatable dancing guys you see in front of used car lots. Cade lets Faith's head rest against his shoulder, and I smile a little in spite of myself when I see his uncomfortable face in the rearview mirror.

Jenna folds her arms over her chest and grunts at me. I look over at her and scowl. This ride cannot be over soon enough. Faith is snoring softly in the backseat, snuggling up against Cade's ramrod straight body while Jenna and I are in some kind of ridiculous standoff in the front. She's been fine —well, occasionally grumpy, but fine—in the kitchen. I'm sure something I've done has annoyed her, though, and it's making for a long and uncomfortable silence as we drive down the back roads to the farm.

Mercifully we pull up the distillery and find no one else there. I'm guessing they've all scattered to their various houses—we're all living here on the farm now—and the promise of additional partying has long been forgotten. We're not exactly kids anymore, anyway.

"I'll drive Faith home," Cade volunteers, already moving her sleeping head gingerly off his shoulder.

"I'd appreciate that." I think we all agree Faith shouldn't be driving, but unless she stays here with one of us, she's going to need a driver. There isn't Uber out here so one of us is going to have to do it. Normally I'd offer to just put her in my guest room, but tonight I need to clear the air with Jenna, and I've got the feeling it won't keep until morning.

"You're going to let your brother take your girlfriend home?" Jenna sounds more than a little drunk. "That's not the kind of manners I would have expected from you, Country."

Cade gives me a questioning look but keeps his mouth shut.

We manage to get Faith to Cade's car. She's groggy and still half asleep. It takes a lot to wake Faith; even when we were kids she could sleep through just about anything. And since she's been working those early morning farm hours, I'm sure she's exhausted. She perks up enough to reach out to stroke my cheek and then do the same to Cade's while mumbling something that hilariously sounds like "so handsome." I'll be sure to tease her about that when she's sobered up and wide awake. Once they're safely down the gravel road a bit, I turn to Jenna, still standing next to me, ready to get to the bottom of whatever has her acting this way.

"Jenna, I—" But that's all I manage to get out before Jenna's mouth comes crashing onto mine.

17

Jenna

At first, I think I've dreamed it. It's that kind of kiss—the kind you would dream about—and so when I wake up in a strange bed with the morning sun coming through a pair of unfamiliar curtains, I convince myself for the briefest second that it wasn't real. It can't have been, because I would never have acted like a petulant child during someone else's celebration, would never have used that ridiculous nickname in front of his brother, and absolutely would not have latched myself onto Charlie's mouth in the distillery parking lot. Not after working so hard to not mess up our working relationship. Not after reminding myself day in and day out that Charlie is off-limits.

But if I'm not in my hotel room, then I've done *something*, and the kiss is probably the least of it.

I remember standing in the parking lot, cursing the gravel under my stilettos, thinking I would give anything to get out of middle-of-nowhere Georgia and away from Charlie's handsome face. Despite what he'd told me about Faith, the way they stood just a little too close and the way she'd lean in, letting her mouth come just shy of grazing his ear, told another story.

Friends, my ass.

But none of that was supposed to be my concern. Charlie's the boy I picked up in the hotel bar, not a man I've set my sights on. He's a one-night stand. Forgettable. Or at least, he's supposed to be.

But somehow he's been worming his way under my skin. And seeing him with perky, sweet Faith had me all tied in knots for some reason.

Well, that and the gin.

But that kiss...

He'd been surprised when I'd grabbed the front of his shirt and tugged him toward me, even more shocked when I'd put my mouth on his. There had been that split-second of resistance before he'd given in, and then we were frantic. I was untucking his shirt and sliding my hands underneath, desperate to touch him. Charlie'd pressed me up against the side of his car, his hands roaming as well. I was dead set on devouring him, and the fact that we were out in the parking lot wasn't going to stop me. In the harsh light of day I might not have been so reckless, but under cover of darkness with the gin coursing through me, I couldn't remember the reasons this was a bad idea.

Until the beam of a flashlight illuminated both of us.

Harlan, the night security guard, had let out a little grunt of surprise before flicking the light away from us and the way we were pawing each other.

"Sorry, Mr. Allen. I didn't know that was you. Thought you all had left for the night." He had cleared his throat and added, "Evening, Chef Bard."

So much for keeping things professional. And private. I doubted Harlan would go around gossiping, but being so impulsive and careless had put us in a situation we would now possibly have to explain away. *I'd* put us in this position.

"No worries." Charlie had extricated himself from the tangle of our arms and legs. "We were just... We were just about to leave."

That's not at all what we were just about to do, but I didn't contradict Charlie, and I didn't stop him when he put me in his car and started to drive me away from mine and deeper into the middle of the farm. I'm sure that gave Harlan something extra to think about.

"Where are we going?" This was not the way back to my hotel. Not even close.

"To my house." Charlie hadn't taken his eyes off the road.

"Oh." That was all the brilliance that I could muster from my addled brain. *Were we going to his house to finish what we started? Was he thinking—*

"You can't drive home, and we should probably talk." He cut his eyes over toward me. "I'll make a pot of coffee."

It was hard to argue with that, especially since I could already feel my eyelids drooping. It was late, and I'd been overserved for sure. And I'd stepped over a pretty bright line, one Charlie seemed more than amenable to a few minutes ago, but without lust fogging his brain, he might be having different thoughts.

I knew all the Allens had built houses out on the property, but other than the quick farm tour I'd gotten my first day, I hadn't really even seen any place but Mae and Sadie's. Their house was older and most certainly lived in. It had been built next door to what was now Chance and Lily's house but had originally belonged to Charlie's grandfather. Those two houses lived large in all the stories of Charlie and his brothers spending summers on the farm—quaint little farmhouses with good porches for sitting. I was sure Charlie's place would be similar. Newer, obviously, but simple. But as we came over a little ridge and the house came into view, I'm pretty sure I gasped.

"Like it? I helped with the design." Charlie's voice was full of pride and as he pulled his car up to the front, I could tell I was going to like the inside as much as the outside. That's the way things were turning out to be with Charlie whether I liked it or not.

The porch light was on, and once we were through the front door, Charlie pointed me toward the living room. "I'll give you a tour later, but for now go and get comfortable and I'll get the coffee going."

Despite the gin, I was still good at following directions and wasted no time making myself at home on the most comfortable sofa ever—although I ended up horizontal pretty quickly. No harm in losing my shoes, right? Or in covering myself with the extremely soft blanket I found folded on the opposite end. It smelled faintly of Charlie, that spicy pine that tickled my nose whenever he and I bumped in the kitchen. The kind of smell that has you closing your eyes for a moment and opening them again to a brand new morning in a strange bed.

The kind of smell that I might not get to experience ever again if the look on Charlie's face is any indication.

"Hey, sleepyhead." He's leaning in the door frame, sweats and a T-shirt replacing the outfit from last night. "You ready for that coffee and conversation now?"

I gulp and try to tame my bedhead with my fingers. I'm pretty sure I don't have a choice.

18

Charlie

Keeping my hands off Jenna last night was one of the hardest things I've ever had to do. And I wasn't even that good at it, really. If Harlan hadn't interrupted us, I would have fucked her right there on the hood of my car. I wouldn't have even hesitated, which tells you everything you need to know about how hard it's been to work with Jenna these last few weeks. Pun intended. She's been walking around in that chef's jacket, and I've been having dirty fantasies about her bossing me around in more than just the kitchen.

Ahem.

That's new for me, and I'm not sure how to feel about it. A one-off in some hotel room? Sure. I'm down for that. But her in charge every night after work? I'm starting to think I'd be down for that too. Which means I'm fucked and not the way I want to be, obviously. I've got Jenna ordering me around all day and a future of freezing cold showers every night after work as long as she's forbidden fruit.

When she'd grabbed me last night, I should have

resisted. That much I know. We had agreed, and she was a little drunk. That's a hard no from me. Until her lips met mine, unfortunately, and then I forgot about all the good guy stuff I've been trying so damn hard to live up to. Taking her back to my house was a big risk, and even though I've put some space between us while I make a show of brewing coffee, the only place I want to be right now is in the living room touching Jenna.

Finding her asleep on the couch gives me another opportunity to clear my head. I sit in the chair opposite her and watch her sleep for a bit. At least when she sleeps, Jenna's relatively still—not the whirlwind she is in the kitchen or the force of nature she is in my brain twenty-four seven. She's turned over on her side, her hair spilling off the couch and nearly to the floor. She's soft like this, and I almost don't want to break the spell, but Jenna will hate waking up on this couch, whether it's the middle of the night or first thing tomorrow morning. I take my time, sipping my coffee, fighting the part of me that still wants to slide under that blanket and wake Jenna with my mouth. That is definitely something I should keep as pure fantasy. No matter how much I want her, no matter how desperate I am for another night with her, we can't risk it. And so I sit like that until it's far too late to take Jenna back to her hotel. I lift her off the couch and take her to my guest room. Jenna protests a little, but ends up with her head leaning against my shoulder. Even that innocent contact has me shaking a bit. I ease her onto the bed in her clothes; there's no way I even think about removing any of her clothing. Hopefully she'll be comfortable enough to sleep through the night.

I make one more trip to get Jenna a glass of water and some Ibuprofen. I leave those on the bedside table and close the door behind me. Then I go back to my own room and stare at the ceiling—I'll never be able to sleep tonight knowing Jenna's two doors down. As soon as the sun starts to peek over the top of the mountain, I'm back out of bed and pacing the kitchen, waiting for any sound from Jenna's bedroom. The second I hear her moving around, I'm at the bedroom door in a flash, a hot cup of coffee in my hand.

God, she's beautiful. Even after a night sleeping in her clothes after a bit too much to drink, she's still got that thing that pulls me in, makes me wish we were waking up together, not about to have a conversation about how that can never happen.

"Ugh." Jenna turns onto her back and throws an arm over her eyes, rolls her neck around. That crick's still there, I'm sure, only today I don't dare volunteer to try to help her work it out. I'm not touching Jenna today. I can't, because once I start I know I won't be able to stop.

"Hey, sleepyhead. You ready for that coffee and conversation now?" I try to sound friendly, even though my entire body is fighting against it. My hands want nothing more than to lose this mug and make better use of this morning. I think of all the things we could be doing instead of talking and have to move away before I do something stupid. "I'll leave the coffee for you." I put it on the dresser by the door and flee down the hall back to the kitchen. I take my time stirring sugar into my own coffee, going through all the things I need to say and all the ones I'm absolutely not allowed to even dream of uttering. *I want you. You're driving me crazy. Just one more time.*

Jenna appears in the kitchen, still mussed up and a little groggy. She blinks in the sunlight. "I think I overdid it," she confesses before taking a big gulp of her coffee.

"Maybe just a little bit."

"About last night, I..." Jenna shakes her head. "I don't

know what got into me. I should maybe apologize to Faith. Did I say anything awful to her?"

"To Faith? I don't think so." I barely noticed the two of them together, and Jenna had been pretty quiet. Sullen, even. But she hadn't been expecting me to show up and, apparently, no one had mentioned Faith. "Why would you think that?"

Jenna seems to weigh her options, her teeth biting into her plump bottom lip in a way that has me averting my gaze. "She just brings out a little bit of competitiveness in me, I think."

I consider this for a second. Jenna and Faith are polar opposites, and there's not a ton of overlap there. Where Faith's sunshine and rainbows, Jenna's a thunderstorm in the best possible way. "Why?"

Again Jenna uses her coffee to cover her face. Takes her time sipping. "Don't make me say it."

"Say what?"

"I know you said you two are just friends, but I get a little jealous when I see you two together. It's stupid." She rolls her eyes.

It's far from stupid. It's brilliant. I swear my chest puffs up enough for people in the next county to notice. Jenna Bard gets jealous. *Jealous when she sees me with someone else.*

"I don't like to lose." Jenna lifts a shoulder, like that tells me everything I need to know.

"And me spending time with Faith means you lost, somehow?" I furrow my brow and wait for Jenna to say something to make this less confusing.

"Let's just forget about it, okay? Let's forget about the whole night—my bitchiness, the kissing, me passing out on your couch. Can we just pretend none of that happened and go back to the way it was before?"

"You want to forget the kissing?" I'm pushing, and I know it. I also know it's dangerous. We both understand we have to forget about the kissing and that it can never happen again. I should be agreeing with her and participating in some super-secret handshake, not trying to get Jenna to explain why she kissed me in the first place.

"Look, Charlie, obviously I like you. And our night was fun." Jenna's eyes meet mine but only for a second. "But trust me when I tell you we cannot let it happen again. I've been at this for longer than you and kitchens can be really volatile places. There's a lot of emotion there and a lot of late nights. That tends to cloud people's judgment. We've already agreed the success of this restaurant is the most important thing. For both of us. We can't let a little attraction get the better of us."

My back stiffens. Jenna may have more experience than I do when it comes to running a restaurant, but I'm no baby. I've worked in enough places to be confident in the fact that, for me, this is more than just a chance to blow off steam. "Is that what this is for you? Just an attraction?"

"Of course," Jenna says, even going so far as to give me a dismissive wave. "What else could it be? You're what? Thirty, maybe?"

"So? What's that got to do with anything?" I snap.

"You've just got things to learn still, that's all." Jenna drains her cup. "Thanks for the coffee. This house is lovely, by the way. I wouldn't have pictured this as your place."

"Thinking it would have a bounce house in the backyard?"

Jenna's mouth puckers. "Of course not. Don't be like that. You're taking what I said the wrong way."

"Am I? I think I'm understanding you pretty well." Jenna thinks I'm some kid who can't see how to prioritize. The kind of man—*boy*—who'd risk it all for a roll in the hay. Fuck that.

"I'll drive you back to your car." I turn my back on her and put my mug in the sink. "We've got a full day today."

"I'd appreciate it. I need to check in with the bakery and confirm the deliveries. Don't want to be short on anything for this wedding."

"No ma'am." I say it on purpose, turning back to face her. If she's going to call me a kid, then I'm going to turn the tables. Jenna winces, but says nothing, all of our usual joking banter a thing of the past. "I'll grab my keys."

19

Jenna

If rain on your wedding day is a good omen, then Hadley and Cooper are about to get their happily ever after ten times over. It was pouring when I made it to the restaurant this morning before dawn. I'd had to run from the parking lot, jumping over puddles as I went. Now, hours later, the rain shows no sign of stopping and the entire road's a sloppy mess. At least that's what I hear from the rest of the staff as they start to trickle in, looking more like drowned rats than the employees of a high-end establishment. I say a silent prayer for the girls from Patty Cakes. Getting a wedding cake in here and set up is going to take some skill. And a whole lot of dodging raindrops.

We've had to make significant changes due to the weather, and everyone is scrambling to try to make what would have been a beautiful outdoor ceremony into one that will now be most decidedly indoors. Cade claimed it was good practice for paying customers and, even though no one wanted to deny that, I'm sure it isn't making the realization that Hadley's dream wedding is a washout any easier. I don't have a spare second to worry about Hadley and her feelings, though. From the moment I unlock the front doors, we're inundated with deliveries. Flowers that were meant for outside are now in, and a million pairs of work boots drag water and mud onto my pristine floors. The ceremony's been moved to the distillery and the reception's been moved here, so there are a million moving parts and that's not counting the thing I'm supposed to be worried about.

And I *am* worried about the food. Even after all the testing and tweaking I've done, I haven't had the chance to make any of these dishes on this big of a scale. Hadley and Cooper wanted a seated dinner, and Charlie told them confidently it would be no problem. We're serving seventy-five people. It isn't even close to some of the parties I've done in my past life, but my staff is inexperienced, and that means I need to be watching them like a hawk. My bravado's floundering a bit as I oversee the kitchen prep.

I'm about to yell for someone to put down more towels by the front door when it swings open again. Charlie stands in the doorway with a full-on thunderstorm behind him.

"For Christ's sake, close the door," I bellow with more acrimony than I intend. We haven't been on the best terms since the night of the bachelorette party. Technically it was the morning after in Charlie's spotless, extremely grown-up kitchen that really did it, but I keep trying to block that whole thing from my mind. The way I sanctimoniously lectured him about restaurant kitchens and how the only thing between us was lust? It's had its desired effect, because Charlie hasn't come near me since, but it's proven once and for all that the relationship I have with him is more than just physical attraction. I've missed the way we had started to get in a rhythm, and I'm not sure if we can get that back.

Charlie shakes off on the doormat, wringing some of the

rainwater from his hair. He's soaked, and I try not to notice the way his wet T-shirt sticks to him in all the right places. He looks up just in time to catch me staring, and the scowl he gives me has me looking intently at the onions I'm chopping.

"How's it going in here?" he asks no one in particular. The waitstaff is scurrying around, trying to get set for an event that keeps changing. One minute I've got them straightening tablecloths and the next they're tearing everything down and moving it all around again. I definitely need Charlie here to run the front of the house.

"We're doing our best." I try to keep a relaxed smile on my face even if inside I'm a bundle of nerves. Fumbling this wedding is not an option, but the universe seems determined to make that happen.

"Where's Justin?" Charlie stalks through the dining room and into the kitchen without even so much as a hello. "Shouldn't he be here by now?"

"No idea. Mike's MIA as well, so I'm two short in here." I try to keep my face neutral. No need for an I-told-you-so about the two guys Charlie insisted on "giving a chance" being the two that aren't here and haven't bothered to call. Justin's technically the sous chef until we can get someone more qualified, so I am going to be feeling his absence as we try to pull this off.

"I'll make a few calls." Charlie doesn't say anything else as he walks away. We're only discussing restaurant business from now on, apparently.

"How's Hadley holding up?" I call after him, even if I can already guess how the bride is probably coping on her wedding day as she watches a flash flood move through.

Charlie stops and turns around long enough to answer me. "Honestly? She seems fine, but that could just be what she's telling us. Lily's trying to distract her while the rest of us try to make this work." Then he's through the office door, slamming it behind him.

I go back to the prep that should have been done hours ago.

"Um, Chef Bard?"

"What, Annabel?" I'm short with her when I've got no reason to be. If anything, Charlie's little band of high schoolers is the most reliable group we've got right now.

"I'm pretty good in the kitchen, if you need an extra pair of hands." She blinks at me. "I think the boys have the rest under control."

I doubt the boys have anything under control, but I'm suffering back here. I look Annabel up and down. "How old are you?"

"Seventeen last week." She straightens her spine.

"Grab one of those extra coats and pull your hair back—wash your hands, too." Lord help me if she cuts herself. "Show me what you know how to do, and I'll put you to work."

Annabel beams. "You won't be sorry." She runs to the hooks along the back wall and grabs a jacket.

I might not be sorry about letting Annabel join the kitchen crew, but I'm starting to be sorry about a whole host of other things: agreeing to this event, letting Charlie talk me into hiring a bunch of guys who needed a second chance, moving to Mint Springs. I cut my eyes over to the office door. It's still shut, Charlie sequestered behind it. He's giving me plenty of space.

And it turns out I don't like it.

20

Charlie

The clouds lift just as the guests start arriving. The road's still a mess, and there'll be more than a few muddy shoes before all this is over, but the rainbow that stretches through the blue sky over the distillery as Hadley arrives makes all of that worth it. She's beaming as Lily helps her out of the golf cart they've driven up from her house. Her mother and grandmother are with them, and when she notices the rainbow, Hadley bursts into tears. Her older sister's quick with a tissue and I'm there to make sure no one steps in a puddle or slips on the way inside.

I lead the ladies in and walk Hadley's grandmother down the aisle. She pats my arm as I escort her to her seat. "Y'all did a great job in here. I know it wasn't easy to make today happen."

"It hasn't technically happened yet," I tell her, a little nervous she's jinxing the change in our luck.

"That rainbow tells me everything I need to know. Don't you worry." I get a wink and another pat as I put her in the front row.

The place does look fabulous. You would never have guessed the distillery wasn't the planned venue all along. Hadley's outdoor wedding with the flower-covered pergola might not have happened, but we made damn sure the alternative was just as magical. There are fairy lights and flowers, and an arch Chance and Cooper built this morning to replace the one Hadley had envisioned for the pasture. A late spring wedding in the sunshine would have been gorgeous, sure, but this wedding isn't going to be second rate, no sir.

Cooper and Hadley have made sure all their important people are here today, and there are plenty of excited faces ready to see them get hitched. They've included pretty much everyone they know in the processional, too, so after I walk the matriarch of the Crawford family down the aisle, we're ready to start. Eddie McDonald is already standing under the arch, nervously pulling on the collar of his dress shirt. Why in the world Cooper and Hadley thought the man who taught them how to make whiskey would be the natural choice to officiate their wedding is anyone's guess. Eddie may have taught Cooper everything he knows about distilling, but I can't imagine he's got some hidden talent for performing weddings. I'm guessing he got his certification online. But, he's one of the few father figures Cooper's got, our own father sending his regards but being too busy to make the three-hour drive from Nashville on such short notice. Yeah, he's not exactly dedicated to this fatherhood thing, even if it means a party.

Hadley's mother floats down the aisle, a mass of sparkles and shine. The Crawford women do not shy away from glitz, that's for sure. When she takes her seat next to her mother they are a blinding mass of sequins.

Unlike my father, my mother has managed to show up.

She grew up here too, although she makes a point of never visiting unless she has to. Apparently Cooper's wedding falls into the category of a must-attend event. We'd all been surprised when she said she was coming. "Wouldn't miss it for the world," she'd actually said, and she nods to people she knows as she makes her way down the aisle, smiling as she goes.

Cooper's been keyed up and ready to go since he got up this morning, and as soon as he's given the signal, he starts his walk down the aisle. He's got Sadie on one arm and Mae on the other, so his march is slower than he'd like. It's like he's been waiting so long for his chance to marry Hadley that these last few minutes are killing him. He gets my great-aunts to their seats and bounds up to the space next to Eddie, one leg doing a constant wiggle once he's in place. At least he looks sharp. Despite running around all day in the pouring rain, Cooper's suit is immaculate, and he's managed to clean up enough to look like he's been sitting on the couch all day, not unclogging gutters and mopping up messes.

I'm hoping the rest of us look half as good.

My remaining brothers and I make our way to the front and get ready for the entrance of the bridesmaids. Lily comes first, smiling like a loon at Chance, who smiles right back. Faith comes next, wearing a dress that's a huge change from the overalls she normally chooses for a work day. I give her a big grin from my spot up front, but she's not looking at me. She's got her eyes trained to my left, locked in tight on the blank face of my younger brother Cade. I give him a glance, and his eyes move toward the floor so fast I'm surprised he doesn't give himself vertigo. A goofy half smile stays on his lips, though. I'm going to have a few questions about that later, that's for sure.

Hadley's sister Mindy comes next. She's smiling, but we all know it's a little forced. She's recently divorced and doesn't always love Cooper. Still, she's done her best to help us get this wedding together lickity-split, so I forgive her for looking less than thrilled to be watching her younger sister get married. We've all known it was only a matter of time before Cooper and Hadley tied the knot.

Finally, the music changes. You'd expect the traditional "Here Comes the Bride," but, of course Cooper and Hadley aren't going to do that. Nothing about their courtship has been the way you would expect. From falling in love as teenagers to hating each other for years after, they haven't exactly been doing things the way you would think. Hadley's appearance at the end of our makeshift aisle to the first notes of Keith Urban's "Only You Can Love Me This Way" has every head turning.

But it's Cooper's reaction I notice. He lets out the biggest breath ever and raises his eyes to the ceiling. I swear his whole body buckles at the sight of her in that white dress coming down the aisle toward him. When he raises one of his hands to his face, I see that he's crying. Cooper is actually wiping away tears as Hadley walks forward. When she makes it all the way up to us and takes Cooper's hand, I hear Cade sniff behind me. Hadley hands her bouquet to her sister, who's also dabbing her eyes with a tissue. Pretty much everyone is crying as we watch Cooper and Hadley gaze at each other.

I scan the room for Jenna. She's been working all morning in the kitchen, but by now she should have come down from the restaurant. Hadley made a point of inviting her to the wedding. She's not just supposed to be "the help" today and we tried to staff things so that none of us would be missing out. The rain's put a wrench in some of that, but

Jenna should still be here and instead of listening to Eddie wax poetic about things that are "meant to be," I'm looking frantically at the faces in the crowd.

No Jenna.

Once the ceremony's done, the plan is to move to drinks and cocktails here before we herd everyone down to the restaurant. After Cooper's kissed the bride—for way longer than comfortable for the rest of us, by the way—and the wedding party goes back down the aisle, I start looking for Jenna again. The food has arrived, and the waitstaff is circulating with plates of small bites.

"Where's Jenna?" I ask one of the teenaged waiters as soon as I get the opportunity. It's Jonah, who technically isn't even supposed to be serving food but seems to be doing a fine job of it.

"Still in the kitchen. Shrimp and grits cake?" He holds the platter out to me.

"No, thank you." Although they do look good, and my stomach is rumbling. "Is she still working?"

"Oh yeah, it's a shit show down there." Jonah's face goes ashen. "Sorry, Charlie. I mean, Mr. Allen, I promise I haven't been cussing in front of the other guests."

Jonah's expletive barely registers. "What are you talking about?"

"A bunch of guys never showed up, I guess. Chef Bard's doing most of it herself. She's got Annabel in the kitchen, and—"

I don't even bother listening to the rest. I leave Jonah where he's standing and take off at a run down the gravel road.

21

Jenna

Just get through the next five minutes. I've been saying that for the last two hours. I'm keeping my head down and trying to think strategically. With the kitchen staff I've got, we're working hard but we're making mistakes. I've gotten the appetizers finished and sent up to the distillery, but now we're hopelessly behind on dinner. In an established kitchen, this might not be an emergency, but in this one, with my inexperienced staff and the completely new menu I'm cooking for the first time, we're at code red.

The ceremony's over, and my little black dress is still hanging in the office. Black might not be appropriate for a spring wedding in the South—or for any wedding, for that matter—but I didn't exactly pack to be able to attend an event like this. I traveled light, and I'm still living out of a suitcase in my hotel room. Which is lucky, I guess, because after this dinner goes down in flames, it'll be that much easier to grab my things and slink out of town.

And that is looking more and more likely. I am sweating

underneath my chef's coat, and it isn't because it's hot in this kitchen. The possibility of failure—with the old one still so fresh in my mind—has me pushing hard, but it might not be enough. Once again, despite my best efforts, I've ended up on the losing end of things. Cooking for seventy-five people basically by myself could have been done, in theory. But this afternoon we are firmly in reality and that reality is that I'm in over my head.

When the front door opens, I groan. *Please, please don't tell me guests are already arriving for dinner service.* But it isn't just any wedding guest who comes bursting through the door. It's Charlie and *damn* does he look good in a suit.

He's already taking off his jacket as he strides into the kitchen. "Put me to work."

"You can't be back here today, Charlie," I argue, but he's already hanging his suit coat on the hooks in the back.

"I'm not going to let you bust your ass all by yourself." He turns to the rest of my motley crew. "No offense." They're all too busy to bother being offended.

"But your clothes," I protest. Charlie's still perfectly pressed, the charcoal suit highlighting his broad shoulders. I am easily distracted by a man in a suit, but there's no time for that today. Charlie's loosening his tie.

"I'll take them off."

"And wear what?" The image of Charlie nearly naked in the kitchen might be something I've fantasized about before, but never in the middle of Hadley and Cooper's wedding dinner.

"I've got a chef's coat, and hopefully another pair of pants in the office. These aren't the best shoes—" He looks down at the shiny wingtips on his feet. "But they'll do."

He starts stripping down while I stand there, mouth

hanging open. The tie comes off, followed by the shirt. He's quick with the buttons, but not quick enough for me to miss what amounts to a strip tease. Once he's bare chested, I cannot avert my eyes. I stare, barely blinking, letting the grits I've got going on the stove start to stick to the pot.

"I would have been here earlier, but..."

"You were a little busy." I try not to look at Charlie's nipples and pretend it isn't a violation of health code—to be half-naked in a commercial kitchen.

"I'm sorry you missed the ceremony, but I'm even more sorry you've been doing this all day." Charlie gestures to the chaos that is our kitchen. "Give me five minutes and I'm your slave."

My mouth quirks up on one side. Involuntarily my eyes travel down the trail of light brown hair on his abdomen. I'm well aware of what's underneath those pristine slacks.

Charlie's head cocks to one side and an eyebrow shoots up. The smirk on his face is hard to miss, and I'm thankful the rest of the staff is too busy to see what's happening between us. "Keep it PG, chef," he says before walking toward the office and, hopefully, a different pair of pants.

If I was hot before, I'm on fire now.

We manage to work side by side without too much more innuendo. Once we're in a groove, there isn't time to focus on anything but the food. Tonight's choices are decidedly more Southern than our regular menu will be, but I've still added a few small touches. There's coconut milk in the grits, so subtle you can barely taste it but enough to keep you wondering. And I've made the tomato tarts a little special. They didn't need much in the way of embellishment; I've begrudgingly had to admit Faith's produce is spectacular. Even the fruit from the greenhouse tastes fabulous. I can only imagine how delicious a real summer tomato will be.

The tarts are coming out of the oven as the guests start to arrive. Charlie had sent word to try to stretch the cocktail hour by another thirty minutes, and somehow those teenagers have made it happen. I'm praying the appetizers were enough to keep people from getting too drunk on the liquor I'm sure was flowing up the hill. Everyone files in looking interested but not ravenous, and only a little tipsy, from what I can tell from behind the fryer. Charlie and I watch as everyone is seated. The restaurant looks magical, and I'm hoping the food can live up to the ambiance.

The first course goes out smoothly, and Charlie's eyes catch mine. He's excited, and I feel less guilty about pulling him away from his family and his seat at the head table. He and I brush accidentally a few times, my already heated skin getting exponentially hotter. I steal glances at him as he mixes and chops, and almost every time I look at him, he's looking right back at me. We're both shouting orders to the line cooks and the waitstaff, but our rhythm together is wordless and automatic, like we can predict each other's next move. Like we can anticipate each other's needs.

Cooper and Hadley wanted things done family style, so we're spared the chore of trying to plate everything. Heaping platters of beef brisket go out with the grits. Serving dishes piled high with my take on chicken and waffles get a few *ohs* and *ahs* from the tables closest to us. But I'm proudest of the simplest dish we're serving tonight. Sadie and Mae had their doubts when I'd shown them the delicate French green beans I wanted to cook. Faith had planted a huge crop of haricots verts in the greenhouse, and I'd snatched them all up as soon as she'd mentioned them. I've left in the required bacon everyone told me green beans absolutely had to have, but I've added it to a light sauce instead of cooking the beans with it until they're a mushy mess. The barely blanched beans tossed together with that sauce at the last minute is chef's kiss—literally. I'm hoping the freshness of the beans cuts some of the heaviness of the other dishes. I even snuck in a touch of lemon zest.

I try not to make it obvious that I'm watching every bite the wedding guests take, looking for a reaction. I want them to love the food, to be transported, even if these aren't necessarily my signature dishes. One day maybe I'll get a wedding where the couple wants me to bring Puerto Rico to their table. Tonight I'm happy to do more of what Cooper and Hadley want, but I still want to wow. I still want everyone to walk out of here raving about the meal they've been served.

"If we're okay in here, I'm going to go and mingle for a bit. You should too." Charlie leans a hip dangerously close to mine on the counter.

"I'm a little nervous," I confess. "Today has been a clusterfuck."

"You did great. Look at those faces." He points out toward the tables.

"*We* did great. I couldn't have pulled this off without you." I leave out the part about Charlie's kitchen hires being the reason we ended up in the weeds.

Charlie shakes his head. "This is all you, Jenna. You should take a second to enjoy it."

"I need to prep the banana pudding, but you go. Spend some time with your brother and the rest of your family. Make sure that lemonade I made for Hadley's working for her."

Charlie frowns but leaves me. He's out at the tables hugging people and slapping backs in two seconds flat. He's still wearing his hastily cobbled together outfit, complete with waffle batter down the front. Still, when he looks up and our eyes lock, that boyishly handsome half-grin looks as devilish as if he was still decked out in his suit. When he lifts his glass to toast me once the wedding cake has been served and everyone's tucking into their itty bitty banana puddings, I have to remember to smile at everyone else because the smile I've got for Charlie is entirely too bright.

And entirely too dangerous.

22

Charlie

"And that's that." I turn the bolt and lock the front door, turn off the lights in the front of the house. I'm still buzzing on this crazy high—the kind you get after winning the big game or fighting a bear. It's part of the reason I love the restaurant business. The lows can be pretty low sometimes, but the highs make up for it. And we've done a great job, despite the whole thing nearly blowing up in our faces. Guests left happy and none of the staff quit. That's a win in my book.

Jenna doesn't look convinced. She's sitting at the bar with her feet propped up on the stool next to her. Her eyes are closed, and for a second I think she's actually fallen asleep there, her back ramrod straight and still in her chef's coat. "If you say so," she finally mumbles.

"Ah, you're alive."

"Barely." Jenna cracks one eye open. "I'm wishing I could transport myself to a bath and then my bed."

"Does your hotel room even have a bathtub?" Images of Jenna covered only by bubbles race through my mind. *Cool it, brain. Not happening.*

"Of course not." The side of her mouth quirks up. "And the shower's got terrible water pressure."

I think about the deep tub I've got at my house. It's only a few minutes down the road. I could have Jenna naked and soaking in it in less than fifteen minutes. Then I could slide in there with her and—

"Umph." It's not the kind of sexy groan my bathtub fantasy needs.

"Your neck still giving you trouble?"

"A little. The new pillows help." Jenna opens her eyes to look at me. "Thanks for those."

"No problem." I move behind the bar to put a little space between us. "Want a drink? Vodka martini, extra dirty?" She smiles at this, and I take my time getting the ingredients together. This kitchen buzz plus Jenna in close proximity is playing with fire and I know it. Plenty of nights I've gone home with someone from work because we were both just excited enough to think it was a good idea and just exhausted enough not to bother looking for a more suitable choice. It hasn't even been three days and already I'm thinking about trying to renegotiate our hands-off rule.

Jenna takes the glass eagerly when I slide it across the bar to her. The way she closes her eyes when she takes a sip goes straight to my groin. Luckily, I'm on the other side of the bar. Unluckily, the groan she lets out now is exactly what my bathtub fantasy was missing.

"So good. Thanks for this." Jenna takes another sip. "Aren't you going to have one?"

"I'm not a big fan of the dirty."

Jenna nearly spits vodka all over the bar top. She's sputtering and choking so much I rush over to whack her on the back. Once I realize she's laughing, not dying, I stop trying to give her first aid and stand there like an idiot, one hand still touching her.

"Oh my God, Country. You're not a big fan of the dirty? You teed that one up for me." Tears are actually running down Jenna's face and she has to use the back of her hand to wipe some of them away. "I needed that." She's still smiling when she finally looks at me. "If anyone's a fan of the dirty, it would be you."

"Takes one to know one." It's ridiculous and not even the right kind of comeback, but it gets Jenna's eyebrow to raise.

"Is that so?" Her tongue comes out the slightest bit between her lips, and the atmosphere in the room changes. All that electricity I'd been feeling earlier is back, only now I can see Jenna's feeling some of it too. My hand's still touching her, and I let my thumb move, tracing a tiny circle on her shoulder. The air crackles between us as we both weigh our options. The right thing to do—the thing we've already agreed on—is to let this moment fizzle out, for me to move away and pretend nothing's happening. Jenna might clear her throat or stand up to leave, and then the spell would be broken.

But neither of us does any of that.

Instead I let that hand slide over her shoulder and down the front of her. She's undone the top few buttons of her chef's coat and that gives me plenty of room to slide my hand inside and palm her breast over the T-shirt she's wearing underneath. I'm not even touching skin, but it doesn't matter, my hand's on fire all the same. When I lean forward and capture Jenna's mouth with mine, she doesn't resist.

We stay like that for a minute, soft and slow, until I get impatient. Wanting Jenna's been taking up a good deal of my time and resisting her has been eating up the rest, now

I'm ignoring the warnings my brain's sending out and letting my body tell me what to do, letting Jenna's reactions lead me. It might be terrible for business, but I'm not stopping.

Jenna pulls away from me, and for a second I think she's going to stop me, remind me of the discussions we've already had and the agreements we've already made, but she doesn't say a word. She reaches over, fishes an olive from her drink, and pops it in her mouth. She chews it slowly, smiling a bit.

"How about you show me how dirty you like it?"

23

Jenna

I was exhausted. More than exhausted. Is there a word for that? I'm sure there is, but all my brain could reasonably do up until a few minutes ago was remind me on a continuous loop: *tired, so, so tired*. Cooking is hard work, the kind that means standing on your feet all day and long nights. You know the meaning of bone tired after working that way for a while, and when I sat down at the bar that's exactly how I felt. Tired in my bones.

But that was before Charlie touched me. All it took was the feeling of his hand on my back and a switch was flipped. Now my brain's focused on one thing and one thing only. Even if Charlie's a terrible choice. Even if we've both said it can't happen again.

When he kisses me, every cell in my body lights up. Was I tired before? Not anymore. Now I'm pure adrenaline, nothing but want and desire. His hand on my breast isn't enough. Nothing's going to be enough until I've had him the million different ways I want him. He's been letting me boss him in the kitchen all day, and that's what I still want—

Charlie giving in and letting me call the shots. He had been fine with it in the hotel room, but that was before. Now that I know more about him, I know he's not used to ceding control, but getting him to bend a little is part of the fun for me. Not big on the dirty, my ass. And I'm about to give him every opportunity to show me how wrong that statement was.

Already the drink he made me is coursing through my veins. It was only one, but it was strong, and I haven't eaten much all day. It's enough to have my limbs feeling warm and relaxed, enough to loosen my tongue and silence all those nagging voices that should be telling me to stop. Liquid courage at its finest. Charlie's not hesitating and neither am I.

When I pull my mouth from his, Charlie's brow furrows. He thinks I'm about to tell him playtime's over. Oh no, honey, we're just getting started.

"You want me to make you a drink?" I'm already pushing my stool away from the bar, already nearly on my feet.

"That's not what I want right now." His eyes are full of heat, and I can't help but smile a little. Of course that's not what he wants. I know exactly what he's thinking, but I like to tease a little. He'll get what he wants—if he'll play by my rules.

"I think I can change your mind." I start to undo the buttons on my chef's coat. I go slow, watching Charlie's face, until I'm down to my T-shirt. This isn't the sexiest outfit in town, and I almost regret never ending up in my dress, but Charlie's face tells me it doesn't matter what I'm wearing, only that I'm taking it off.

I pull the T-shirt over my head and slide the loose pants I wear in the kitchen down over my hips, step out of my clogs and pull off the cotton socks I'm wearing. Yes, any of the grandmothers probably out sexed me in the clothing department tonight, but I've always got one secret weapon.

No one knows the kind of things I wear under my dowdy kitchen outfit. And, oh boy, do I like to have that little trick up my sleeve.

Charlie's eyes nearly pop out of his head when I end up standing in front of him in nothing but my underwear. It is far from sensible—a matching set in a dark emerald green, lacy and pretty close to see-through. It covers barely enough to make taking it off another layer of reveal, but leaves enough covered to have Charlie moving toward me.

"Charlie." It's a warning, but it's also a promise. *Try it my way, you'll like it.* He stops. "Grab one of those bottles."

He still can't tell what I'm planning, but he does what I tell him, reaching out for one of the bottles of whiskey he can most easily reach without putting any more distance between us. It's a fine choice, although just about anything would work for what I've got in mind. I pull the pins from my hair and give it a shake, letting it fall on my shoulders.

"Come a little closer."

Charlie moves slowly, like he isn't sure if he should be excited or frightened. He's probably right to be a little of both. Plenty of people will tell you I bite, although most of them enjoy a little teeth. We'll see if Charlie's one of them.

He's letting his eyes roam all over me, but he doesn't try to touch me. His fingers flex against the neck of the bottle and his lips part. He stays quiet, though, not even so much as a gasp or a groan from Charlie yet, just that hungry look I'm coming to love.

I reach out and take the whiskey from him and pull out the cork. The *pop* startles him and he manages to tear his eyes away from my chest long enough to look me in the eye. I tip the bottle and let a drizzle of the amber liquid trickle onto my chest. Charlie's eyes follow the path the whiskey takes over the swell of my breasts. It disappears into my cleavage, some of it making its way down my stomach to my navel.

"Lick it off."

Charlie is more than happy to comply. When his tongue makes contact with my skin for the first time, the groan he lets out reverberates through my whole body. There is nothing like having a man take his time and Charlie goes slowly, tracing along the edges of my bra with a reverence I wouldn't have guessed he had. He looks up at me as a hand snakes around to the clasp. He's asking permission, and that deference alone has me getting weak in the knees. I nod and he frees me from the lace that's been holding me tight all day.

"God, these tits," he murmurs as he takes one nipple into his mouth. His teeth give me a little nip, dragging lightly along the skin, and I close my eyes for a second. I tilt the bottle again and let more of the alcohol cascade down the front of my body. Charlie keeps working, licking every last drop from my skin, the flat of his tongue moving over every inch of me.

His tongue circles my belly button and dips lower, finding the edge of my panties. I'm more than ready to take those off, but I make him wait a few seconds longer, prolonging my own suffering a bit but keeping as much control as I can.

"Jenna." He's not quite begging, but there's an edge to his voice. It's enough desperation to make me give in.

I take two steps back, separating myself from Charlie's magical tongue and strong hands. I put the bottle on the bar top and hook my thumbs in the top of my panties, wiggling a little as I slide them down my hips. Charlie's chest rises and falls as he watches me. I keep my back against the bar and beckon him to come closer. He's in front of me in less than a second, so close I can feel the warmth of his breath on my collarbone.

"Up." I don't need to explain. Charlie lifts me onto the bar, nuzzling me a little with his nose against my neck. It's more familiar than I'd normally like, but I let him get away with it. I give him a little shove to put some space between us again.

The cold wood of the bar is unyielding, pressing against the back of my legs and the flesh of my ass. I move a little to get more comfortable and then spread my legs. Charlie sucks in a sharp breath, his eyes transfixed on the space between my thighs. I slide a hand down and run a finger through the wetness there. All this teasing has been torturing me too. I find my clit and grind a little against my hand.

"Get over here and help me out, Country."

The bar's too tall for Charlie to go down on his knees, but he makes the best of it, squatting down until his face is even with my pussy. Again his eyes flit to mine to ask permission. Already he knows what I expect. I smile and thread my fingers through his hair. I give him a hard tug and his mouth makes contact with my skin.

Heaven.

24

Charlie

There are a million things I want to say, but Jenna seems to prefer the silent treatment. And it's difficult to talk and do my best work. I'd rather keep my mouth where it is, my tongue circling Jenna's clit. She groans and leans back on her elbows, letting go of my hair. She writhes against me, and I slide one finger in. The noise she makes lets me know she approves. I'm in danger of coming in my pants at this point. I'm still fully clothed—T-shirt and the pair of baggy houndstooth pants I was lucky enough to have found in the office. I lost the chef's jacket as soon as the last guest was ushered out. Jenna's eyes lit up when I came into the restaurant wearing my suit. I'd have loved to keep that on if I could keep getting her to look at me that way a little longer. Still, the way she's looking at me now is hard to beat. When her eyes flutter open, she looks at me with nothing but lust—comical outfit be damned.

"You want to touch yourself, Country?"

She has to know I'm dying to, my erection's pressing against the front of my pants, begging for attention.

"Get your cock out."

The order is sweet relief. I pull the front of my boxers down and shove a hand inside, freeing my dick. I'm hard as a fencepost, and my fingers brush against a drop of precum on the tip.

Jenna props up enough to get a better look at me. "Stroke yourself while you eat me. Do it slow."

My body doesn't want slow. It's begging for release and keeping my hand from going on autopilot is difficult. I try to concentrate on Jenna, hoping the distraction will keep me from finishing things before they really get started.

I keep working Jenna's clit and add another finger. When I graze her with my teeth, her hips shoot off the bar. I do it again and she moans so loud I imagine the bottles behind us clattering together. Her pussy tightens around my fingers, and she arches her back, coming apart right here under the soft after-hours lights of my restaurant. I don't think there can be anything sweeter until Jenna sits up.

"Fuck me."

I have never been so relieved to keep condoms behind the bar. I know several people would be sending up prayers for my wayward soul if they found out, but none of them are here now, which means I can fish around behind the bar until I find what I need. I suit up as quickly as possible, Jenna's eyes on me the entire time. She licks her lips, and I have to start running through football statistics in my head to get my body under control.

Her naked chest has the faintest sheen of sweat on it, and I still get the occasional whiff of whiskey when she moves. I desperately want to be skin to skin. I rip my T-shirt over my head and launch it back behind the bar, yank my pants down to my knees, and reach for her. She slides her ass to the edge of the bar top, and I get ready to bury myself in her.

Of course, that's not how things work with Jenna. Her hand comes up to my chest, basically stopping me from doing what I want most in this world right now. I let out an impatient moan, which only garners a wide smile from Jenna.

"What's the rush, Country? You have someplace to be?" She lets her fingers slide ever so slowly over my right nipple. The skin there pebbles, and goose bumps rise on the rest of me. I might have wanted fast, but Jenna calls the shots. As much as I like the eventual reward, following orders at a time like this takes more self-control than I've got.

"You told me to fuck you. You not going to let me?" I'm lined up with her center, nearly touching her. With barely any effort I could be inside her.

"Well, I don't want to make it too easy."

I bark out a laugh. Nothing with Jenna is easy.

"But I guess it is getting late." With that she grabs my ass and pulls me forward, impaling herself on my cock. The height of the bar makes it hard for me to get the kind of leverage I want, but that seems to suit Jenna just fine. She controls the pace and the angle, wrapping her legs around my waist and throwing her head back. I contort myself to get at her breasts and put my mouth back on her nipples. The appreciative murmurs that Jenna makes have me trying to keep that up for as long as possible.

But I know I'm going to be faster than I'd like. I'm too keyed up from the day I've had. Still, Jenna persists at staving off my orgasm by slowing down right when I start to speed up. It's infuriating, but effective, and when Jenna finally gives me the chance to finish, it's the most intense orgasm I've ever had. It leaves me shaking and sputtering, holding onto Jenna for dear life.

Pressed up against me, I feel Jenna's smile against my skin—right before she sinks her teeth into my earlobe.

"You could go back to my house. Shower."

"I can shower at the hotel." Jenna doesn't bother to look at me as she grabs her pants from the floor and slides them back on. "Where did my panties go?"

"You could take a bath. I've got a great tub." I reach over to the bar stool next to me and pick up the scrap of lace she's looking for.

"I really shouldn't." She takes the panties from my outstretched hand. "Thanks."

"You could stay over."

Jenna pulls her T-shirt over her head. "We're not making a habit of this, Charlie. Staying over at your place would be... We're not going steady, okay?"

"I didn't say we were, I just thought—"

"Well, don't. This is already going to make it harder to work together." She puts her hands on the hips I had my fingers wrapped around only a few minutes ago. "And we have plenty to work on."

"We had nothing but compliments, and I think we managed to keep the staff from quitting." It isn't an A-plus, for sure, but it isn't the funeral she's making it out to be. "My brother's hitched and your dinner managed to outshine even the bride."

"We did it by the skin of our teeth. You know that, right? We've got to get this place organized before we try anything like that again."

"Come on, it wasn't that bad."

"Are you kidding? We were lucky the kitchen didn't catch on fire. Or that one of the kids I had to rope into working with me didn't cut a finger off or something. Charlie, we were exceptionally close to having the whole thing blow up in our faces." Jenna fumbles around with her shoes.

"Well, we'll try to make sure that never happens again." I'm acting like it was no big deal, but my pride is having a tough go of it. I know Jenna was the secret ingredient here. Without her, nothing works. "The staff left happy and the guests too."

"But we can't run things like this every night. I can't bet everything on a place that—"

"A place that what?" I bend down to pick up her chef's coat. It's slightly damp with whiskey.

"A place that's going to mean failure." Jenna pauses and reaches for her coat. "Again."

"We're not going to fail. We're going to iron out these wrinkles. Trust me."

Jenna's laugh startles me. "Trust you? Oh, I've heard that before."

I don't know how everything went down in Boston, but I know enough. Jenna's restaurant isn't hers. She put her blood, sweat, and tears into something, and she lost it. That's more than enough to make her hesitancy understandable. "We both know this business isn't easy."

"I'm not worried about the business, Charlie. If you'd start listening to me, the business part of this would be fine. I'm concerned about the personal. You're asking me to trust you. *You*. The last time I did that I ended up out on my ass. I'm not willing to have that happen again."

"Look, I'm not trying to take advantage of you. Whoever did that to you, I'm not that guy." I'm confident in my assessment. Jenna can trust me; she just needs to see that. Of course, me standing here naked isn't making me seem all that professional.

"You might not think you're that guy, but I'm sure he didn't either. Things with Frank started out all puffy clouds and rainbows, you know." Jenna points at me. "You can't promise me things here won't go south too."

"Frank was your husband?" I've got the edges of the story. I heard what she told my aunts at dinner, and I've heard rumors.

"Yep. And I trusted him with the business decisions. I was focusing on the food. It made sense at the time." Jenna shrugs. "Until he decided he'd rather fuck one of the hostesses. I'm sure she's doing a great job running the place." The bitterness in Jenna's voice is hard to miss. "And we can't let this happen again either." She gestures between us like we're talking about a delivery mistake and not me having my dick inside her. "It was a good stress reliever, but that's all it was. That's all it can be. I know a little more about this than you. Once you've got a little more experience running things you'll see."

"Are you calling me inexperienced?" She's doing it again. Pulling rank. I'm not sure if that's a reference to work, play, or both. I'm younger than Jenna, but that doesn't mean I haven't had my share of life's bumps and bruises. And only a few minutes ago she wasn't exactly complaining about what I was bringing to the table.

Jenna gives me a disappointed look. "Be reasonable."

"Yes, ma'am." I fold my arms over my chest, my annoyance starting to bubble over.

"I have to get going." She's got her keys in her hand already. "I'll see you tomorrow." She gives me one more glance from head to toe. "And you might want to go ahead and put your pants back on."

I don't move. I'll be damned if I'm going to let her be in charge of me now.

"Suit yourself." Jenna comes toward me and plants a kiss on my cheek. And she's out the front door, leaving me standing there naked as the day I was born and probably not any smarter.

25

Jenna

"Once again, a slave to your libido."

"It's not funny, Addison." I pull on a boot and try not to lose my balance.

"You're right. It sounds absolutely tragic to have pulled an event completely out of the crapper by sheer force of will and then celebrating with martinis and sex with a handsome man on top of the bar." I can hear the sound of a knife hitting a cutting board.

"Are you working right now?" I can picture Addison's immaculate kitchen in the Back Bay. The restaurant where she's the executive chef is right off Newbury Street. It's small, but perfect, and Addison does great work there.

"I'm multi-tasking. Don't worry, you're not on speaker."

I should hope not since I just detailed my entire evening in extremely vivid terms. It was thirty minutes of the kind of confession I should probably save for a priest. Addison can't exactly give me absolution, but I'm hoping she can help me get my head out of my ass. "I have to quit though, right?"

"What?" The chopping stops. "Why do you keep asking

that? Absolutely not. You don't think Charlie's going to be angry, right?"

"I was pretty short with him when I left," I confess, trying to wing my eyeliner and button my shirt at the same time. I'm not very successful. "But he was fine before. With the sex, I mean."

"Of course he's fine with the sex. What red-blooded American male isn't fine with sex, especially the way you do it? He got a repeat performance. Not many men have been so lucky." I hear the sound of running water, the gurgle of a pot filling.

"Yes, but the first time we didn't know we had a connection. I had no idea he was going to be my boss, and he had no idea I was going to run his kitchen. Now... Now I think I crossed a line." I don't regret sleeping with Charlie again, but I know there will be repercussions. He might try to act like he's a playboy, but I haven't seen a flock of women hanging around. Except for Faith, of course. *Grrr*. For some reason that still gets under my skin.

"But you both broke the agreement. So now make another agreement. Shake on it." Pots clank. "Be grownups. Or keep screwing each other after work. Separate spheres."

"I don't know if he's a separate spheres kind of guy." More and more, Charlie's striking me as the kind of man who tries to be good. He might fail, but he tries. I wipe another crooked attempt at eyeliner off my face.

"Oh no, Jenna. Is he a feelings boy?" I can hear Addison's wince through the phone line. "I thought we both agreed we weren't doing feelings."

"I'm not. I'm worried he is." My heart does a funny little flop. *We're not doing feelings*, I remind it.

But I'm not sure it's listening.

The flop happens again when I walk into the restaurant. I see the back of Charlie's head, bent over his laptop. He reaches around and gives his neck a squeeze in a move I've come to know signals frustration. It's eight in the morning and Charlie's already doing the back of the neck squeeze. Not a good sign.

But when Faith comes up next to him and hands him a cup of coffee, all that stress seems to melt away. Charlie smiles up at her and she smiles down at him, ruffles his hair a bit, and then settles herself in the chair next to him. It's all happiness and bliss from where I'm standing, Faith—somehow still cute in her overalls and Charlie looking well-rested despite spending most of the night here.

With me. Naked.

I try to put all that behind me and tame the flutter in my heart. It's more of a pounding now, anyway, not nearly as romantic and more threatening. Oh, Charlie didn't spend the last few hours worried about anything. What does he have to worry about with Faith sitting next to him? She's probably fifteen years my junior and sweet as pie. Maybe not a firecracker in the sack, but most certainly wife and mother material—two things I never really was and will never be again.

I clear my throat once I get closer to them. The fact that they don't notice my approach tells me quite a bit. They're in their own little world, huddled up over whatever they're looking at when they aren't staring at each other.

"Jenna." Charlie seems genuinely surprised, like having me walk in this morning is completely out of the blue. "I wasn't expecting you until later."

"I told you last night we had things to get started on

early. It's early, so here I am." I cut my eyes over at Faith's shiny blonde head. "I see you've already got things going on this morning. Didn't sleep in?"

"I was up most of the night." There's none of the teasing that might come with innuendo. He's not talking about being here with me last night. Not referencing our time together at all. It's what I told him I wanted, but it stings a little just the same.

"And I work farmer's hours, so obviously I'm up." Faith shifts in her seat to look at me. "Coffee? I made a fresh pot."

"I can get it, thanks." I let my mouth settle into a thin line. No smiles for Charlie or Faith this morning.

Charlie joins me at the coffee pot. "There's really no need for you to be here this early, especially after the day you had yesterday." His hazel eyes are kind, crinkled at the corners. I don't let myself get sucked in.

"Am I cramping your style?" I look pointedly at Faith. "Were you expecting a little private time? Make use of the bar again before any of the rest of the staff shows up?"

Charlie's brow furrows. "Faith's here to go over the planting schedule. See if we need anything extra before everything's finalized. We're coming down to the last few weeks for summer vegetables."

"She couldn't do that over the phone?" I pour the hot coffee into my mug and add a little cream and sugar. "That's extremely personal service."

"Jenna..." Charlie's voice lowers to a whisper. "Don't."

"Oh, trust me. I won't. Not ever again." And I march myself into the kitchen and pretend to be extremely busy until noon.

26

Charlie

"Do you think Jenna would want to make something with the apple brandy?"

"I don't know. You could ask her." I fill my glass again with some of Cooper's wedding moonshine. Only my brother would think he needs to distill something special to commemorate the last of his bachelor days.

"I'm asking you. Why don't *you* ask her?" The look Cooper gives me isn't one I like seeing.

"I'll try to remember to ask her the next time I see her." I take another sip. God, my brother's gotten good at this. It's so smooth I barely notice it going down. That's dangerous, especially if this conversation's turning to Jenna.

"The next time you see her? Don't you see her every day?" Cooper's face is serious. "I was gone for a week, and you've already messed things up with the new chef?"

"I didn't mess anything up." I reach for the bottle again, but Cooper slides it away from me.

"What did you do, Charlie?" He slides his new wedding ring around on his finger. It's actually got a strip of whiskey barrel running down the middle because Hadley knows what he likes. I'd bet she's never called him inexperienced even though she's known him since he was a literal kid.

"I didn't do anything. I swear." I leave out the part about having sex with her before I knew who she was and I most certainly don't mention how I fucked her on the bar just a few hours after Cooper's wedding dinner. That would not go over well, not to mention how awkward it would make drinks at the restaurant. "She thinks I'm green, is all. We're not seeing eye to eye."

"You been acting like a baby?" He's joking, but I don't laugh.

"Of course not. She just likes to play that card." I'm a grown-ass man. I do not need Jenna or my brother to try to make me feel like I'm not.

"You two looked to be getting along pretty well before we left."

"That was an emergency." I think back to the rush of adrenaline I had that night and the way Jenna and I kept bumping into each other in the kitchen. "She was pissed the guys I hired didn't show up."

"Well, I don't blame her for that. I know you want to give people a chance, particularly if they're local, but you can't have them messing things up at... Do we still not have a name?" Cooper hands come up in frustration. "We aren't going to be able to get a sign made before the grand opening."

"I'm kicking some things around. Maybe I should poll everyone at dinner tomorrow. Are you and Hadley coming over to Mae and Sadie's or are you still technically on your honeymoon?" I'd much rather talk about Cooper's week at the beach than my troubles with Jenna.

"I think Hadley will be happy to see some faces other

than mine." He gives me a grin. "You should invite Jenna. She might want to have a say in the name of the restaurant she's going to be trapped in."

I let out a frustrated breath. "I'll see if she's free, I guess. And she's not exactly stuck, you know. She's still living in the hotel." I assume that's so she can disappear at a moment's notice.

Cooper raises an eyebrow. "You'd better get things nailed down, Charlie. We can't have the chef bailing on us. Invite her to dinner. She might not appreciate seeing you outside of work, but she'll get to hang out with the rest of the family. Maybe we can remind her that all the Allens aren't pains in the ass."

"Good luck with that." I finish my drink. And good luck getting Jenna to do anything I ask her to.

∽

Jenna says yes immediately.

So much for her being the stubborn one. Or maybe Cooper hit the nail on the head and she's fine with spending time with my family but not with me. I could ask her, could lean out from my seat at the bar and call out. I won't, though. We've started exclusively texting to the point that I can hear the messages I send her arrive on her phone. Conversation between us is a constant symphony of beeps and buzzes.

Once I send the dinner invitation, she replies right away. Normally she makes me wait, has me watch her open the message and read it, and then I get to witness how she ignores it for a bit. Twenty minutes, an hour, the end of the shift—those are all options when it comes to getting a response.

Obviously I've started doing the same thing to her. Yes, I was just telling Cooper all about how mature I am. The irony's not lost on me. I had even made things more juvenile by waiting until the last minute to send the text. A four o'clock invitation to dinner at six seemed like one with a good possibility of rejection. Jenna might have had other plans or been too tired to think about socializing. We're both here at the restaurant working from sunup to sundown, but she's still in for dinner tonight. Great. I send her a thumbs up emoji to seal the deal.

Later, once the plates are cleared and my family's out on the screened-in porch for whiskey tasting and restaurant naming, I've almost forgotten Jenna's there. Mind over matter is working. Or it is until she walks a little too close to me and I get a whiff of one hundred percent pure Jenna. It's a mix of spice and coconut. I can't imagine Jenna spritzing on perfume, but the way she smells is like something out of a tropical vacation. It matches her in a way I could never confess to anyone—spicy, but still a little sweet. Delicious but with a bite.

She almost touches me as she walks past, and I notice a few raised eyebrows and concerned looks as Jenna takes the seat the farthest away from me. We've barely said two words to each other since she showed up, looking like a super-model with her hair cascading down her back and her ass encased in what look like leather leggings. She'd brought more wine and some kind of a plant for my aunts. They'd fussed over her, of course, and raved about the way she pulled things together at the wedding.

"Well, Charlie helped too." It was the one sliver of a compliment I'd gotten all night, and I'd quickly been forgotten once Cooper and Hadley started telling us all about their trip. I'd tuned out all the discussion of sun and sand and concentrated on my plate. If anyone noticed, no one said anything.

"Have the two of you been talking about possible names already?" I think Sadie must be asking Cooper and Hadley. They've got something important to name too, after all. But when I look up from my shoes she's staring at me. Everyone is staring at me.

"Me?" I point stupidly at my chest.

"Yes, you, Charlie. You and Jenna. It must come up at least occasionally," Mae coaxes, looking from me to Jenna.

"We haven't really talked about that."

"We're usually busy with other things. We're working separately a lot." Jenna's attempt to explain doesn't seem to clear anything up for my family.

"I thought y'all worked pretty closely together." Cade rubs his chin. "Looked like you were pretty familiar the other night."

"What are you talking about?" I sound defensive at best. I absolutely cannot look at Jenna. One glance will give everything away, and I'm starting to sweat at the possibility that Cade already knows. How easy would it have been for him to notice something the night of the bachelorette party? Or—even worse—for him to have noticed lights still on at the restaurant when we were together? It wouldn't have taken much effort to peer in a window and see—

"When you had to jump behind the line and sous chef the shit out of that wedding dinner. Y'all worked great together, and I don't think that's because you never talk to each other." Cade looks to my siblings for confirmation. "Y'all saw that too, right?"

Looking at the faces of my two older brothers, I'm pretty sure that's not all they're seeing. Chance's lips twist in annoyance, and I know a brutal conversation's in my immediate future.

"I think I misspoke." Jenna leans forward, trying to divert attention away from me and my big mouth. "Charlie and I work together very well. Just since the wedding we've been working on some things separately, so we haven't talked about the name *recently*. But we've obviously had conversations. Go ahead, Charlie, tell them what we talked about." I know she's not a saint, but she seems like one now. Jenna and I have never had a conversation about naming the restaurant and she's letting me off the hook instead of calling me out on that. "But we should make sure everyone's got drinks first." She's even buying me five extra minutes.

The clinking of bottles and the procuring of ice only takes a second, and then I'm back in the hot seat. I clear my throat. "I keep trying to make it more farm."

"And I keep thinking it needs to have a twist," Jenna interjects like we're rehashing an old argument.

"Right. So why don't we tell you our ideas and then if y'all have a few we can put those out there too?"

"Yes, great idea. But tell them that idea you had first. The one I liked." Jenna gestures for me to hurry up and get on with it. That would be a lot easier if I had any idea what she was talking about.

"Do you mean Back Forty?" I ask hesitantly. I've got a list of possible names as long as my arm, but Jenna doesn't know a damn thing about them.

"Was that my favorite? I thought it was Pasture." Jenna looks at me questioningly.

"But there was one of those in Richmond, remember?"

"Well, that is too bad because I like the sound of that," Mae tells us. "Keep going." All of my siblings are waiting for more of the brilliant ideas Jenna and I have allegedly come up with.

"I liked Harrow. You know, like the thing with the tines that you pull behind the tractor." Jenna nods enthusiastically.

"And I was surprised you even knew that word." I don't even have to pretend to be surprised now.

"The same way you were surprised when I suggested Sickle and Scythe." Jenna points at me like she's remembering.

"Were we going to use those separately? Or was it supposed to be the two of them together?" I ask, pretending to think.

"It has to be together. We talked about that. Alone, Scythe is too murdery, I think."

I snap my fingers. "That *is* what we decided." I nod. "Y'all feel free to chime in with your own ideas." It doesn't take much to get the ball rolling and before long Sadie's rushing to grab a pencil and paper to write all the ideas down.

"See, you two do work well together." Mae pats my arm. "You had us worried there for a minute."

Me too, Mae. Me too.

27

Jenna

"So what do you think for the test days? Is the weekend too much?" Charlie leans a hip onto the stainless steel counter.

"Do you feel comfortable having the cast of *High School Musical* handling a high-volume night?" I keep chopping, but enjoy the sound of a slight chuckle at my joke. Of course he's not going to really laugh. This is a truce, but not a complete cease fire.

"They're going to have to do it some time. Might as well be while we're still in the testing phase. How are you feeling about those new kitchen guys?" Charlie reaches out to snag a strip of bell pepper and I consider chopping off his finger.

"You have to quit giving me every sob story and stray in town." Who knew Mint Springs had so many down-on-their-luck guys who needed just one more chance? "I notice you aren't trying to keep all those prize winners for the front of the house."

"I'm trying to keep the neck tattoos to a minimum out

there." Charlie's joking, but I'm not laughing. My kitchen does have an exceptionally high number of neck tattoos.

"I don't have anything against the tats, but if we want to attract quality talent, we can't keep picking up all these dudes who can barely hold a knife. We need experience." I was hoping to be able to convince some talent to move here and, eventually, I'd like to be able to take a night off and think the kitchen was in capable hands.

"That'll come," Charlie assures me.

"Only if you let me run things my way." I point the knife menacingly at him. "And keep your hands off the ingredients."

"Yes, ma'am."

I give him my best cat impression, hissing for him to leave the kitchen. "Don't you have something to do? Somewhere else to be?"

"Actually, no. This is the main thing left on my to do list. Help me nail down our test dates and I'll be out of your hair." He gives me one of those boyish grins which is simultaneously attractive and cautionary. They are cute, but remind me he's got a lot of growing up to do. He's a thirty-year-old man-child, and I can't spend my time entertaining any illusions that he's something other than that.

Fantasies though? Those I'm still letting myself entertain. Often to the detriment of a good night's sleep.

"Maybe one Saturday to see how we do? We can always add extra dates or take a break between tries. We could do three, then a regroup, and then three more. How does that sound?"

"That'll work. I've got the menu close to ready. We won't do any specials, but I'll eventually work those in. Text me the dates and I'll confirm once I'm done here and can get to my calendar. We'll need to check with Faith too. Make sure she can handle an actual order." It's bitchy, and I know it, so I make it worse with a big, toothy smile.

"She'll be fine. You just make sure you've got the order ready to go. She needs a little notice, but soon we'll be on a regular delivery schedule. Easy as pie." He reaches out again and this time manages to get a pepper strip. He pops it in his mouth and then walks backward toward the dining room, hands in the air.

I scowl but decide against stabbing him. We're making too much progress to ruin it all with me getting arrested. But I do growl as he turns, and I'm pleased to watch him quicken his pace.

Can't have him too relaxed.

∿

"I was thinking some more about the name."

"Hmmm?" Charlie doesn't look up from his laptop. He's moved from the office to the bar now that the rest of the staff has left for the day. We've both been busting our asses to get them all trained up. He's set up camp as far away as possible from the site of our last brush with temptation. He never sits down at that end now. I've noticed, but I don't say anything. That's a subject where teasing is dancing with the devil.

"The restaurant name."

"You have a favorite? We've got a pretty big list now." Charlie's brothers keep adding more and even Lily and Hadley have started showing up at random times during the day to shout possibilities from the front door. "Or are you adding a new one?"

"I'm wanting to revisit one that didn't make the list." I

pull out the bar stool next to him, hoping this isn't going to put me too close. I don't want any accidental knee knocking or shoulder brushing. "I think you should still consider naming it after Mae and Sadie."

Charlie shakes his head. "They acted like they hate that idea."

"Well, of course they *acted* like they hate it. Everyone does that. That's why you don't ask. It would have to be a surprise. We would unveil it at the grand opening." They'd waved the idea away when it had come up before, but I saw the way Sadie and Mae reacted to finding out my restaurant had been named after my grandmother. And Sadie loves having her own gin. They might have acted like they weren't interested, but they'd done it in that self-deprecating way that told me they would probably be thrilled.

Charlie doesn't seem convinced.

"It's like telling someone you're going to name your baby after them. It feels a little awkward. But we're using so many of Sadie and Mae's recipes for the start of our menu here. Even if we're jazzing them up a bit and I'm putting my own spin on them, their ideas are the backbone. And from what you've told me of your summers here, Sadie and Mae were the backbone then too."

Charlie considers this. "That's probably true. We certainly wouldn't have eaten as well."

"Or had the kind of experience where you didn't have to think about anything but being kids. They're a big part of why you and your brothers are all here now." I take a chance and touch Charlie's hand. "You know them better than I do, but they don't seem like the kind to demand the spotlight, even if they deserve it. Just think about it."

"Was that why you named your restaurant after your grandmother?" His hand stays under mine.

"Pretty much. She was the biggest influence on my cooking for sure. And she always made me feel like a princess, even when it was clear other people might not agree." Thinking about my grandmother pokes at the hollow place I've got inside now. Naming my restaurant after her had felt like a triumph. That hadn't turned out the way I'd planned.

"I'm guessing she acted like she didn't want the attention but then loved it?" Charlie's eyes meet mine.

"My *abuela*? No. She acted like it was her birthright from the start. You should have heard her when she came into the kitchen at my grand opening. You would have thought she was Gordon Ramsay with her criticisms. She said she couldn't have her name out front of anything less than the best." I smile thinking about her antics. "She was barely five feet all, but she could scare the shit out of the biggest guys. My entire staff was terrified of her."

"And your ex didn't think he should change the name?"

"It wouldn't have been worth as much. People know Ana's. If he had changed the name, he would have lost the name recognition." And people would have known for sure that I wasn't the one in the kitchen. "Frank's lucky my grandmother wasn't around to see that. She died a few months before I lost the restaurant for good."

Charlie's forehead wrinkles. "I'm sorry, Jenna."

I shrug and move my hand from his. "Think about ways we can include Sadie and Mae. Talk to your brothers if you aren't sure how they'd take it. Cooper's using family names for the liquor, I think everyone would agree we could do the same here. It's a big honor, I think, and one they deserve."

Charlie nods, and I stand, ready to grab the rest of my things. "I'll see you tomorrow."

"If you're lucky," I tell him.

"Then I'm pretty sure I'll be seeing you because nobody's as lucky as me."

I walk away from that cocky grin before I get sucked in.

Jenna

"When are you going to move out of that hotel? You need a kitchen of your own."

"This is my kitchen." I don't bother looking at Mae, I already know I won't like the face she's making.

"You know what I meant. Don't you want a more permanent place? Living there isn't exactly comfortable, I wouldn't think." She looks to Sadie and I half expect her to elbow her sister. I know a planned attack when I see one. These two are masters of the ambush, but so stealthy you never suspect a thing.

"I like the hotel." That's not entirely a lie, but it's certainly not one hundred percent the truth. The things I like about the hotel are all the things I shouldn't confess. I'm enamored with its anonymity and the fact that even here in Mint Springs they don't seem to care one bit about what I'm up to. While plenty of other guests have come and gone, I'm still camped out in room 215 with only one suitcase and an addiction to late-night TV.

"It doesn't seem very..." Sadie looks at Mae and thins her lips. "Permanent."

"Mae mentioned that." I reach for the sugar. "Should we make a batch or two with a little something different?" I'm hoping talking about the jam we're making will distract Sadie and Mae enough to drop the subject of my living arrangements.

"I like the classic, but I'm sure you can come up with something delicious. Have you even looked at apartments? Hadley used to live in a cute little place. Where was that building, Sadie?" Mae hands me the sugar, but she couldn't care less about the work.

"Was it over on Bramblett? It wasn't in town exactly. We can ask her tonight. Lily lived there with her for a bit. Two bedrooms." Sadie nods as I measure the ingredients.

"We could try a little balsamic. I think you'll like that with the strawberries. Black pepper is nice too, gives it a little bite." I'm not sure if they're even listening to me.

"I'm sure there are places in town, too, if that's what you like. Too loud for me, and I'd miss my chickens, of course." Mae taps her chin. "Too bad we don't have a place out here."

"She could move in with Charlie," Sadie suggests. "His house is too big for him anyway. All that space to wander around in."

"With Charlie?" My voice raises two octaves.

"Sure. He doesn't bite." Sadie's not even joking. "And it's not like he's going to be settling down any time soon. He'll have plenty of extra room forever."

"That wouldn't be permanent either, though," I protest. "And I see plenty of Charlie at work already. I don't need to live with him too." I'm already fighting off my attraction to him, I don't need him sleeping down the hall. I imagine running into Charlie in all sorts of compromising positions.

I'm already starting to sweat, and it has nothing to do with the giant pots of water we have boiling to process our jars. "I'll start looking for a place soon. Let's concentrate on finishing up this jam." The season's first strawberries wink at me from the bowls on the counter.

"Fine. We'll leave you alone. For now." Mae emphasizes the last part. "And pepper? Are you crazy?"

~

"I know we're prepping for the test days, but what would you say to me borrowing the kitchen one night next week?" I resist batting my eyelashes.

"Borrowing? What does that mean?" Charlie's hazel eyes bore into me.

"I would like to cook for your family, but I don't have any place to do it." The idea had struck me after my interrogation with the aunts. Normally, I'd show my appreciation the same way I show my love—with food. Hell, that's the way I show pretty much everything. There's not an emotion I don't work out over the stove top. Sadie and Mae had already done that to welcome me and to make me feel included. I could return the favor, if Charlie would agree.

"You want to use the commercial kitchen for that?" He was building up to a no.

"It's not the best compromise, but until I have a place of my own..."

"When are you planning on taking care of that, anyway?" He pretended that the question was a throwaway, but he was paying too much attention to really not care.

"Soon." Vague, sure, but true. I'd get to that eventually, if I decided to stick around. If things managed to stay just on the right side of reasonable. "I'd like to make some of the dishes my grandmother used to make. Share my family recipes in the way they were originally made. The same way Sadie and Mae have done for me. And I'd like to invite your brothers. And Lily and Hadley, of course."

"You don't need the restaurant for that." Charlie stares at me, and I can see him weighing his options. He's going to shoot my idea down. I can see why. There really isn't any need to have my own private dinner party here, not when we're so close to the soft opening. "You can cook at my house."

"Your house?" That is not at all what I wanted. It isn't moving in, but it's making myself at home.

"You've seen my kitchen; it should have everything you need. I've never hosted family dinner there. It'll give Sadie and Mae a break. Pick a day and we'll let everyone know." He seems to think that settles it.

"Are you sure you'd be comfortable with me in your space like that? I'd be there most of the day." I'm already dreading the mental gymnastics I'm going to need to perform to avoid Charlie in his own house.

"It shouldn't be a problem. And it'll win me kudos with everyone. It'll be more comfortable than having it here." He's full of good points, and I did ask him for a favor. Unfortunately, he's giving me what I want. Sort of.

"Okay," I say brightly. I'm nothing but sunshine about this new arrangement. "I'd love to borrow your kitchen. Thank you." I stop short of extending my hand to shake his. Charlie regards me with confusion.

"You're welcome. It'll be fun."

I nod. That's not the word I would have used.

29

Charlie

"Whoa there, you tryin' to pull weeds or decapitate someone?"

I look at the ridiculous gash I've put in the ground in front of me.

"You know you don't have to help me if you'd rather be somewhere else." There's no malice in Faith's voice. She's not like that. Her sunny disposition even applies to firing me from my offer to help her out with her chores. "We can go do something else, if you think you're going to be too dangerous with that spade."

"Sorry, I'm a little distracted." I take one gloved hand and try to pack the soil back flat. "There, good as new."

"A *little* distracted?" Faith gives me one of her patented looks of disbelief. She's been handing them out to me since elementary school.

"Fine. A lot distracted." Ever since Jenna showed up at my front door this morning, her arms full of more food than we'll ever be able to eat, I haven't been able to think about anything else. I'm not thinking about the food, of course, although I'm sure whatever Jenna's making is going to be hands down one of the best meals I've ever had the pleasure of eating. No, I'm thinking about the way her eyes had gone wide and her lips had parted like she had been somehow surprised to have me be the one opening the door to my own house.

I'd tried to stay out of her way, but the pull of her in my kitchen was too strong. There was nothing on TV that was going to be able to entertain me for long when I knew she was working in there. No chef's coat today, and Jenna's combination of leggings and baggy T-shirt should not have been as mesmerizing as it was.

After my tenth time interrupting her, she finally kicked me out.

Of my own house.

"Jenna's making dinner tonight at my house."

"Oh?" Faith bends down to pull a weed from between two plants. They're still small, and the ground is still soft from when they were planted.

"She doesn't have a kitchen, so she's using mine." I lay out the facts. This is all just fine. Completely normal.

"That sounds cozy." Faith's blonde head bobs between the rows of tomatoes, straightening stakes and pulling tiny blades of grass from the ground. "Bet that's not driving you crazy at all."

I sigh loudly enough to have Faith standing up again. "I can't shake her, you know?"

"I know. It's worse than the time you had a crush on Hadley's big sister."

"I never had a crush on Mindy Crawford." I put my hands on my hips, indignant.

"Are you kidding me? You used to try to spy on her and her friends, riding around on your bicycle. Used to make me pretend we were going down to buy things at the Piggly Wiggly so you could bike past Hot House Flowers. I've never spent so much time at the beauty salon in my life." Now Faith's got her hands on her hips, mimicking my pose, the early afternoon sun shining down on her. "Go ahead and try and deny it. I knew exactly why you wanted to take all those trips into town."

I lower my head. "I'd forgotten about that." We couldn't have been much older than twelve and Mindy Crawford had to have been closer to sixteen or seventeen.

"Always have liked 'em a little bit older," Faith teases. "And I could see it with Jenna from a mile away. She's got that mean streak you like."

"She's not mean. She's…" I don't dare try to explain this to Faith. She'll be able to see right through me. Yes, Jenna's a bit on the bossy side, but I don't need to try to convince Faith how great that can be.

Faith waves me away with her hand. "I know how she is."

"But you don't. She comes across as cold sometimes, maybe, or distant, but once you get to know her…" I don't know why I'm pushing this with Faith. She may be my best friend, but she and Jenna don't need to be buddies. It would probably be easier if they weren't.

"I have tried to get to know her, tried to be nice. But she's too Boston and I'm too Mint Springs, I guess." Faith shrugs. "It's not like you're going to marry her; she's just working at your restaurant."

I pause.

"Charlie?" Faith's stricken face peeks out from the plants. "Oh, no. Seriously?"

"What? No. No, I'm not in love with her. Don't be stupid." But the way my chest tightened at the word isn't a good sign. Jenna and I are a terrible match. We're like oil and water. Which, if I think about it, can still make a good salad dressing if you blend it well enough and add a few more ingredients. The same way Jenna and I take a little mixing, but once it happens—

"Good Lord, Charlie. You're going to get yourself into a heap of trouble, you know that, right?"

Faith has no idea how much trouble I've already gotten myself into. And how tempting that trouble really is.

"Think about the future here, okay? Nothing good can come of you fooling around with the chef at your restaurant. Things will end badly, and you're not exactly known for being able to gracefully exit a relationship. Or whatever this would be." Faith is exasperated. "This is the ultimate broken record situation right here."

I startle. "No it isn't."

Faith rolls her eyes. "You are always going after the messiest of choices. Why can't you pick a local girl and settle down? Or not even that. Pick a local girl and squire her around for a bit?"

"Squire? What does that even mean?" I'm already defensive, and Faith doesn't even know how messy things with Jenna already are.

"You'd better hope Cade doesn't find out. He and I were just talking about how you—" Faith clamps her mouth shut.

"You were talking to Cade?"

"Sure. At the wedding." Faith tries to play it off, but she and Cade have never been buddies. They don't "talk" and never have.

"I see. And what exactly were you talking about again?"

"Nothing." Faith moves away from me and starts working farther down the row. "But mark my words, Charlie. If you can't keep it in your pants this time, there's going to be real trouble."

I'm pretty sure there already is, but I keep my mouth shut. Instead, I try to focus on the work, mindlessly yanking at every stray weed that shows up in my path. It doesn't work though, because my empty mind keeps going back to Jenna in my kitchen, in my bed, in my hands.

And I'm going to have to go back to my house eventually. Where all those thoughts will be harder to ignore.

30

Jenna

I have officially made too much food. So much food, that I'm almost embarrassed to have Charlie's family come bursting through the door in an hour and see the spectacle I've got going on in his kitchen. The counters are piled high with the bowls and pans I've used and the ingredients I've been digging into. One big advantage of a commercial kitchen: a giant sink to hide all of your dirty dishes. Another? A person you pay to wash all those pots and pans for you. Charlie will probably kill me when he gets home and sees this mess.

If he comes back, that is. He left in a rush this morning, mumbling about having so much to do. He hadn't seemed all that busy camped out on the couch flipping through the million sports channels he's got on the giant TV. But he'd been quick to jump up and come into the kitchen if he heard even the slightest noise. Before I even had a chance to ask where he kept the can opener or if I should have brought the mortar and pestle from the restaurant, he was right next to me, opening drawers and pulling out equipment. He seemed to want to help, but he never said as much, and I was hesitant to ask for a whole host of reasons. Several of them X-rated. I'd had to get rid of him.

Now, I'm getting to the point where I can take ten minutes and think about cleaning up—the house and myself. The plan is to make the kitchen presentable and then do the same for myself, so I fill the sink with soapy water and get to work. Standing in the silence of Charlie's kitchen doing something so domestic is actually kind of nice. I relax into the feeling of the warm water on my hands and enjoy the view of the mountains out the window. Another woman might imagine having Charlie come home, 1950s style, and for a moment I entertain that idea. It isn't me, though. If I'm imagining Charlie coming home and finding me here at this sink, up to my elbows in suds, it is going to end up decidedly more slippery. No chaste kisses for me as I think about getting soaking wet up against this fancy granite countertop.

By the time I'm done with the dishes, I'm worked up enough to be glad Charlie isn't here. I have always had an active imagination, and I can easily picture Charlie pressed up behind me, his wet hands on my breasts. My nipples ache to be touched, and my panties are damp. Damn, it would be nice to be able to take care of that before dinner. I'm not about to touch myself in Charlie's kitchen, but in that little half bath? I do need to change clothes, after all. And I'm sure I can be quick.

I've brought a dress to change into. It might only be the Allens coming tonight, but I wouldn't ever try to present my food looking sloppy. My pride wouldn't let me and neither would the memory of my abuela. My grandmother took pride in her cooking and her appearance, and that was a lesson I learned early on. People treat you differently depending on the way you're dressed, and even a beautiful woman can use a little sparkle. My oversized T-shirt and leggings might be comfortable, but they don't exactly scream "competent business woman." Hell, they don't even say "domestic goddess," and I'm not even interested in that label, no matter what my earlier kitchen fantasy might indicate.

I slide out of my slouchy outfit and get ready to pull on the form-fitting dress I've brought for dinner. It's nothing special, but it shows off my curves and requires very little wrestling to get into. That's a plus, it turns out, because this bathroom is on the small side. I take my hair down out of the ponytail I've had it in all morning. I only cook with my hair pulled tight in a ponytail or—even better for work—a bun. When I release it, it falls over my shoulders.

When my hair is down, it's one of the first things people notice. It's fuck-me hair. Long and glossy and made for running your fingers through. Or pulling, let's be honest. And it seems to attract men like bees to honey. I take a look at myself in the mirror over the sink. I'm not photo ready by any means, and the lighting in here leaves a lot to be desired, but it works. I slide one hand over my chest, and my nipples pebble through the lace. I let the other hand drag down my belly and past the elastic of my panties. I know it won't take long for me to come, even if I'm only working with my fingers. I let them slip over my clit and even that brief bit of contact has me purring. I lean over the sink, imagining Charlie behind me, pretending it's his hands on me and not my own. That gets me hotter than almost anything these days, thinking about Charlie while I touch myself. It's even hotter that I'm having to do it quickly. It makes it seem even more taboo, more forbidden, to be sneaking around to get myself off in his house.

I squeeze my eyes shut and furiously work my clit. I pull a lacy cup down under one boob and tweak the nipple, fantasize about Charlie's tongue there instead. I'm panting. My hand is a poor substitute, but I can feel myself getting close. That familiar hum has me groaning a little, pushing first one and then another finger inside myself, using my thumb to keep the pressure on my clit. My head lolls forward a bit as I rock against my hand, letting my orgasm overtake me.

"Jenna? Are you alright?" Charlie's question is followed almost immediately by the doorknob turning. It happens like a slow motion scene from a movie—me, already too far gone to stop, and him in the room before he realizes what he's walked in on.

Charlie's eyes widen as they take in the scene in front of him. I'm nearly naked, with my hand down my panties, my face already fixed into an expression he knows better than most. His mouth drops open as he stammers something about hearing me moaning right before he backs out of the bathroom and closes the door behind him.

31

Charlie

Holy hell. What in the name of high school football did I just walk in on?

I pace back and forth in my bedroom, running my hands through my hair hard enough to pull some of it out by the roots. I had expected to find Jenna in the kitchen still working away on dinner. I'd managed to stay away most of the day, but after working with Faith I smelled a little too much like manure and sweat to be a reasonable guest at any dinner party, even one being held in my own house. I'd tried to time it so I had the opportunity for a shower and a quick change of clothes.

But then Jenna hadn't been in the kitchen, and I'd heard a whimper and then a moan from the bathroom off the front hall. I'd thought maybe she was hurt—she could have cut herself or burned her hand, something like that. But she wasn't hurting at all. Sweet Jesus, that was a sight to walk in on. Despite the angel on my shoulder telling me I should try to wipe those images from my brain, the devil on my other side's pretty sure he's keeping those forever. Jenna in her underwear, making herself come? That's going to be pretty near impossible to forget.

Although now I have to go out and look her in the eye. Even worse, in a few minutes I'm going to need to keep doing that with my entire family here. I put myself in the shower and turn the thing on full blast, as cold as I can get it.

By the time I come out of my bedroom, Jenna's dressed and sitting at the kitchen island. She's got a drink in front of her and her head in her hands. She startles when I come in the room, and her cheeks flush pink. One thing I have never seen Jenna do, no matter the circumstance, is blush. She's really off her game.

"Charlie, I..." She looks miserable.

"Don't worry about it." I go to the liquor cabinet and grab a bottle of whiskey. We're both going to need a drink to get through this conversation.

"I thought you'd be home later, which doesn't explain why I was doing that here in the first place. You let me borrow your house, and I act like a pervert." Jenna's upset enough that her voice is rising with every word.

"That's not the most perverted thing I've ever seen you do." It's true even if it doesn't help the situation.

Jenna's mouth hangs open a bit, but then it slowly morphs into the tiniest smile. "That's probably true."

"And that's the most action that bathroom's ever seen." I grab a glass and pour myself a double. No need for ice or anything elaborate. The whiskey burns my throat a bit as I take a swallow, but it takes my mind off other parts of me that were too invested in half-naked Jenna.

"I don't normally make a habit of doing that in other people's houses."

I start to press her for more details, but the doorbell

rings. My family's here just in time to keep me from getting to the good stuff. "You look beautiful, by the way. Not that you didn't look pretty good before." I manage to keep my hands to myself as I pass her surprised face on my way to the front door.

"Well, I could not eat another bite." Sadie pushes her chair away from the table for emphasis. "I'm full as a tick."

"I went a little overboard, maybe. I wanted you guys to taste so many things." Jenna's face has been lit up like a candle all night. With each dish she brought out from the kitchen, she had a story to tell. Every bite was full of memories. My family can appreciate that like none other. It didn't hurt that dinner was also delicious.

"We always appreciate overboard." Cooper looks at Hadley. "And it looks like someone's really gotten their appetite back."

Hadley smiles. "That lemonade you made me really helped, Jenna. The ginger did the trick. Well, that and getting further into the second trimester."

"That's an old home remedy the women in my family swear by." Jenna's in her element. "Does anyone have room for dessert?"

"Dessert?" Lily groans. "I don't, but I'm gonna make some."

Everyone else nods while Jenna jumps up to get the next course from the kitchen.

"This is nice, Charlie," Mae says. "We've never really spent much time in your house." She looks around the table for confirmation. Already I can feel a setup.

"Yes," Sadie agrees. "And it was lovely to walk into a

house that smelled like a home cooked meal! Has Jenna been here all day?"

"Most of it. That pernil takes an entire day to make, but she prepped it yesterday at the restaurant." The pork had been fork-tender, falling apart in a way you can only get from hours of cooking. "I wasn't here, though. I tried to stay out of her way."

"You weren't here?" Chance seems to think that's the weirdest part of this situation.

"I went to help Faith pull some weeds. Jenna didn't need me here."

"You were with Faith?" Cade's question is sharper than I'd like.

"Sure. What's your issue with that?" I can't believe Cade's in on this too. My entire family ganging up on me to, what? Start something with Jenna? My brothers can't think that's a good idea.

"We all thought you were in on this dinner," Mae clarifies.

"This was all Jenna. She wanted to cook for y'all, and I let her use my house. I don't know how to make any of these things. We spend plenty of time together during the work week. She didn't need me to help her; she needed a place to do it. I don't understand what all the confusion's about." I grab my plate and stand. "I'll see if Jenna needs any help."

She's standing at the kitchen island, prepping the most gorgeous bowls of rice pudding I've ever seen. I've already told her it's my weakness, but watching her hands move and the tiny smile playing on her face makes me realize I've got another weakness I hadn't fully realized.

"Can I help?"

Jenna's head snaps up. "You can get ready to run these out. We should probably clear first, though." I didn't bother grabbing anyone else's empty dinner plate when I rushed in here to avoid more interrogation.

"I can go back and do that."

"Mofongo and pernil was too much, wasn't it?" Jenna makes a face.

"It was the *pasteles* that put it over the top." I smile in a way I hope she recognizes as teasing.

"I was worried I wouldn't get another chance, so I basically threw the entire canon of Puerto Rican cuisine at them in one evening."

"Why would you think you wouldn't get another chance?" I move closer to her. The smells of the kitchen mix with the smell of her skin. Sadie was right about how good it feels to walk into a house that smells like this, but she missed one crucial ingredient—Jenna. It has to have this right here.

"Charlie, we both know this is fraught with obstacles. Restaurants are hardly ever successful, and you and I working together is..." Jenna's brow furrows.

"Great?" I offer, pairing it with a grin.

"I was going to say volatile. One minute we love each other and the next it's hate."

I startle. "I don't hate you. I could never hate you." *Jenna thinks I hate her?*

"Oh, you could, believe me. Eventually you might. I'm trying to be realistic."

"Is that why you won't find a permanent place out here? Because you think I'm going to send you packing any minute?"

Jenna doesn't answer.

"We have plenty of time, Jenna. And it's all going to work out fine." I take one more deep breath of rice pudding plus Jenna. "At least you only made one dessert."

"I made two. There are thumbprint cookies with guava paste over there on that tray." Jenna scrunches up her face. "Sorry."

"Don't ever apologize for feeding me, Jenna. Or the people I love." I don't wait to see her reaction to that. There's a table that needs clearing.

32

Jenna

"You really don't need to stay; I've got it all under control." I might be fine with letting people help me clear the table and serve a bit, but I am not ever going to let guests start a dishwashing conga line. I know at Sadie and Mae's house everyone pitches in, but tonight is my first and—possibly only—Allen family dinner party. There's no way I'm going to have pregnant Hadley wilting on her feet or eternal good sport Lily up to her elbows in roasting pans. I've done a decent job washing as I go and my last hit of dishwashing, while leaving me incredibly horny, also kept the kitchen fairly clean.

"I do not feel okay leaving you with a mess, Jenna. After cooking all day? At least let the boys stay and help." Mae's eyelids are drooping but she's still got the energy to volunteer her nephews.

"I've got Charlie. He can't leave the kitchen a mess, otherwise he'll wake up to more work." I wink at his elderly aunts. "He'll help."

"If he knows what's good for him," Sadie interjects, and

both she and Mae fall all over each other laughing. We've obviously given them too much of Cooper's apple brandy.

"Let me escort you ladies to the truck." Cooper comes alongside Mae and offers his elbow. "Thanks again, Jenna. It was all delicious. I'm excited to talk pairings and recipes next week."

"Me, too." Over dinner Copper and Hadley were full of innovative ideas about how we could source local ingredients for both our menu and their future offerings. The apples are merely a start, and I can't wait to brainstorm with them. "Are you sure you've got that under control?" I cock my head toward Mae and Sadie. They're already moving into the front hall.

"Cade's helping." Cooper nods in the direction of his youngest brother, who gives us a little salute before chasing after the senior citizens. "We can handle those two if you're sure you can handle Charlie."

"Charlie?" I scoff. "He's easy." That's the world's biggest lie. He may seem easygoing and fun, but he can also be incredibly stubborn.

Cooper knows this, of course, and gives me an incredulous look. "If you say so." And then he's off chasing Mae before she ends up in Charlie's flower beds.

Chance and Lily file out next, with hugs and compliments. I will never get tired of hearing about how good my food tastes. Sometimes people are blowing smoke up your ass, but by now I can tell a true reaction from a fake one. The ones tonight were genuine and made even more significant because they came from Charlie's family—a family I'm becoming attached to whether I like it or not.

Charlie's already at the sink when I come back into the kitchen.

"You don't have to do that." My dishwashing fantasies

have already gotten me into trouble, and I'm more interested than I should be in the way Charlie's rolled his sleeves up. I'm looking at entirely too much forearm in all that soapy water.

"You shouldn't have to do dishes. The cook doesn't clean. House rules." He smiles at me over his shoulder. "Get a glass of wine and go sit on the couch. Put your feet up."

I start to protest. I shouldn't linger in Charlie's house. I should make an effort to get out of here as soon as possible. But the pull of a nice glass of wine and the chance to be off duty for a bit wins out. I grab a fresh glass and reach for the open bottle of red on the island. In truth, it's one of many consumed tonight. Those Allens can drink.

"Do you want a glass?" I ask the back of Charlie's head. "I try to be nice to the help."

"Sure. I can take sips in between pots here. Scullery maids need to stay hydrated." He doesn't stop working even as I come up next to him and put the drink on the counter. "I was serious about you sitting down. You went all out tonight. You've *been* going all out. You deserve a break."

The living room suddenly feels too far away. "How about I sit in here with you?"

Charlie stiffens. "If you want." The only glimpse of his face I can get is from the reflection in the window. I pull out a stool anyway, hoping he's wearing a smile and not a grimace at the thought of me in here with him.

I sip my wine and watch Charlie's back as he washes, rinses, and dries. Even through his button down shirt I can see the muscles from the farm work he does flexing under the fabric. The couch in the living room is starting to feel like a much safer choice, but too late now.

I slide off the stool and move toward Charlie. "Are you sure I can't help?"

My proximity surprises him, and he jumps a little. It's a slight movement, but enough to have the platter in his hand falling back into the sink and water splashing up onto both of us.

"Oh, I—"

"Oh, God. Sorry—"

We both reach for the slippery platter at the same time, hands touching in the water.

"Did it break?" I ask, my face too close to his.

"I don't think so." Charlie's not looking at the tray in his hand; he's looking at me. "Jenna…" I can see the fight he's having with himself in real time. It's written all over his face. We're too close but not close enough; we're not supposed to keep doing this, but we keep giving in.

I don't break eye contact and neither does he, even when he drops the platter again, letting it clank against the sink. One wet hand comes up toward my face and threads into my hair, holding me firm at the scalp. Then Charlie's mouth slants over mine. His other hand snakes behind me and pulls me close, pressing our wet fronts together. Any reticence I had dissolves.

Finally.

Charlie

I'm doing it again. Letting my selfishness take over, letting what I want be more important than what I know is best. Ever since I walked in on Jenna earlier, I've had to fight extra hard to keep my hands to myself and my mind out of the gutter. It's a superhuman effort now with her in the same room and no one else to see, no one to stop me.

The dishes were a good distraction, but one that only works if she leaves the room. Feeling her eyes on me as I work actually has the opposite effect, and as I try to concentrate on finishing the last of the serving pieces, it's like I'm in a snow globe, constantly being shaken again and again. When Jenna comes up next to me, I'm already well past the point of being able to resist her.

She ends up wet—soapy water trickling all down the front of her. The dress that's been torturing me all night has a deep V-neck, and one tiny droplet starts at her collarbone and travels all the way down, taking a path I've taken before with my tongue. My eyes track it until it disappears in between her tits. It slows as her chest rises and then disappears.

Jenna's face is full of surprise, her lush mouth opening from the shock of the water and then closing again as she leans closer. Once our hands touch, I don't have an excuse anymore. It's too late before I've even really made a move; in my mind I'm already taking Jenna to bed, already using every available surface in this house to put us farther over the line we said we weren't crossing again.

I kiss her hard, and the way she moans against my mouth tells me she's been waiting too, trying to ignore the pull. She doesn't stop me—if anything she presses tighter against me when my hand finds her ass. My other hand is holding her face the way I want it, and I enjoy that for a few seconds. Jenna's not one to be controlled, but she's letting my tight grip stay, which in a way is still her being the boss. I'm very aware that she could shut all of this down—hell, she probably should—but I keep her where she is and get ready to push my luck even further.

"Tell me what you were thinking about." I whisper it into the shell of her ear. When she takes her time answering, I push her further. "When I came home. When I saw you in the bathroom."

Jenna shivers, presses closer.

"Tell me." I let my voice stay firm in a way I never do with her. Even at work, I seldom try to dominate when it comes to Jenna. We're working together most of the time and the rest I let her take the lead. When we've been alone, I've liked deferring to her, being the one who's controlled. This is what Jenna seems most comfortable with, but tonight when her eyes flash at my tone, she doesn't seem angry.

She seems turned on.

"You," she answers, her voice deep and low. "Your hands on me."

"Like this?" My hands are on her now, moving along her curves.

"Just like this. Right here."

"What else?" This is the best kind of torture—the sweet feeling of Jenna telling me what I want to hear while I skirt along the edges of what I want to do to her.

"Your mouth." Jenna moves to kiss me but I turn my head a bit. Her frustrated grunt pleases me to no end.

"My mouth where?" I lick my way up the column of her neck.

"Everywhere, Charlie. Everywhere." She's pliable in my hands—soft—and she's letting me go on for longer than I would have expected.

"Everywhere?" I move my roaming hand from her ass and let it find its way up under her dress. I've already seen that Jenna's wearing something lacy and sheer under there. When my fingertips find the fabric of those panties, I'm not surprised they're already damp. Jenna wiggles a little, pressing against my fingers, and I slip under the barrier between us to touch bare skin. "Were my fingers here?"

"Yes," Jenna hisses out. "Inside me." She pulls her head from my hand and puts some space between us—enough for me to be able to see her face when I increase the pressure and slide two fingers deep inside her. She clutches at my shoulders, moving on my hand. I curl those fingers forward and find her clit with my thumb. Jenna moans again and puts her head against my chest. Her dark hair falls to cover her face, and I pull it back. I want to be able to look at her as I make her confess her dirty thoughts to me.

"Tell me the rest of it." I make it an order, and Jenna's

head comes off my chest immediately. For a second I think I've gone too far, but she only smiles a bit.

She keeps riding my hand but manages to whimper out, "Your cock."

"What about it?" It's basically screaming to be freed from my pants.

"I need it, Charlie." Jenna's eyes are closed, and she's biting her bottom lip.

"Tell me," I order again, and the fire in her eyes this time makes it unmistakable: Jenna isn't minding this one bit.

"Bend me over. Please." Jenna is not one to beg and, holy shit, do I like the sound of it.

"Come here." I bring Jenna to the edge of the kitchen island, where I'd had my family gathered less than an hour before. At the loss of my fingers, Jenna whimpers again, bouncing a little. She's impatient and not at all in control, and I'm prepared to enjoy it while it lasts. I slide those fingers between my lips and lick the taste of Jenna off of them. She watches, eyes dark, her lips parted. I begin to move her upper body over the countertop before I have a stroke of genius; I straighten her back up and pull the top of her dress down, exposing her breasts. I free each one from the lacy cups, looking far longer than necessary at Jenna's tits. The dusty rose of her nipples against the tan skin makes it impossible not to touch them for a bit. Her nipples pebble under my fingertips.

Now when I lean her over, her breasts are pressed against the countertop. She turns her head to look at me, but I keep one hand on her back to make her stay flat. "Turn your head this way." Jenna does it without hesitation. I smooth the hair off her face, letting my thumb graze her bottom lip.

I move behind her, grab the hem of her dress, and pull it

up. Jenna takes in a sharp breath but doesn't protest. I run my hand over the globes of her ass, feeling the lace under my palms. It's not what I want, so I pull the panties down and let them pool around her ankles. The softness of her skin has me humming, not sure I can wait even though I'd like to prolong this as much as possible.

"Wider," I command, and Jenna moves her legs farther apart. She's still wearing the heels she put on before dinner, and her legs look impossibly long. Now she's completely exposed to me, and I run a hand between her legs, teasing her a bit, enjoying the way she shivers.

"Charlie." It's a plea.

"Shhh. I need to get a condom. Stay exactly like that. Don't move." I expect some complaining about that—a little push back, at least—but Jenna stays the way I've positioned her as I walk away. Once I hit the hallway, I basically fly to my bedroom. The faster I get back to the kitchen, the more likely Jenna is to maybe still be in there.

I'm expecting her to have turned the tables somehow, and my heart's racing at the thought of walking into some kind of Jenna-orchestrated trap. She's been too docile, too compliant tonight, and as I fumble through the drawer of my bedside table, I'm sure she's not going to be doing what she's been told. Not a chance.

But once I slow my run back down to a walk and turn the corner into the kitchen, I'm shocked to find her exactly where I left her. She hasn't even turned her head, and I can stand in the doorway to stare at her all I like. Her bare ass is still up in the air and her breasts are still pushed against the cold granite.

I walk in slowly. I know she can hear me, because her breathing speeds up, coming in short shallow bursts until I'm right beside her. "You look so hot like this." I run a hand down her back as I use the other one to unbutton my shirt. Going slow is killing me, but by the way Jenna's legs are shaking, it's killing her too. I'm willing to suffer if it gets her worked up like that. I am willing to *torture* myself for that reaction.

Jenna's whimper almost makes me reconsider. "Charlie," she whines. There is nothing like my name on her lips, and having the roles reversed is making this almost disorienting. I've forgotten what it's like to be able to pull the strings, and I still can't believe Jenna's letting me.

"Hold on." I get my shirt off and toss it on the floor, start on my pants, sure to let the clinking of my belt buckle linger for a minute. "Let's make sure you're still warmed up." I walk behind Jenna and put a hand on her backside. She flinches, and I think about giving her a slap. I don't push my luck, though, partly because I'm desperate to be inside her. Her dress is still bunched around her waist, the fabric twisted. I want the whole thing off, but I'm afraid to break whatever spell Jenna's under.

Jenna groans as I let my fingers glide lower.

"Fuck." It comes out low and slow, sounding about as Southern as I ever have. Jenna is soaking wet. I barely touch her and her hips jerk in response. I get the condom on faster than I ever have in my life.

"Charlie, please," Jenna whispers, and I don't waste any more time messing around. I plunge myself into her, both of us moaning.

I have the idea that I'm going to be able to go slow, that I'm going to be able to tease Jenna for a bit and take my time, but once I'm buried in her it's obvious I'm about to embarrass myself. My salvation comes from an unlikely source. On my second thrust, I feel Jenna's pussy start to tighten around me. Her prolonged *oh* clues me into the fact that Jenna's already well on her way to an orgasm. I let the feel of her body take me with her and I go right behind her, calling out her name as I pump into her. Still bent over the island, Jenna pushes back against me, keeping her chest pressed against the counter.

I collapse on top of her as we try to catch our breath.

"Sorry that was so fast," Jenna says in between pants. "I'll make it up to you."

And although you can bet I'm going to take her up on that offer, I laugh all the same.

34

Jenna

"You can't say things like that and not explain them."

"What is there to explain? Annabel said she'd rather stay with you than work with a bunch of Neanderthals. I can see her point. I don't think she was talking about me, though, for the record. Give me your foot." Charlie reaches out his hand.

"Don't try to smooth this over with a foot rub." I make a stern face but still offer him my right foot.

"This isn't an attempt to placate you, this is good business. I can't have my chef standing on her feet all day and not offer a foot rub." Charlie pushes hard on the ball of my foot and I groan. "It's also a play to get in your pants."

"Well, that shouldn't be difficult." I'm already naked and in Charlie's oversized bathtub.

"I don't like to assume." Charlie's hands keep working. "I'm giving you a heads-up because Annabel's going to come and talk to you tomorrow. I think it's a little late to change teams, although I'm open to having her train with you after the test days if you're okay with that."

I lean my head against the edge of the tub. Water sloshes over the edge a bit, but I don't freak out the way I might have before. Charlie's bathroom is made for splashing. "She does a good job, and she's old enough. She really showed her skills when she jumped into the kitchen at Cooper and Hadley's wedding. If she wants to change from the front of the house to the back, I'm fine with that. I can't say I blame her."

Charlie shoves his bottom lip out in an exaggerated pout. "But we're in agreement about waiting until after the test days? And you have to take Jonah, too."

"What?" I give him a little splash. "I'm not taking Jonah. You keep the flunkies you hired. No offense to Jonah, since he's marginally competent." Charlie's been working over-time to get the people he trained ready. He's a big believer in effort over experience. I, on the other hand, have tried to be adamant about my hires meeting basic requirements. You want to work in my kitchen? You'd better have worked in one already. I don't have time for many newbies.

"You're too tough," Charlie complains.

"And you're not tough enough. You want to argue about that again?" I know he doesn't. It's the kind of fight no one wins. Charlie tries to be the good guy, and I try to be the hard ass. We're never meeting in the middle on that. It's the same as the hotel fight we keep having. I've spent the past five nights here, but I refuse to give up my hotel room. Charlie's argument that I can always get another room doesn't stop me from telling the front desk to book me for another week. It's something that's unspoken now. My suitcase might be here, but that doesn't mean anything. "How are the reservations looking for tomorrow night?"

"It's a little sparse, but I think some people are just waiting."

"For what?" It's not like there are going to be a bevy of better offers for dinner here in Mint Springs, and we need a full dining room to be able to really see if things work.

"They want to see what their friends do, find out if we're worth the money. They can get what they like at Ham & Eggs; they don't know yet why they should let us make their dinner." Charlie shifts to grab my other foot. "Give it time."

"Are they really our target demographic? I thought we were trying to get people to drive down from Chattanooga or up from Atlanta?" I slosh the water around again, trying to seem competent while Charlie's strong hands knead the bridge of my foot.

"Eventually. But be careful what you wish for. We'll have plenty of those people for the grand opening. We don't necessarily want them to try to break in the staff." Charlie's fingers keep working my foot, distracting me from my arguments. When his hand moves a little higher, I try to pull my leg back, but he holds firm. "Want to see this other kind of massage I'm working on?"

"You feeling good about things, chef?" Miguel is one of the newer guys on the line, and one of the reasons I can confidently answer the way I do.

"I am. I think tonight's going to go well." I don't even have to fake a smile. I've got the usual first-day jitters, but it's more excitement than anything else. "You nervous?"

Miguel shakes his head. "Not at all. We know our stuff."

He's right about that. I've got my side more than ready. Sure, things can still go wrong, but I've got a trustworthy team. Most of them are experienced, and all of them jump when I say jump. Charlie complains that I run my kitchen like a dictator, but I'm not apologizing. If anyone screws up tonight, my bet's on Charlie's team.

Looking out to the front of the restaurant, I can still see him trying to work out a few kinks. He's way more forgiving than I am, but I'm hoping his last-minute pep talks keep the waitstaff from messing up things for my guys. Right now Charlie's showing Chandra how to use the POS system. Again. Her face scrunches up in concentration as Charlie's fingers move on the touch screen. She's not brand new to restaurant work, but Chandra's only worked at Ham & Eggs before. That place is as mom and pop as it gets. They still write orders on paper slips and hand them back to the kitchen. Nightmare. But Chandra's picking up a few shifts here now, so she has to get up to speed.

Charlie looks up and sees me watching him. I tilt my head and wait for that hint of a smile he gives me at work. We've been keeping things low-key, especially here. No one needs to know we're anything more than co-workers. I don't know what we'd even tell them; how to define our relationship is still a mystery to me too.

And I'm not about to ask Charlie for his take on things. That would only confuse the situation. I'm fine with casual and undefined, and I don't need that to get muddied up with Charlie's interpretation. I'm willing to see how things play out, but I'm keeping my cards close to the vest for now.

"Hey." Charlie pokes his head into the kitchen. He's a little breathless. "You getting excited?" He runs a hand through his hair, making it stick out in all sorts of places. I resist the urge to reach out and put those strands back in place.

"A little. You?" I already know he's about to burst out of his skin. This morning he bounded out of bed like he was expecting Santa Claus.

He pretends to calmly consider this. "Fuck, yeah, I am." That smile is contagious. "Can I help you with anything?"

"I'm good. Worry about Chandra." I nod in her direction. She's still bent over the computer screen, occasionally cursing under her breath. "Is she going to be okay tonight?"

"She'll be fine. Got to jump in sometime."

"If you say so." There's no use in disagreeing. "What time is Lily coming by?"

Charlie looks at his watch. "Any minute now. Don't know that we need her, though."

"She'll still want to walk through one more time." Lily's like me. She wants things to be perfect. Of course she's going to come and make one final inspection of the restaurant before we open it up to outsiders. Her name's on this too, and she wants the place to look fabulous.

"I'll take care of her. I'm guessing you're still prepping?"

"A little bit. We're actually ahead of schedule." Already there are delicious smells wafting from the work stations. The sofrito's mixed and waiting, and all of the elements to make Mae and Sadie's signature dishes are chopped and ready. All that's left is to have diners love it.

And they do love it.

When we open the front doors, it's a steady stream of customers until nearly closing time. The food comes out looking magazine ready, and the feedback is all positive. I even get comfortable enough to come out into the dining room to chat with the brave souls of Mint Springs who've taken a chance on us tonight. Again and again I look up to see Charlie looking at me, our eyes meeting over the heads of families in conversation and couples out for a romantic evening. I can see the happiness on his face, each and every time, as the rest of the world fades away for a second. In those moments there's only me and Charlie and the way his dream's coming together.

Which doesn't feel as casual as I'd like. Not at all.

35

Charlie

"Have you got a swimsuit?"

Jenna doesn't look up from her book. "Like, in general? Or are you asking if I have one here? Because, yes, I have a swimsuit, but, no, I didn't pack it." She does not look thrilled when she finally makes eye contact. "Why?"

"Because you need a swimsuit for what I've got planned for today. Preferably a teeny, tiny bikini, but I'm not picky."

"No, thank you." Jenna goes back to reading her book.

"You don't even know what we're doing," I grumble into my coffee cup. "It's going to be fun."

"If you have to tell me it's going to be fun, I already know all I need to know." Jenna's smirk makes me even more determined.

"I'm surprised you even recognize that word, Miss Taskmaster."

That gets her attention. "Be careful what you wish for, Charlie." Her eyes glint. In the last two weeks, Jenna's taken back the reins. Now that we've fallen into this easy routine of her ending late nights in my bed instead of driving to the hotel, I've learned to appreciate the way she gets things done. She's unstoppable at home and at work, and that's had nothing but benefits for me. In times like these, though, I wish she'd relax a little.

"On what will probably be our only day off for the next few months, I would like to do something awesome."

Jenna's eyebrow raises. "Now it's *awesome*, is it? I'm spending the day the way I want to, Charlie. I've got this book and my coffee and, possibly, a hot, naked man to have my way with later. I don't need a swimsuit for any of that."

"As much as I like the sound of that last part—believe me, I do like that idea very much—I made some plans with my brothers and I told them you'd be coming." I brace for the unhappiness I'm about to endure. "I can promise ice cream and blueberry picking."

"Charlie." Jenna blows out a breath, but then she surprises me. "Blueberry picking?"

"Yes." I tread lightly. "There's a place not far from here. We're also planning a float trip. That's the swimsuit part."

"What's a float trip?" Jenna's actually interested.

"Kind of what it sounds like. We use those inflatable tubes and float down the river. We can actually stop right out there." I point out the window toward the river.

"There's a river out there?" Jenna squints. "You never told me that."

"You haven't heard about the Allen brothers and their legendary river adventures?" I don't have to pretend to be shocked. Summers on the farm always meant time at the river, even if it meant sneaking out in the middle of the night to make it happen. We gave the grownups plenty of gray hair that way. "There's a rope swing and everything."

"And people get in the river and float? I didn't think that

was a real thing." Jenna closes her book, and I know I've got her.

"People *pay* to do that and we've basically got it in our backyard."

"Well, I guess I've got to do it now. Where's the best place to get a bathing suit at the last minute in Mint Springs?"

It turns out there isn't a great place to get a bathing suit in Mint Springs, especially if you bring a girl who's used to shopping in Boston. If you do that, you end up in Walmart buying the only plain black bikini available in town after over an hour of trying to figure out where women actually shop.

"There must be places. I probably should have asked Hadley and Lily," I sheepishly suggest from the driver's seat.

Jenna looks like she could have told me that, but she doesn't call me out on it. "At least it's cheap. Who knew you could even buy a bathing suit for fourteen dollars?"

And she looks hot in it, although I tried to keep that to myself after she called me into the dressing room to give my opinion. That little cubicle did not have room for the reaction I would have liked to have. Jenna would look great in a potato sack, so a tiny bikini nearly blinded me.

"Now we just go float down the river?" This still seems like a joke to Jenna, like she thinks this is all some elaborate ruse.

"Something like that." I roll my eyes. "We're meeting my brothers and their lady friends at the put in."

"The put what?"

"The *put in*. That's the spot where you start, you know, you put your boat in the water." I realize how ridiculous that sounds as it comes out of my mouth. "I swear that's a real thing."

Jenna's pulling her hair back, braiding it as she looks at me incredulously. "It had better be because if I say that and everyone laughs..." She mimics cutting her throat by dragging her index finger over it. "That'll be it for you, Charlie Allen."

"I don't doubt it. Hey, come here." We're stopped at a stop sign on one of those deserted country roads, nobody out here but the two of us. I lean toward Jenna and hope she'll move toward me too. She makes me wait for a second, of course, but then puts her torso over the center console. I slide one hand over her cheek and let my thumb rest on her jawline. She blinks for a second, but then closes her eyes and lets me kiss her, slow and deep.

"What was that for?" she asks when her eyes flutter open.

"Probably my last chance for a little while." Once we're with my family, there'll be no more kissing. It was their idea to invite Jenna today, but I'm sure they didn't think I'd have to just roll over to ask her. We haven't actively denied anything, but we haven't made a show of it either. I'm positive all three of my brothers would have something to say about me sleeping with the chef we worked so hard to convince to come out to the boonies, and Jenna doesn't need or want any drama. It's been harder than I thought it would be, the past two weeks, switching off all the intimacy unless we're alone.

A horn honking behind us makes us both jump. This road's not so deserted, after all. At least it's not anyone we know. I wave apologetically to the elderly man in the pickup truck to keep him from laying on the horn again. If he understood the situation, I doubt he'd be rushing me. Pretty much everyone can understand how hard it is to keep from kissing a beautiful woman when you know she's about to be out of bounds.

We're the last to arrive, but if anyone thinks it's suspicious we're showing up together, no one breathes a word. I'm much more concerned about who I see walking up to us with her inner tube and floaty cooler of beer.

Faith.

"I didn't think you were coming today," I call out to her, if only to make certain Jenna knows this wasn't a detail I "forgot" to mention before I convinced her to come with me.

"Is that because you forgot to invite me?" Faith's tone's teasing, but I know she's serious. I do usually invite her along on these kinds of things. A trip to the river, the blueberry picking, ice cream after—all things I would normally have Faith with me for. "It's a good thing I ran into Cade yesterday."

I shoot my little brother a look, but he only shrugs. "Even numbers is better anyway." That's nowhere near true, and now I've got to act even less interested in Jenna or risk getting called out by Faith. Great.

"Is this safe for a pregnant woman?" Jenna asks, and we all turn to look at Hadley. She's also wearing a bikini, and her new little bump is easy to spot.

"This is so gentle. No real rocks or anything. Besides, I've got Cooper to fish me out." Hadley beams up at my oldest brother and his sunscreen-coated face. "Oh, can you get my shoulders?" She hands him the bottle of SPF 30 and turns around.

"Can I borrow some of that? I didn't think to bring sunscreen, or a hat. I should have grabbed one when I bought the swimsuit."

"Of course." Hadley hands the bottle to Jenna, who

starts to strip down to her bikini. I look away so I won't be caught staring.

"You had to go buy a swimsuit?" Lily's in it now, digging through her bag.

"Yeah, I didn't bring one. Didn't expect to need one, I guess." Jenna starts the process of coating herself in the lotion.

"And you had to go with Charlie?" Hadley asks doubtfully as Cooper slides his hands over her shoulders the way I'd like to be doing to Jenna.

"He did okay. And I managed to find something in my size that works." Jenna's starting on her legs now, slathering the sunscreen on all the places I'd like to be touching.

"It sure does. Check out that booty." Hadley and Lily give Jenna several compliments I try to drown out by whistling to myself. Totally inconspicuous.

"Charlie, can you do my back for me?" Jenna did not think that question through.

I clear my throat. "I, um...of course." And I proceed to put sunscreen on her like I'm applying it to my grandmother. My brief, quick strokes are sure to leave Jenna's back with a few streaks, but I don't dare try to do a better job.

"Look at that." Chance's confused whisper at least makes everyone look away from what I'm doing. I follow the tilt of his head to see Cade doing an exceptionally thorough job on Faith's shoulders.

"He is really getting in there," Cooper comments as we all watch Cade's fingertips deftly lift the strap of Faith's bikini and slide underneath. "You know anything about that?" The question's directed at me, but I'm too dumbfounded to answer.

"Leave Cade alone." Lily's saving him from the embarrassment only older brothers can dish out. "Are we getting on the river or what?" She hands Jenna a baseball cap. "Sorry, this is the only thing I've got."

Jenna pulls the hat on. The logo for the local auto body shop sits proudly on her forehead. "Okay, Allens. Show me how this is done."

36

Jenna

If a year ago you had told me I'd eventually find myself floating down some obscure Georgia river wearing a trucker hat with a cheap beer in my hand, I'd have told you to take your meds. The fancy Boston chef with her own restaurant and her exploding culinary career would have laughed until she cried. But now I'm basking in the sun on an inflatable inner tube, my toes dragging through the water.

Charlie's been floating next to me, although there's quite a bit of movement between the tubes I hadn't expected. We've got two floating coolers full of drinks—something I didn't even know existed before today but now I'm sure I can't live without. The beer's plentiful and already making me relax. Hadley was right about this river; there's hardly a rock to interrupt the flow of water. When I think I see a snake, Charlie gives me a little shrug and paddles back enough to get me another drink.

It's the perfect lazy day, and I don't do lazy.

I get to spend time hearing all about how Hadley's been feeling and listen to the plans she's got for her nursery. It's a conversation I wouldn't normally be having with my usual girlfriends, but the dappled light of the trees overhead and the gurgling of the water keeps me from putting my guard back up.

"Do you have kids?" Lily asks as she drags one hand through the water.

"Me?" The question startles me a bit. "No. I like them, but there was never a right time." Frank and I had had that discussion, but both agreed the restaurant was more important. Neither one of us was particularly keen on kids so the decision had been easy.

"But you've still got time, right?" Hadley's concern isn't something I'm expecting.

"Well, I'm already forty, so that ship is kind of sailing, but I've never been particularly maternal so I don't think it's something I'm going to regret not doing." I let the sun warm my face a little. I've never wanted kids, but for some reason no one ever believes this. I get ready for the inevitable laundry list of reasons I should think about having a baby.

"Forty? I had thought you were younger." Hadley kicks until she's closer to me and inspects my face through her oversized sunglasses. "Hardly a wrinkle."

"It's genetics." Lord knows it isn't anything I'm doing. Leave it to Hadley to decide to focus on my face and not my uterus.

"What are you ladies talking about?" Charlie's interruption is a welcome one. Not that I'm in need of rescue, exactly, but we were in danger of getting more personal than I'd like.

"Hadley's thinking about a gender neutral color for the nursery." I reach out for Charlie's hand to pull his tube closer, and he threads his leg through my inner tube. We wobble for a bit, but, luckily, don't topple out. Lily's eyes focus on Charlie's leg so close to mine, but she doesn't say anything.

"That is *fascinating*, but I paddled up here to remind y'all that we're almost home." He points up toward the next bend in the river. "Don't want anyone to miss the spot. Get ready to disembark."

Once we're all out, after carrying our tubes up the muddy side of the riverbank, I expect everyone to scatter. But there are cars to retrieve, so the boys all pile into Cooper's truck and take off down the road. I stand there awkwardly, unsure if I should pretend to be going to the hotel to wash the river dirt off or if I can make my way to Charlie's for a fresh pair of panties without attracting too much attention.

"Why don't y'all come to ours for lunch?" Hadley offers. "We're the closest."

"I think Charlie and I are supposed to go blueberry picking." All eyes turn to look at me.

"Blueberry *picking*?" Faith's question holds a million other ones. "Are you taking him at gunpoint?"

"No, he suggested it." Why do I suddenly feel like the new girl who doesn't know a damn thing?

"That is interesting." Hadley says, looking at Lily. "But you'll need to eat first, right? Just come up for a minute. The boys aren't even back yet."

"Are you sure you aren't too tired?" Lily asks, but we're already walking toward the house like it's a done deal.

"If y'all don't mind sandwiches. I've got plenty of produce from Faith too." Hadley looks over at Faith. "She just dropped off some of those crazy striped tomatoes I love."

"Zebras," Faith offers, walking along beside me but most certainly keeping her distance.

"You should taste these, Jenna." Ah, Hadley. Always the peacemaker.

Thankfully the boys get back quickly and don't have any trouble finding the rest of us. Charlie shovels in a sandwich and then motions for me to come with him. "Thanks for the hospitality, Hadley, but I promised Jenna some blueberries."

"We heard you were going picking? We could all go." Lily looks ready to make this a family trip, but Charlie cuts her off.

"We are, but we've got some work stuff to do first." He grabs my hand. "We wouldn't want to keep people waiting."

Cooper and Chance's eyes cut to where Charlie and I are attached. I drop his hand. "I'm fine with everyone going. Our work things can wait until tomorrow." Especially since they're a figment of Charlie's imagination. He is not doing well with the "we're just co-workers" act.

"I'd love to come blueberry picking," Faith chimes in, and I can see there's some kind of standoff happening here.

Charlie looks at the faces around us and finally relents. "Fine. Meet up in half an hour? Does that give everyone time to change out of their swimsuits?"

There's general agreement and before I even have time to tell Hadley thank you for feeding me, Charlie's dragging me out the door. You'd think we were participating in the Indy 500 the way he speeds to his house along the gravel road, skidding to a stop once we make it to the driveway.

"Charlie—"

His mouth comes down on mine hard. "I really need to get you out of this swimsuit," he says against my lips. "And I've only got thirty minutes."

"Twenty-eight," I correct.

The desperate groan he lets out has all the irritation

from earlier evaporating. The discussion about Charlie's impetuous behavior can wait a little longer.

"You'd better get started then." It's meant to be a tease, but Charlie's face changes instantly.

We never even make it out of the car.

37

Charlie

I don't think I'm ever going to be able to wipe this grin off my face. It's hard not to smile when you wake up to blueberry breakfast rolls. Oh, and to a beautiful woman in your bed. The pastry definitely takes a backseat to barely-dressed Jenna and the things I did to her tits with that cream cheese icing. I will never look at pastry the same way again.

That's all after the nearly perfect day yesterday. Jenna in a bikini until I basically tore it off of her, watching her fill bucket after bucket with blueberries from Miller's, and then getting to see the sunset from my front porch as we sipped on blueberry margaritas. I did have to spend some time putting aloe vera on Jenna's back after discovering my sunscreen application had been pretty near useless. I made that worth everyone's while, though.

Her face is all sun-kissed this morning, and I keep sneaking peeks at her as I try to organize the schedule for next week. Things could not be better for me right now. I'm making this restaurant go from a wish to reality, and I've got Jenna next to me, killing it in the kitchen. We've got the grand opening coming up fast, and I should be thinking about that instead of thinking about Jenna climbing over to the driver's seat of my car and impaling herself on my—

My brothers walk in right as my memory's starting to get good, all three of them looking like something out of a mafia movie as they come through the front door. That cannot be good. They're all stone-faced as they approach me at the bar.

"Charlie." Chance is curt. "Can we talk to you for a minute?"

"Well, good morning to y'all too," I drawl out. It's probably not the time to be a smart ass, but, as usual, I can't seem to stop myself. "Pull up a stool. Coffee?"

"We should probably talk in the office." Cooper looks at Chance and Cade, and they both nod their agreement.

"This sounds serious. Somebody die?" I take another sip of my coffee.

"Let's just go into the office." Chance gestures with his hand, as if I need him to point me in the right direction. "I know damn well where my office is, and I don't need to be frog-marched in there. Give me a second." I save my work and shut the laptop. My brothers trail behind me as I stomp to the back of the restaurant. Jenna looks up as we pass, her face clouding as she watches us.

I shut the door with a bang once we're all inside. "Alright, what's got the three of you going all *Sons of Anarchy*?" I do not like the feeling of being ganged up on.

Chance folds his arms over his chest. He might not be the oldest, but when it comes to this business, he's got the biggest stake. It's the money he made from the sale of his tech business that keeps everything afloat. He's good at acting like we're all in this together, but when the rubber meets the road, it's Chance who stands to lose the most. "Don't get defensive, Charlie."

"I'm not defensive." But I say it in the most defensive way possible, already preparing for a fight with my brothers.

"We need to talk about yesterday." This time it's Cade getting ready to tear into me.

"Yeah, we do. What possessed you to bring Faith?" I spit the question at him like it's a legitimate concern, like it's the obvious issue from our time together.

"Faith always comes with us. I was surprised you hadn't invited her yourself." Cade's not about to be contrite.

"And the way you put that sunscreen on her? What in the hell was that? You two looked pretty familiar." I cross my arms now too, daring Cade to deny it.

"We're not here to talk about Faith, Charlie," he deflects. "We're here to talk about Jenna."

I've known from the second they walked in what this was about. "What about her? She's doing a great job."

"She is, and we don't want you to screw that up." Cooper's firm, like he's talking to a kid, and it flies all over me.

"Screw it up? What do you mean?"

"It was obvious to everyone yesterday that you're interested in Jenna in a way that might make things messy here. We're here to warn you that pursuing that would be a bad idea."

"What are you, my lawyer?" I lash out at Cooper, knowing it makes me look even more guilty than I am. How can I explain the thing between me and Jenna to them when I can't even explain it to myself? My desire to protect this little kernel of possibility—to protect her—makes me even more furious that they're sticking their noses in my business. "I don't need y'all coming in here acting like I need a babysitter."

"If Jenna leaves, Charlie, we'll all be screwed. And she'll leave if this gets uncomfortable. This isn't one of the waitresses. She's an integral part of this operation; we can't do it without her. In the past—"

I cut Chance off. "In the past, what?"

"Let's not focus on that, okay?" If Cooper's trying to keep this conversation civil, he's too late. "We all want this to work, and we want to be sure we're on the same page. Whatever you're feeling for Jenna, you have to put the brakes on."

"You can't tell me what to do." Have I ever said a more juvenile thing in my life? I'm proving their point, making it even easier for them to assume I'm going to fuck things up. "Things here are going great, so maybe y'all should work on staying in your own lanes. Come talk to me when I actually mess up instead of assuming I will—for a change." I glare at each of them in turn. "I've got work to do." I storm out, leaving them standing in my office. It's the most unsatisfying exit I could have orchestrated, but I can't stand there another second and be lectured.

Eventually they leave, grumbling as they go. They all wave to Jenna, whose brow hasn't unfurrowed since they came in.

"What was that about?" She's obviously concerned. Everyone in here is on eggshells now, afraid of whatever my brothers came to discuss. But it's a thin line I've got to walk here between Jenna and my brothers. This is important to her, too, and I can't have them squawking in her ear about what a bad bet I am.

"Nothing. Family shit." I try to pretend nothing's wrong. I'm not about to tell Jenna what my brothers have said, not about to jeopardize anything just for the sake of their baseless concerns. I know what's at stake if Jenna decides to leave, and I'm not about to give her any reason to. I'd like for things to stay the way they are with us professionally even if I selfishly want more from her personally. I can have both those things. My brothers will see. Eventually they'll understand why I'm taking the chance. I can keep my relationship with Jenna private. In public I can be all business. She and I have already talked about that. I just need to turn it up a notch.

"We need to go over some of the details for the grand opening. Want to do that tonight? I'll cook if you make more of those margaritas." I think about touching her, but worry about who'll see. I give her a raised eyebrow and hope she can tell I'm talking about more than dinner.

"I think that can be arranged. Come back to the kitchen in a little bit. I'm making blueberry ginger jam. I'll need your opinion." Jenna sashays back to the stove, hopefully forgetting all about Cooper, Chance, and Cade and their visit. I try to put it out of my mind as well.

What the hell do they know anyway?

38

Jenna

"They're both coming?"

"They're both on the list. Is that bad?" I look up from my clipboard at Charlie's stricken face.

"How did they both even get invited?" He's pulling out his phone and mashing his fingers on the screen.

"I didn't put the list together. You'd have to ask your brothers. Or Lily, maybe. I don't know who had final say." I'm not sure why this is such a big deal.

"I'm asking them now." Charlie pauses and his eyes fly over the screen. "Everyone's coming down here."

"Now? Everyone? Why?" We've got too much to do to have an impromptu family meeting.

"Because if both my mother and my father are coming to this event, we need to get ready for World War III."

"It cannot be that bad. Even if they're both here—"

The front door flies open. "How in the hell did they both get invitations?" Cooper's voice booms through the empty restaurant. He's made it down the hill from the distillery in less than a minute.

"Did you run here?" I ask as more Allens start to pile through the door.

"Basically. Hi, Jenna." He gives me a smile but then goes right back to frowning.

"I told you this was an emergency." Charlie's pacing, doing that thing with his hands in his hair.

"Should I get snacks?" Everything around here is an excuse to eat, and I've learned Charlie's brothers tend to yell a little less if they've got their mouths full. I don't know much about their parents, but from what I can tell, this conversation might have a little yelling.

"If you've got some, that would be great. And coffee. This might take us a while to figure out." Charlie's noticeably colder now that his family's here.

I know it's serious when Sadie and Mae come walking in the door. Now everyone's in the restaurant and I'm passing around cups of fresh coffee and some of the tartlets I've made with the rest of our blueberry haul. I have to admit I've loved making things with fruit I actually picked. I was an idiot the whole time we were at the blueberry farm, smiling from ear-to-ear despite the prevalence of about a million bees, which kept city-girl me running for her life.

Sadie takes a bite of her tart and gives me a surprised look. "Ginger?"

"Do you like it? Next round is more traditional." I clasp my hands in front of me like a first-grader. Pleasing Sadie and Mae is more important to me than I'd like to admit.

"I love it. Delicious, Jenna. And the crust...to die for." She reaches for another, and I now know I've gotten it right.

"Can we get back to the real issue here?" Cade asks, and they all settle down again, frowns on all their faces. "How did they both get invitations?"

Lily slowly raises her hand. "I did that." She grimaces. "I

thought it would be rude to not invite them. I never dreamed they'd both want to come. Your dad didn't even come to Cooper's wedding. Neither of them came to ours." She looks at Chance with hurt in her eyes. "I really thought they'd probably throw the invitations into the trash, but y'all have been working so hard. I wanted to show them how well things are going."

"It's okay, Lily." Chance takes her hand. "None of us would have thought they'd both say yes either. We need to figure out how to have them both in the same room without having to hide all the knives."

"Will it really be that bad? They'll be able to keep it together for one night, won't they?" I probably shouldn't interject anything here, but I can't believe two adults can't be civil for a few hours, especially for their kids.

The laughter that comes from the table of Allens is uproarious. Sadie and Mae are even wiping their eyes. I stand there wide-eyed as they all laugh and laugh.

"Our parents couldn't put aside their differences if the fate of the world depended on it," Cooper explains. "They were always a little fiery, but toward the end of their marriage it got downright combustible. Those two will burn everything down to hurt each other."

"They'd ruin the grand opening?" My mouth hangs open. My own family isn't always perfect, but no one would have dared come to my restaurant and make a scene. In the end Frank and I managed that all on our own, but my family? Never.

"They wouldn't do it on purpose." Cade doesn't seem to think that's an excuse. "They wouldn't be able to help themselves."

"We need to figure out a way to keep them from ending

up anywhere near each other without locking them both in closets somewhere." Charlie doesn't invite me to sit even though I'm one of the major players in this event. He steeples his fingers and closes his eyes.

"I guess I'll go and get more snacks," I offer, hoping he'll realize his error and tell me to pull up a chair.

"That'd be great, Jenna." He doesn't even look at me as he says it.

"Thanks for your help today." Charlie reaches out a hand. It lands on my arm where he rubs his thumb over the skin in the crook of my elbow.

"You're welcome. It is my job, after all." I don't pull my arm away, but the smile I give him is wooden.

"Is something wrong?"

We're alone in the restaurant, and now Charlie's back to touching me, talking to me in that low voice I have trouble resisting. As soon as his family cleared out, a tentative plan in place, it was like a switch was flipped. I don't expect him to act like a teenager with a crush in front of his family or the rest of the staff—we've both agreed that's not a good idea—but I expect him to be friendly. Today he was noticeably distant when they were around.

"I'm just tired, I think. Getting a little stressed about the opening." I chicken out and say nothing. It isn't like me to avoid confrontation, but battling it out with Charlie right now is about as appealing as week-old fish. And I don't like positioning myself as the victim, begging him for attention. That's not me at all.

"Yeah, me too." Charlie reaches out and wraps me in his

arms. "You want to take it easy tonight? I could go grab a pizza. I know you don't love the local place, but it's easy."

"I've actually got a bit more work to do here tonight. You can go, though. I can lock up." I pull away from him.

"I can wait." Charlie starts to open his laptop back up. "I can find something to do until you're finished."

"Don't." My hand comes out to keep his computer shut. "I'm thinking I'll be here for a little while and then go to the hotel tonight."

"What? No." Charlie shakes his head. "Why would you want to do that?"

"To give you a little space. And to take some for myself. I don't need to stay at your house every night. You could go and spend some time with your brothers."

"I spent plenty of time with them today," Charlie argues.

"I know. I was here." I move farther away.

"If you want a little space, fine, but I'll miss you." Charlie gives me puppy dog eyes, and I falter. So much for the bad-ass bitch who isn't going to let a man run her life. One sad look and I'm reconsidering the hard line I was planning on taking. "And my house is closer. You'd be five steps from pizza and a warm bed instead of a car ride away from a lonely night on a lumpy mattress."

"That mattress isn't lumpy." I'm wavering and Charlie can tell.

"Come back to my house. I'll open a nice bottle of wine, run you a bath. Be your stress reliever."

I like the sound of that and the way Charlie's looking at me. This is a defeat I can never tell Addison about. I might get to take out some of my frustration on Charlie tonight in bed, but it doesn't make me feel any more appreciated at work.

"I am very stressed."

"Come on then."

And I follow him to the front door, forgetting all about the work I had pretended to need to finish.

39

Charlie

Perfect. Everything has to be perfect.

And it will be. I'll be damned if it's anything less, and I'll string up anyone who screws it up. I straighten my tie. I look pretty good, considering my stomach is threatening to make an escape via my throat. So much is riding on today, and all of our preparations are going to come down to this. That's an exaggeration, I know. If it all falls apart tonight it won't literally be the end of the world, but it'll put a dent in our reputations. Mine and Jenna's. Even if I was willing to risk mine, I would never take that chance with hers.

All morning there's been constant prep. The distillery's as shiny as can be and open for drinks and nibbles. Jenna's outdone herself, with a menu up there and one for dinner down here. The wedding was a good first run, and we've had several tries at getting things right, but tonight will be the ultimate test. Things might go wrong, but it won't be because Jenna's food wasn't on point.

And it won't be because of our relationship. It's killing me not to be able to be upfront with everyone about how I feel about Jenna. Having to make sure it looks like we barely know each other is taking a toll. It's easier to work together when we've got some banter going and we don't have to be so guarded. I try to make up for it when we're alone, but Jenna's less enthused lately with me whisking her away to the privacy of my house the second we get done with work.

I make my way down to the restaurant, happy to see the rest of the staff already there for the most part and doing what they're supposed to be doing. Even Brian and Jonah look sharp in their neatly pressed shirts and ties. I had to teach them how to tie them, but they're pros now. Taking a chance on those kids is going to pay off in the end.

Jenna's in the kitchen barking orders to her guys. I love watching her in her element. She's the boss back there, and she gets results. She looks up and makes eye contact with me, smiling before she goes back to work. I keep my cocky grin to myself. I'll give her plenty of that later.

"Charlie!" The unmistakable bellowing of my older brother makes me quick to stop looking at Jenna. He's also wearing a suit and looks like he's about to throw up. "Lily says we've got two last-minute RVSPs. Heavy hitters. Can we accommodate that?" He's actually sweating.

"Should be fine. We're getting close to capacity, though. If we get too many more of those it won't matter who they are. We won't have any chairs left." I've been watching the numbers closely. We're packing the place. I've got every single member of my staff working tonight.

"I'll let her know. And Cooper wanted me to make sure you knew they could stretch the cocktail hour for longer if you needed to. Is it hot in here?" Chance wipes his forehead.

"It's sixty-five degrees. I can put it down to sixty-two, though." I'm actually enjoying seeing my usually cool, calm, and collected brother freak out a little.

"I can't believe I'm this nervous. Do we have a handle on Operation They Ruin Everything?" Chance lowers his voice like he's telling me something straight from a James Bond movie.

"Cade's on it. I don't think you need to whisper. Even if Mom and Dad heard you, they would never think that's about them." Each other? Maybe. But our parents still don't have any idea how much their own fighting messed us up. "He might need a break eventually, though. Even Cade can't keep his laser focus on that all night."

"We'll let him have a minute to enjoy himself." Chance smirks a little at this. Cade isn't known for cutting loose. His idea of really enjoying himself will probably mean hiding out in his office. "Is everything else ready to go? Anything I can help you with? How's Jenna?"

"She seems fine." I act like I haven't been speaking to her obsessively about tonight. Granted, we've been doing most of it in bed—the real reason I'm not excited to tell my brother anything more than exactly what he needs to know.

"*Seems*? Go and check. Let me know if she needs anything." He holds up his cell phone and waves it at me as he walks away.

I ignore the implication that I'm not taking care of things. I've got Jenna all sorted. The restaurant looks amazing. I double-check on my front of the house staff one last time before sending half of them up to the distillery. Before I know it, it's time for guests to start arriving for dinner. When they do, they arrive happy. I make it my mission to keep them that way.

I know we've got a handful of restaurant critics, local celebrities, and influencers in attendance tonight. I'm noticing plenty of phones coming out for selfies and snaps of Jenna's beautiful food. I'm circulating among the crowd when I hear it.

"Of course, it was my idea. What better way to make use of the family farm, right? Lucky for these boys I've got deep pockets." My father's voice booms out through the front of the restaurant. I try to ignore it, but his boasting doesn't stop. It's the first time I've seen him in years, and though his hair's thinned a bit and he's put on a few pounds, there's no mistaking that voice. Or the way he's making himself the center of attention. No matter what you've done, my father's done better. No matter where you've been, he's surpassed it. It's all smoke and mirrors—he'd even gouged Chance on the price for the farm when he'd finally agreed to sell it. Deep pockets? If he's got them now it's because of what Chance put in them, and you can bet none of us will ever see that money again.

I could go over and tell him to shut the fuck up, but I'm well aware it won't do anything but cause a scene. He's talking to Matt Sullivan—former professional baseball player and current owner of the nursery down the road. The only reason my father's even bothering to talk to Matt— other than having an audience—is the fact that he's deemed him worthy. Most people in Mint Springs don't qualify for that label, according to Jeff Allen. Despite sharing a name with my grandfather, Jefferson Allen Jr. never picked up any of his better traits. Of course he'd glom onto someone he thinks knows his worth. Lucky for the rest of us, Matt already knows my dad is full of shit.

My mother's across the room with Cade, and she focuses in on my father like a hawk that sees a mouse. She'd love the opportunity to make a fool of my father in front of everyone, and it wouldn't take much effort. Cade's trying to keep her occupied, but he's failing miserably. It's not his fault; our parents are drawn to each other in a way that defies logic. They spent years trying to get away from each other but somehow end up pulled together over and over again. I'm plotting the quickest route to intercept her when Jenna comes out from behind the warming lights and stainless steel of the kitchen.

She walks through the restaurant, greeting people as she goes. To anyone else it might look like Jenna's taking her time, meandering between the tables, but she's on a collision course with my bombastic father, and I doubt that's an accident. When she interrupts their conversation, the look of relief on Matt's face is plain. He may have made it to the major leagues, but he's no match for my dad's overbearing personality and his tendency to run his mouth. Jenna, on the other hand? There isn't much Jenna can't handle, and the way she looks at my father as she offers her hand is both commanding and amused.

My father looks at Jenna and smiles, holding her hand a little too long. He probably thinks he's found another willing victim to listen to his tall tales—another ear to bend while he's here eating and drinking on our dime. He has no idea what he's just run up against.

Jeff Allen is about to run into a brick wall of Jenna Bard, and I cannot wait.

40

Jenna

I could hear him all the way in the kitchen. Loud. Obnoxious. Unforgivable.

To come to the grand opening of your sons' big venture and then try to take all the credit? No, sir. From what I can tell, Charlie's father provided little more than genetic material when it comes to how his boys turned out. It's hard to miss the fact they're related. The elder Allen is blond and tall with the hazel eyes Charlie and his brothers all have, but his eyes don't have the sparkle and he doesn't have their manners, that's for sure. I can see why Charlie's mother is basically foaming at the mouth from the other side of the restaurant. I'm sure she's had enough of this crap to last a lifetime. After being married for a while to my own version of this, I know I have.

It's understandable that Charlie and his brothers don't want to cause a scene, and confronting their father in the center of the restaurant is absolutely going to do that. But I can't have anyone ruining this night and that includes jackass fathers. We've got the official naming of this place coming up, and people have worked too hard to have this be the bitter taste in their mouths. I want nothing but good memories tonight, and this man is making that impossible.

Matt Sullivan looks close to tears when I come up beside him. I'm sure he's been biting his tongue hard enough to draw blood. These Southern boys and their manners can keep the peace but don't fix the problem. No wonder there are so many fist-fights at Bootlegger. If you hold it all in, it eventually has to come out. I'm not one to keep my feelings to myself. Blame it on my Puerto Rican roots or on my Boston upbringing, but either way I'm happy to be the bad guy here.

"Sorry to interrupt, gentlemen." I use the term loosely in this case. "Are you enjoying everything?" I let Matt give me a few compliments before I tell him his wife is looking for him. He excuses himself from our conversation so fast I'm surprised there aren't tire marks on the floor.

"I don't believe we've met." I offer my hand and Charlie's father readily takes it, rubbing his fingers along my skin instead of giving me a firm handshake.

"No, we haven't had the pleasure. I'm Jeff Allen; I'm the reason you have a job."

That surprises even me. "Excuse me?"

"This whole thing was originally my idea. I'm too busy these days to handle something like this." He swings his arm out wide. "Luckily, my boys are good at doing the legwork."

"That is good." I give him a smile. "They have been working hard. It's difficult to get this kind of business off the ground, but they're all incredibly driven."

"They get that from me. Always told them hard work is the way to go." He takes a sip from his drink. "They didn't tell me you were so pretty, though. I would have made a trip down here."

Is he flirting with me? I try not to shudder. "I *am* a little surprised I've never seen you before. What with all you've put into this. You're pretty hands-off, I guess. I would have thought you would have at least come by to make sure things were going well. I thought you'd have at least shown up for Cooper's wedding. We had it here, you know."

His face changes a bit, losing some of its good humor. "I was sorry to miss it." He motions to Chandra, holding up his empty glass. "Sweetheart, I need another of these." God, he is a piece of work. "You're doing great work back there. Everything's tasty. I've got a few suggestions, though. Ways to really punch things up. We could talk about those later, maybe. Or tomorrow. I might stay a few days. We could visit a few places in Chattanooga. Or Nashville, even." He lifts an eyebrow.

"And to miss Chance's wedding too. You must be *awfully* busy." I say it a little louder than necessary.

"I have my own businesses to attend to." Chandra delivers his drink and doesn't even get a thank you.

"I thought I heard you saying *this* was one of your businesses?" I make a stupefied face, like I really don't understand how the pieces all fit together. "But that doesn't make sense, really, does it? Not after you sold this farm to Chance. And what he paid for it! I think people'd be surprised how much you thought it was worth."

"Now listen here—" His face contorts a bit, redness spreading from his cheeks to his neck.

I lower my voice and lean in close. "No, *you* listen. I know exactly how little you've done to make this place and your family a success. You were invited here tonight as a *guest*. And if you want to stay that way, you'll sit down and enjoy your dinner and say nice things like everyone else. I know plenty more I could broadcast tonight, so I advise you to put a smile on your face and act gracious." I smile brightly as he sits, scowling. "So glad you're having a good time."

I'm sure he's shooting daggers at me as I walk away, but I don't mind. Only good karma tonight in this restaurant. Particularly since we're coming to the part of the night I've been anticipating the most. Once I've made a loop and glad-handed as many people as possible, I go back to the kitchen to check on dessert. There's not much for me to do now that I've got competent staff. Miguel's got the line completely under control, and the first round of our sweets samplers are ready to go. Everyone's going to get a tiny taste of what they can have if they come back and, by the looks of things, plenty of them will.

But first, we've got champagne coming out for a toast. Charlie and his brothers all come forward as the guests get their glasses of bubbly. In the low light, everything sparkles. Chance is the one giving the speech tonight, talking about how great it is to work with his brothers and how much they appreciate everyone's support. Hadley and Lily get a mention as being the most supportive spouses in the entire world. They both blush and smile, looking gorgeous and happy. And then Chance turns things over to Charlie. He's nervous, straightening his tie and clearing his throat, but so undeniably handsome in that suit I forget to breathe for a second.

"And I'd like to call Chef Bard out here."

I start to shake my head no. We're in the middle of service, and I've already taken a victory lap. But the entire family's beckoning to me, so I go, ending up next to Charlie as he sings my praises. I get some whistles and a good round of applause, but I don't hear much of it. I'm only looking at Charlie, lost in a moment no one knows I'm having.

"And another one of Jenna's brilliant ideas has to do with the name of this restaurant. We've gone back and forth about what we should call this place. We all agreed we wanted something that really showed you not only the kind of food you would get here, but the way you would be treated. We wanted you to get a taste of what it was like for the four of us coming here every summer and being made to feel like the most cherished kids in the world. Our grandfather isn't here tonight, but Cooper's first whiskey is named after him. We're hoping to have that ready for tasting next year. Some of y'all are already drinking Sadie's gin and Hadley's moonshine. Mae's apple brandy's hitting the shelves in a few weeks. My brothers and I have made a commitment to being part of this community and to honoring our family. That's why we've decided to name this restaurant after the two ladies who really taught us about food and family and farm. Welcome to Sadie Mae's, y'all. The sign goes up tomorrow."

I'm almost afraid to look at Sadie and Mae as everyone lifts their glasses. I want so badly for them to love this idea, but I might have been wrong to push so hard for it. I let my eyes travel over the tables in front of me until I find them, both crying a little but smiling big. Sadie gives me a wink.

"They like it," I whisper as Charlie's hand comes to rest on the small of my back.

"They love it," he whispers back, looking down at me. "You done good."

And then he kisses me full on the mouth for everyone to see.

41

Charlie

Of course the three amigos are in my office bright and early the next morning.

"I don't have time to accept all of your heartfelt congratulations right now. I've got a restaurant to run." I try to shoo them out of my office, but they don't budge.

"As much as we'd love to take a day to really enjoy last night, Charlie, that little stunt of yours needs a conversation. We figured we'd get it out of the way early." It's Cooper leading the charge today, looking a little tired and with noticeable bedhead.

"What stunt?" I get to work opening my laptop and trying to look busy. In truth, I'm as exhausted as they probably are. After finally getting the place cleaned up enough to lock the doors last evening, I ended up staying up most of the night pretending to be Jenna's naughty assistant. It turns out she liked the suit. A lot.

"Kissing Jenna like that. It almost overshadowed the announcement of the name. You had tongues wagging for sure. I bet if we went to Ham & Eggs right now there'd be people talking about it." Cade's probably right. I hadn't planned the kiss; it just sort of happened. Cooper and Chance got to thank their wives, and after the way Sadie and Mae reacted to the name, I got kind of swept up in the moment. I wouldn't take it back, though. I've had enough sneaking around.

"Maybe you guys should go to the diner and check it out. Do a little investigative reporting. You could go by Patty Cakes, too. See if there's any gossip over there. Get me a cinnamon roll while you're at it." I am not about to give them the possibility of telling me Jenna's off-limits again.

"This isn't a joke, Charlie." Chance gives me a serious face to prove his point.

"I never said it was. Jenna is great. We like each other and we work well together. What's the problem?"

"You know what the problem is. Things are great now, but what happens when they aren't? When the two of you break up or stop seeing each other or whatever, we'll be out a chef. We cannot afford to have that happen." Cooper's voice booms through the room and I hope no one else can hear us.

"Why do you automatically think something's going to go wrong?" I glare at my brothers.

"The longest relationship you've ever had lasted three months, Charlie. You aren't exactly known for your prowess in this area." Chance leans forward in his chair. "Your past behavior isn't exactly all about settling down."

"So? Why does everything have to lead to a wedding and a picket fence? Y'all are all getting married and having babies. That's fine. That's not how I see myself, and I don't think that bothers Jenna." I pretend I'm confident in this, despite never having had a conversation with her about it. It isn't their business how unsure I actually am. Maybe Jenna does want a picket fence and a house full of babies, but I wouldn't bet on it.

No one wants to touch that assertion with a ten foot pole. We all sit in silence for three beats, all three of them staring at me.

"I'm not going to screw this up, but I'm not going to pretend it isn't happening. It's fine y'all—more than fine. You'll see."

But things are not exactly fine when Jenna comes into the kitchen a few hours later. Next week's our first real week of dinner every night. Lunch will follow, if there's enough of an appetite for it. Jenna's been talking nonstop about what it will take to get things ready for the days ahead, and it doesn't sound like anyone's going to be having leisurely mornings for a long, long time.

And I left her sleeping this morning. Turned off her alarm to make sure she took a break.

She's mad as a hornet when she rushes through the front door, pulling her hair back as she stomps in.

"That is not good," Miguel mumbles under his breath, careful not to make eye contact with her. He's concentrating exceptionally hard on trimming the pork chops in front of him.

"Why didn't you wake me up?" Jenna whisper-hisses at me once she's close. "I should be setting an example for these guys, not laying around like the lady of the manor. I told them all to be here on time or I'd have their asses, and here I am waltzing in late."

"I thought you could use a little extra sleep." I go in to kiss her but she pulls her head back. "Are you crazy?"

"Yes. I thought we'd already established that." I try again to kiss her and end up with a mouth full of air.

"Can I speak with you in the office, please?" She's suddenly all sugar and no spice.

I let her lead the way in case she's planning on stabbing me or something. Once we're in, I close the door and try for the third time to land my lips on her.

"You absolutely cannot be doing that here." Jenna's hands push on my chest enough to have me taking two steps back.

"Everyone knows."

Jenna doesn't seem to think that's a positive development. "I *know* everyone knows, and I won't have them snickering about it behind my back or questioning how I got this job. We still have to be professional, Charlie. *I do.*"

"No one cares." That's a bald-faced lie. The chairs where my brothers were sitting this morning are barely cold.

"I care. And you should too. Yes, you can stop giving me the cold shoulder at work, I guess, but that doesn't mean you can start kissing all over me now." Jenna's hands go on her hips—a sure sign she's not going to back down.

"When did I give you the cold shoulder?"

"Give me a break. You only have two temperatures, Charlie. There's no in between. But you're going to have to figure out a way to be friendly with me here without trying to hump my leg all day. And you can't undermine me in front of my staff or sabotage me by making me late. My reputation is about all I have left. I cannot let whatever's happening with us destroy it."

I don't know what to say to that. I open my mouth but then quickly shut it again. "I have no intention of destroying your reputation, Jenna." So much for out in the open being better than top secret.

She lets out a breath and her shoulders sag. "I didn't mean it like that, exactly. I know you wouldn't do that on purpose, Charlie. But other people's opinions matter in this industry. I can't simply ignore that."

"Okay." I give in. What's the use in fighting about something I know to have some truth to it?

"Don't make that face. We have to keep things separate. I didn't say you couldn't kiss me ever again." Her smile's the kind that usually gets me into all kinds of trouble.

"Can I kiss you now?" I push my luck.

"You can give me the one you would have given me this morning, if you hadn't snuck out without me," she teases.

"I wouldn't have put that one on your mouth." I swallow, hoping she'll take the bait even though it's only ten in the morning and the walls here are thin.

Her eyes glitter but she keeps her distance. "Save that one for later."

42

Jenna

"We're going to need a steady stream of tomatoes if you want to keep the tarts on the menu." Miguel's standing in the door of the walk-in refrigerator. "And it would be nice to be able to keep them out of here. It really affects the flavor."

"I'll have Charlie talk to Faith. This should be prime tomato season right now, shouldn't it? I can't imagine we'd have trouble getting plenty of homegrown tomatoes." I add that to my list. Really, I should have a direct line to Faith, but Charlie's still the one she likes to deal with. I didn't exactly make a friend there with my earlier antics, and now that there's something between me and Charlie, Faith's even more standoffish.

"And we could use a few more guys back here. I know you don't want to be overstaffed, but if things keep moving at this pace we're going to need them sooner rather than later. And it might be hard to find anyone with much experience. I'm thinking at least one more line cook and one more guy on prep." Miguel looks at me over his shoulder. "We're still not in a position to lure too many people to drive an hour each way."

"True." I add that to the list as well. "Keep an ear out for anyone you know who might be interested. I'll have Charlie post an ad or something. Will you help me weed out the bad ones?" I hope Miguel will help me interview and train any new hires. I need things to gel with my staff and buy-in is the best way for that to happen.

"Of course. Annabel's really coming along. She filleted all that fish from last night. Not even a nick once she got the hang of it." Miguel's pride shows through. He likes being the mentor, and I'm happy to let him.

"She seems to like it."

"Maybe we've got a miniature Chef Bard on our hands?" he suggests, and I can see he means it as a compliment.

"We'll see." I gather up my things. "I'm going to check out that possible beef supplier with Charlie. I should be back in time to help with the end of the dinner prep."

"Got it," Miguel says, and I know he absolutely does.

"I thought this place was close by?" I'm looking out the window at nothing but green fields and fences as far as the eye can see.

"We're taking the scenic route." Charlie grins at me from the driver's seat.

"I don't have time for the scenic route, Charlie," I warn. "I need to be back to help with the dinner prep. They'll be short if I'm not there."

"Sometimes you have to make time for the scenic route. You'll be back before they even miss you. I just wanted to have a little adventure with you away from the restaurant."

He reaches for my hand, lifting it up to his lips. "Plenty of deserted back roads out this way."

"You do know that's how almost everyone gets killed in horror movies, right? Parked out on some dirt road getting busy. It's almost guaranteed."

"You want to get busy on one of these dirt roads? Jenna, I am surprised." Charlie brings both our hands to his mouth in mock shock. "This is a work trip."

I roll my eyes. "Charlie Allen, you know if I offered to do just about anything to you right now, you'd happily accept."

"Like what? Give me some options." He lets go of my hand and slides his palm up my thigh. "We're actually only going to that farm right up there, but save those ideas for the drive home." He gives my leg a squeeze.

I know very little about cows other than how to make them taste delicious, but I'm here with Charlie to muck about anyway. I've got a new pair of boots that ride the line between impractical and practical, but I still try my damndest to keep from stepping in anything. I will never be a fan of that part of living out in the country.

I let Charlie do most of the talking, discussing the specifics of any deal we might make with Dan Rayborn, the farmer who meets us at the front gate. I only care about the kinds of cuts we'd be getting and how steady that supply might be. In that way, Charlie and I make a pretty good team. Our strengths combine in a way that gets things done. I'm starting to appreciate how opposites can complement each other some of the time.

"How many cows do you actually have?" It's a basic and possibly stupid question, but no one laughs.

"We've got two herds—one beef and one dairy. Neither of them very big, really. We try to run a lean operation. I don't like to have stressed land or animals," Dan explains as we walk the property. "I can show you the milking barn and let you know about that too, if you're interested."

I give Charlie an excited look. "Have you got more than cow's milk?"

"Goat and cow for now. Sheep eventually, maybe." Dan points us in another direction. "Walk over here with me and you'll see."

By the time we're ready to leave, I've nearly convinced Charlie to put one of the baby goats in the back seat. I've never been much of an animal lover, but those little maniacs won my heart. Now I can see why goat yoga is a thing. I can only imagine what my friends in Boston would think seeing me today, feeding a tiny goat from a bottle. If they knew I was loving every minute working in the herb garden Charlie's got thriving behind Sadie Mae's, they'd most likely want to have me committed.

"You can come back to see the goats any time," Dan assures me, probably a little afraid I might actually try to steal one.

"Be careful offering that to this one." Charlie points at me. "You'll never get rid of her."

"You wish," I say and give him a little shove.

Charlie's face does this funny thing I haven't seen before, a little twist of his mouth and crinkle of his eyes. He blinks a few times and then it's gone. He's shaking Dan's hand and telling him we'll be in touch before I can get another look at him. He reaches for my hand on the walk back to the car, and I let him take it, threading our fingers together.

"So if I want to win your heart, I need to steal one of those goats." A tiny smile plays on his lips.

"Maybe not steal. You could buy one. Then it would be all on the up and up." I swing our arms a little between us. "And who said anything about my heart?"

The way Charlie's hand tightens around mine has my stomach clenching a bit. "Nobody," he says, but his face tells me something different. The aforementioned heart nearly stops for a second. He can't be serious, can he? Fun and casual is what we're doing here. I'm not supposed to be falling for Charlie or his family, or Mint Springs even.

But on the car ride back, with the sun on my face, Charlie's hand in mine, and a sweet summer breeze blowing through the open windows, I realize I might be doing exactly that.

43

Charlie

"What the hell is this?"

I could have maybe ignored the yelling coming from the kitchen, maybe even the string of colorful expletives that followed closely behind, but the loud banging was something I probably shouldn't let go unexplored. Jenna's team ran a little hot sometimes, but this was over the top, even for them.

"Is there a problem?" I crane my head around the corner.

"Yes. Several." Miguel's frustrated face is not what I like seeing at two in the afternoon. A real problem this close to dinner service is never a good thing.

"Anything I can do to help straighten things out?" I'm not a complete idiot in the kitchen. If there's a minor issue, I can hopefully make it go away before Jenna gets back from the yoga class I convinced her to take. Hadley needed a little exercise, and Jenna always needs a little *ohmmm*. She's wound pretty tight on the best of days. Convincing her she was doing Hadley a favor was the only way I got her to leave this kitchen.

"I think we're past that point right now." Miguel runs a hand through his hair. "Jenna is going to flip out when she sees this."

"What?" I can't have Jenna flipping out.

"That new guy—the one who's officially forty-five minutes late, by the way—he fucked up the entire order of produce that Faith brought over last night."

"You're kidding me." Even I know how bad this could be.

"I wish I was. Come and see." Miguel invites me into the kitchen with a flourish. "He was supposed to do prep last night before he left. I showed him exactly what to do. Basic stuff. Dice a ton of onions. Nothing fancy or complicated. But he's not great with following directions. See for yourself."

I look at the plastic bins that line the walk-in. Every single one of them is filled with diced vegetables. Oh, there's onion in there all right, but there's also peppers and carrots, all mixed together. And Jenna's coveted tomatoes. Those are supposed to be sliced for the tarts she makes and she's always nervous about having enough.

"What can you even make with this?" I look at Miguel, hoping he's got a fabulous suggestion.

"Nothing that's on the menu."

"Fuck."

"Exactly." He rummages around in a few other bins. "There's some stuff left, but not much. He probably even stayed later to chop all of this."

"Which guy is this?" *Please, please don't be—*

"Your guy."

"Fuck."

"Exactly."

Jenna comes tearing in wearing extremely distracting yoga pants. I know better than to say anything about that now that I've completely ruined her day. Well, technically not me, but the flunkies I hired when I, once again, tried to help her out. She gives me a look that has me cowering a bit as she marches into the kitchen.

I overhear her talking to Miguel. He's doing his best to calm her down while giving her an accurate assessment of the situation. When she finds out the guy never even showed back up today, she roars. There are some combinations of swear words I've never even heard before coming from back there. And that's saying a good bit since I spend a fair amount of time with Maggie Gentry. Lily's grandmother all but invented cussing.

I linger outside her space. There's no way I'm going barging in. I hear Miguel trying to help her decide what to do next, speaking the Spanish I know they use together to brainstorm. It frustrates me to not know exactly what they're talking about, but I do hear a few obvious curse words. I've been working on my Spanish, but Babbel never teaches you the important stuff. There's no chapter you can skip to about how to grovel to your girl when you've messed up her sacred space.

Jenna throws her chef's coat over her exercise outfit and I know there's no coming back from this. My plan to get her all blissed out has backfired one hundred percent. I should hide out in the office for the next year or so at least, but I brave the edge of the kitchen instead. "Is there anything I can do to help?"

Jenna turns around so fast I swear I see smoke. "Yes, in fact, there is. You can stop hiring fuckups and sending them to work in my kitchen. I do the hiring and I do the firing, Charlie. This guy, if we ever see him again, is absolutely fired, and you—" She points at me menacingly. "You don't get to hire anyone else. Not one more goddamned person. Got it?"

"Absolutely." It's the only way to answer a question like that.

"Now go and get on the phone to see if Faith can help us out with another order. Miguel and I will see what we can do with the rest of this mess." Jenna turns her back on me, effectively shutting me out.

Faith has a few things, but not enough to make us whole. She makes the delivery herself, probably so she can see my face as she drops it off. She's not usually one to rub things in, but the look she gives me is more effective than any words could be.

Dinner is the disaster anyone could have predicted. The dining room is full for most of the night, and we're out of a good number of things before we even get started. The tubs of diced veggies sit in the cooler while patrons ask for menu items we would have had if only we could surgically repair tomatoes and zucchini. I give away more desserts than we sell and I plunder the bar more than once for free drinks to soothe unhappy customers. Through it all Jenna grits her teeth and stares at the tickets still hanging in the window. No visiting with anyone tonight to see how they liked their meal. I'm paying for a good deal of those too, comping things left and right.

The kid I'd hired to wash dishes quits mid-shift. You might think the dishwasher's the least important member of the team, but I'm here to tell you, there's nothing worse than a restaurant with no clean dishes. We find his uniform shirt later, clogging up the commercial dishwashing machine.

The way Jenna screams then beats anything I've ever heard, and I'm sure if that kid was anywhere within spitting distance, I'd be bailing Jenna out of jail.

Miguel leaves at the end of the night with his shoulders hunched over and remnants of the crazy vegetable sauce for tonight's special all over the front of him. "I don't know how you're going to fix this, but you'd better do it fast, Charlie."

"I'm working on it," I assure him, even though I don't know how to repair what I've broken. Jenna's team was solid, and I didn't break it on purpose, but we can't afford any more defectors.

That night Jenna leaves without so much as a goodbye. She sleeps at the hotel and doesn't seem inclined to move back over to my place. I have officially fucked it up, as predicted.

44

Jenna

It doesn't take much to ruin the flow of a restaurant. Things can be perfectly calibrated and one tiny change can throw that all off. At Sadie Mae's it isn't so much a bunch of small things as one large one.

Charlie.

He's got plenty of experience, but he doesn't seem to learn from his mistakes. And interjecting himself into my team when things are going well is his superpower. I've let it happen twice now, and it warrants a conversation, but the very thing I'd told myself I needed to avoid is sitting in my way. I want to have a conversation with my boss—one that in plenty of places might get me fired—not with my would-be-boyfriend. Or whatever Charlie is. The "keep it casual" idea has left us without defined parameters at work or at home.

But for the sanity of myself and my team, I have to clear the air, and set some hard and fast rules for Charlie and the kitchen. Even if it means having the fight I'm bracing for.

I come into the office and shut the door behind me.

Charlie looks up from behind his laptop and gives me one of his big smiles. "Hey, I missed you this morning."

"I needed a little space." And time to plan this landmine of a conversation.

"You back on track?" It's a genuine question and implies the breakdowns of the past few days are something I can fix.

"Not exactly. I need to talk to you about that." I want to sit, but not across from the desk. I want to be equals in this, even if I know Charlie's technically got the power. I've got some too—they need me here to run the kitchen. But right now the balance is all off, and I've done that to myself by blurring the lines with Charlie. "I need you to respect my authority in the kitchen."

"You made that clear yesterday. In front of everyone." He's not smiling now. Charlie tends to let things roll off his back. He's a forgive and forget kind of guy, but he hasn't forgotten the sharp words I had for him in the heat of the moment yesterday.

"I'm sorry I wasn't more professional—"

"I need the staff to respect me too, Jenna. I need *you* to respect me." His eyes focus on mine, giving me a stare down I wouldn't have thought he could pull off.

I don't have a ready answer for that. I'd love to tell Charlie I have the utmost respect for him here in the restaurant, that I trust him to be able to run things and take charge. But, honestly, the way he does things makes me nervous, and the proof's in the way the last few days have gone. "I'll try not to disrespect you in front of the staff again."

Charlie's face clouds. "Thanks, I think. Is that it?"

"No. I was hoping we could talk about some ground rules, make the chain of command a little clearer."

"I think it's pretty clear already." Charlie isn't going to budge.

"If it were clear, I don't think we'd have had as many of the breakdowns we've had in the past few days." I stand a little straighter, daring him to ignore me.

"Those all happened in the kitchen, Jenna. The front of the house is running well. I don't know how setting up a bunch of arbitrary rules is going to help any of that." Charlie says it like it's a challenge, and he knows I never back down from a challenge.

"Those were all the result of things *you* did, Charlie. That's what I'm talking about. If I tried to make arbitrary decisions for you about who to hire and what they should do, that might not be great for your team. I'm asking you to keep your nose out of the kitchen. Stick to your part and I'll stick to mine." Before I finish, I can see I've made a miscalculation. The mix of personal and professional's too much for Charlie to navigate.

"What I think you're forgetting here is the fact that the kitchen is also my responsibility. All of this is my responsibility, whether you like it or not."

"You know that's not what I meant." My lips threaten to curl into a snarl. "All I want is for you to let me run the kitchen. I need to do the hiring and the firing. I need to be able to have enough autonomy to control the outcomes."

"Is that all you want?" Charlie slams his hand on the desktop. "You want me to call a meeting and tell everyone you're the real boss around here? Make sure none of your guys listen to me or check with me first on anything? How is that showing me any kind of respect, Jenna? How is that showing them I deserve any respect? I guess you'd like me to tell them all the past few days is all on me, right? Those are Charlie's mistakes, guys. Not anybody's fault but his."

"Some of those *were* your mistakes. I'd love for you to take responsibility for them. I'd love for you to see it works better when you let me do my job. When I fuck up, I make changes. We have to make some changes." I'm not yelling, but my voice is firm.

"You can't run everything with an iron fist. Maybe your way isn't the best way. Maybe what you need to do is learn to adapt. You're not the boss here, Jenna. I am. My brothers are. Either you get on board with that or we have a problem."

"That has never been an issue." I blink in confusion. Charlie pulling rank to put me in my place is not what I expected.

"Then let's keep it that way." He's dismissing me. He even gives me a little wave toward the door before he lowers his eyes back to the computer screen.

I wander out of the office on autopilot. There's plenty of mindless work I can do in the kitchen without using too much mental energy. My brain stays focused on Charlie and our conversation. I'm not even sure when things went wrong, but I have a bad feeling in my gut about how this turns out. I can't back down if it means this restaurant fails. And I can't take another failure. That will be it for me and my career. If things can go from great to terrible in the span of a few days, maybe this isn't the place for me. I've learned another hard lesson, unfortunately, but unlike Charlie, I learn from my mistakes.

Mint Springs might have grown on me, but I can't let that stop me from taking care of myself. Time to start putting out feelers for another job. Good thing that suitcase stayed packed.

45

Charlie

Never let it be said that I can't take a bad situation and make it worse. What could have been a normal work conversation with Jenna went sideways in two minutes flat. I know the best way out of this mess is to apologize to her, but giving in and admitting I was wrong feels too raw. I plan on making things right, but after I've had time to cool down. Maybe tonight back at my place I can explain to Jenna why I couldn't just give her what she wanted.

She was right to ask me to back down and let her run the show in the kitchen. I can't possibly do her job, even if she could probably do mine with one hand tied behind her back. Hell, she could do her job and mine and still have time left over in the day. She's smart and capable and makes me look like an amateur. Which is a big part of the problem. It isn't Jenna who needs to adapt, it's me.

I try to catch her eye during the day, but she keeps her head down. The usual laughter and chatter from the kitchen isn't happening today, but I figure that'll come back once things calm down. No one on the other side of the counter is happy with me today, and it shows in the scowls I get instead of smiles. Not one cheery hello for me today. I deserve it, but it still stings.

Dinner is fine, although that's not an adjective I would have chosen if I had a chance. Everything runs according to schedule, and other than Jonah dropping a plate, nothing goes wrong. But Jenna doesn't smile unless she has to and the rest of the staff is just as dejected. As soon as the shift is over, Jenna's heading toward the door.

"Can I talk to you for a second?" I try to sound contrite.

"I really need to get out of here. Can it wait until tomorrow morning?" Jenna sounds like she's talking to a stranger.

"I'd like to do it now, if you don't mind." We're exceptionally cordial when all I really want is to reach out and touch her, pull her up against me, and tell her how sorry I am that I'm a massive jerk with a chip on my shoulder.

Unfortunately for me, Miguel comes to the door as we're standing there, awkwardly trying to get past us without interrupting. "Sorry," he mumbles. He undoubtedly knows I've been a dick, and even if today's new infraction hasn't been explained, my mistakes from the past few days are still messes he's cleaning up.

"I'll walk out with you." Jenna pulls the front door open and walks through, careful not to touch me. "We can talk tomorrow, Charlie." She's not about to be swayed.

I let them go, watching as they get into their cars in the parking lot and drive away. Jenna's off to the hotel again, leaving an empty spot in my bed for another night. I consider having a drink, but I don't want to sit at the bar by myself. Not only will I feel pathetic, but I'll do nothing but think of Jenna. My house won't be much better, but at least

I'll be suffering in private. There's no danger of anyone walking by and seeing my sad face over there.

I stare at the ceiling for hours once I'm home, wishing I'd had the balls to fix this before Jenna walked out tonight. But I'm determined to make things right in the morning. First thing. I'll make sure Jenna knows how wrong I was and get her back to her old self at the restaurant and back in my arms at night. I fall asleep confident things will be better after a good night's sleep.

But things go from bad to worse from the moment I step foot in Sadie Mae's. There's an issue with the freezer and a missing delivery of linens. Every opportunity I have to talk to Jenna gets swallowed up by the minutiae of running a restaurant. When I finally get a free second, Jenna's already having her dinner meeting with her team. I give them all a nod and ask her for a minute of her time.

She looks at her watch. "Can't now. Maybe if there's a lull tonight?"

There isn't, and we work straight through to closing, even having to wait on a few tables that are having such a good time they don't notice we should've locked the doors an hour ago. Normally, I'd have considered that a win—I want people to lose track of time here in Sadie Mae's—but tonight I'm itching to get them out and lock the door. Jenna's closed the kitchen and is ready to leave long before I will be.

"Hey." I touch her arm. She's left her chef's coat in the kitchen, and I can get a quick hit of silky skin under my thumb. Jenna's T-shirt is worn and blue and usually lives on the floor of my bedroom. "Have you got a minute?"

"I'm pretty worn out. Can it wait?" She's not going to make things easy.

"About what I said the other day..." I look into her eyes, hoping she can see how sorry I am.

"Don't worry about it. You were right. You're the boss." There's no warmth there, no hint of all the other things I hope I am to her. "Have a good night." She pushes past me and out into the parking lot. I'd follow her out there to try and make my case, but I've still got patrons inside.

"Jenna—" I call out to her, but she only gives me a wave over her shoulder, never even turning to look at me. I had expected angry, but I'm not sure how to deal with this. She can't ignore me forever, can she?

It turns out she can. Jenna is a master at staying busy. She keeps her head down and the kitchen runs with more efficiency than ever. It doesn't look like a fun place to work, but that might be because all the smiles slide off their faces when I dare to cross into the space. Jenna will talk to me about deliveries and specials, nightly reservations and food costs, but she will not let me apologize, and she's not about to let me plead my case for why she should let me touch her. She stays an arm's length away, always keeping it professional no matter what I try to say.

When she finally does decide to come into the office and shut the door behind her, I breathe a sigh of relief. After more than a week of the cold shoulder I think she's finally come to her senses. Maybe now we can get back to normal. But Jenna doesn't look like she's come in here to kiss and make up.

"Here." The envelope she hands me has my full name written on the outside.

"What is this?" I take it, but don't open it.

"My resignation, effective at the end of the week. Miguel can step up until you find another executive chef." Then she turns her back on me and walks out.

46

Jenna

The regret sets in just a few steps from the office door. *Maybe I'm being too hasty, too impulsive.* I shake those thoughts away. I've made my bed and now I have to lie in it. Actually, it's Charlie's bed that's been the problem this time, and I'm not about to fall back in it. He'd looked shocked when I'd handed him the letter, but he can't have been entirely surprised by it. He'd told me in no uncertain terms that if I couldn't adapt we'd have problems. I can be flexible, but I'm no pretzel. And letting myself get involved with Charlie means leaving this job. I should have known from the second I walked in that he and I couldn't make this work. Lesson learned.

I'd phoned Addison as soon as I'd realized how wrong I'd been. She'd tried to convince me to stick it out a bit longer, but agreed to keep an ear out for any jobs with potential. I needed to have a plan B before I cut ties here. I never imagined something would open up so soon, or that they'd be interested in hiring me, but Addy found me something I could only have dreamed of before.

Beacon Hill, with all the freedom I want. The chance to own a little piece of the pie if I can come up with the money. And my empty apartment waiting for me, a just-in-time coincidence since I had been about to put it on the market. I'd been ready to pull up stakes in Boston for good and put down some tentative roots here in Georgia. Lucky for me, I hadn't pulled the trigger on that yet. Still, it feels a little bittersweet to be giving up on Sadie Mae's and the potential there.

"Are you sure you want to leave? You were starting to seem kind of happy there." Addison's question isn't one I really want to answer. This isn't about what I want. If it was, I'd be talking about more adventures with Charlie, more time in the kitchen with Sadie and Mae, more Georgia sunsets on the back porch.

"I can't have whiplash at home and at work." Those things are true even if a new job doesn't mean any less of that, necessarily.

Addison isn't going to let me get away that easily though. She turns on the sarcasm. "At least the sex was good, though. And you can make buttermilk biscuits and pimento cheese now. Those are some pluses. And you didn't get too attached. Still able to give outrunning your feelings a shot." I ignore Addison's tone. The mention of Sadie and Mae's recipes gives me a little pain in my chest. I'll have to tell them I'm leaving in person, no matter how much it hurts.

"That's true." I can try to look on the bright side. I would never have been able to grow my understanding of Southern food without my time here. I would never have realized how sexy a little drawl can be on the right person, either. I probably would have been better off never knowing that.

"Now you can come back here and get back to that work

life balance you're so famous for." Addison sighs. "Did you book your plane ticket? I can pick you up from the airport." She's not happy with my decision, but she's going to support me anyway. I can always count on her for that.

"You don't have to. There'll be plenty of time for us to catch up." Once I'm back in Boston I can see Addison as much as our schedules allow. We can be right back to boozy brunches and late-night bar meet ups on the days we aren't slaving away in our respective restaurant kitchens. This new job will be another step up for me and on a scale I hadn't imagined I'd ever get to see. I should be thrilled at the opportunity.

Instead, I keep picturing Charlie's face and the shocked look he'd given me, like it'd slapped him right across the face. I can't imagine his brothers were thrilled when he'd had to tell them about my letter of resignation. I should have given it to them all as a group, but I knew I didn't have the stomach for that. Having all four Allens look at me the way Charlie had would have been too much. I was starting to think of them as more than employers, that much is true. And that's how I get myself into trouble, trusting people to be family and friends. Crossing the line the same way I did with Frank and getting burned again.

"Are you finishing out the week?" Addison's question cuts through my mental fog.

"I think I owe it to them. As it is, they'll be scrambling to find someone else. I've got a strong team if Charlie can leave them alone and let them work. Who knows what will happen when the new chef comes in?" I do feel bad to be abandoning my guys. I made some promises I would have liked to have been able to keep. Hopefully their jobs stay secure even with a new chef taking over. "I would give them more time, but the new job can't wait."

"If I know you, you don't want to be hanging around, not with things going the way they are. It's not like you're going to start holding hands and singing Kumbaya with Charlie. If it's over, it's over. A fast, clean break is the best for all of you." Addison exhales. "I've got to go, but let me know how I can help."

"You've helped me plenty. Really, Addy, who knows where I'd be without you?"

"Stuck in Mint Springs with a petulant man baby as a boss, according to you."

I think we both know that's not the whole truth.

Working dinner that night feels a little like attending a funeral. I haven't formally told anyone but Miguel, but everyone knows something's up. There's a pallor over the kitchen that spreads out to the dining room. Charlie keeps his distance, although I occasionally catch him staring at me from across the room. I make good use of the separation provided by the stainless steel counter and the rest of the line cooks. I don't want to have any kind of an altercation, and I keep getting misty when I see how visibly Charlie's hurting too.

I'm almost tempted to take it all back, to try and soothe the sadness in Charlie's eyes. I start to consider if we could work things out and make a clean slate of it when he comes stomping into the kitchen.

"I'm going to give this back to you." He holds out my letter of resignation, the edges of it now frayed.

"Why?" Dinner isn't quite done yet, and I have to keep moving around the kitchen to talk to him.

"So you can throw it out or rip it up or whatever. I don't

accept your resignation, Jenna. I won't." His voice rises over the sounds of the kitchen.

"You don't have a choice, Charlie."

"I haven't told anyone else yet. You can still take it back. You can still stay at Sadie Mae's. You can still stay with me." That last part breaks my heart a little but I realize I absolutely have to stay firm. Nothing's changing if this is how he's coming to me now.

"It's too late. I've already accepted another job. After this week, I'm done here, Charlie. There's no taking it back."

Charlie's face falls but when he looks up again there's an angry glint there. "You were looking for something else all along, weren't you? Letting me think you were committed when you had one foot out the door. Don't bother finishing up the week. Tonight's your last night." Then he walks away.

The kitchen is silent.

"You heard the man. Miguel, looks like your promotion starts tomorrow." Then I go and spend five minutes in the walk-in so no one can see me cry.

47

Charlie

The bottle of whiskey was a bad idea. I had bought it for a special occasion and figured ruining the best thing I've ever had was probably occasion enough. I didn't drink the whole thing, although I could have if I hadn't had to report to family dinner at six. I've gone through enough of it that making my way up Mae and Sadie's front steps is a bit of a challenge. I curse under my breath and use the handrail to help pull myself up.

All heads turn when I fall through the front door. And I do literally fall because my legs don't seem to like the change from outside to inside. Cooper's helping me up before I can crawl back out to the porch.

"Are you drunk?" He peers into my eyes. "God, you reek."

"I was celebrating," I slur. My tongue feels too big for my mouth.

"Oh my, Charlie. Whatever you're celebrating, you're not going to sit at our dinner table without sobering up first." Mae looks disapprovingly at me. "I'll put on a pot of coffee."

Chance comes over to help Cooper get me on the couch, grabbing me under one arm while my oldest brother takes the other. "Jesus, Charlie. Have you been drinking all day?"

"Just since I got up." Which sounds worse than it is. I stayed in bed long past noon, dreading having to tell my family that they were right all along. I promised things with Jenna would be fine, and they are decidedly not. I've ruined everything, and they are going to be more than disappointed. I've put the business at risk and left myself pining for a woman who wants nothing to do with me.

"That doesn't sound good." Cade regards me from over Cooper's shoulder. "Should we get some water in him?"

"Don't bother." I want this hangover to hurt. If it were up to me, I'd keep drinking until there wasn't a drop of liquor left in all of Mint Springs.

"You gonna tell us what you were celebrating?" Cooper's laughing a little bit, but he won't be for long.

I try to sit up straight on the couch, but still end up listing to the side some. It doesn't matter anyway, there's no way to look dignified. I lost most of my dignity when I tried to convince Jenna to stay. She'd told me then what I'd refused to believe all along—that she was never going to stick around. I was a fool to get attached.

"Jenna's new job. Who else wants to drink to that?" I raise my hand in a mock toast even though it's empty.

"Jenna's what?" Chance leans in closer like he's misheard.

"Job. J-O-B. She tried to quit, so I went ahead and fired her." I nod my head. "I got a little ahead of myself there, I think."

"You *fired* her? When?" Cooper's pulling out his phone, undoubtedly trying to get in touch with the woman who was once our executive chef.

"Last night. I was trying to give her back her letter, but she wouldn't take it. Said she already had another job lined up." I'm leaving out big chunks of the story, but my mouth and my brain aren't communicating well.

My brothers look at each other. Cooper's leaving Jenna a message, asking her to please get in touch as soon as possible. None of their expressions look particularly thrilled with the news I've just given them.

"Why would Jenna have been looking for a new job when she's got one here?" Cade asks. "Charlie, what in the hell did you do?"

"Me? She's the one who was looking for something else. Probably never planned on staying anyway. Maybe she's been looking for other jobs this entire time. Did you ever think of that?" I congratulate myself on my excellent powers of deduction and my presentation skills. Clear and concise. Jenna is not to be trusted. Period.

"I knew something like this would happen. How do we fix this?" Chance isn't asking me. He's only looking at Cooper and Cade.

"Hello, did you not hear me? I tried to fix it. It's too late. She's already gone." I make a motion with my hand like a plane flying away.

"Gone? Where was she going? Charlie, I so want to wring your neck right now." Chance looks like he's not speaking metaphorically.

"Go ahead. It would be a relief." They can't make me feel any worse than I already do.

Cade shakes his head. "Maybe we can still convince her. Cooper, try calling her again." He looks at me with a mixture of pity and disgust. "You couldn't keep it in your pants, could you? Millions of women in the world, and you have to start screwing the one we needed to keep."

"You think this was about screwing? This was more than that. *She's* more than that." I stupidly try to stand and take a swing at my youngest brother. I miss and go down hard on the living room floor just as Mae comes in with a cup of coffee.

"Boys! Not inside the house," she scolds. "What in the world is making y'all act like that?"

"Charlie fired Jenna," Cooper volunteers, and Mae gasps.

"I had to. She was going to quit," I explain from my spot on the rug.

"That makes no sense." Mae shakes her head. "Where is she now?"

"He doesn't know." Chance takes the cup from Mae. "We'll figure it out."

"Well, I can't imagine she'd leave without saying goodbye." Mae's voice wavers a bit.

"She might. She isn't the kind to do what you tell her." I keep my head on the floor.

"What does that mean?" Cooper pokes me with the toe of his boot.

"I told her I was the boss, and if she couldn't accept that then we'd have a problem. You know how she is."

"Seriously, Charlie? You got in a pissing match with Jenna? About what?" Chance's angry voice is hurting my head enough for me to go ahead and blurt out the facts I had no intention of telling my brothers.

"She doesn't like me hiring people without consulting her. She thinks I'm too nice. Too lenient on the staff. That I try to be their friends." I wait for someone to defend me, to take my side and agree that Jenna's in the wrong, but no one does.

"I thought we hired Jenna because she knew how to run

a kitchen? Wasn't that the plan? Why in the world would you go around trying to mess with that?" Cade is exasperated. I'm lucky no one's given me a kick in the head.

"I was trying to help." It sounds lame even to my ears.

"Well, you've done a great job, champ. Top notch." Cooper puts his phone back up to his ear. "She's not answering. Should one of us go over to the hotel? See if we can talk her out of this?"

"I'll go," Chance volunteers. "Y'all stay here and try to get the full story out of this one." He's halfway out the door already. "And think about what we're going to do if Jenna isn't coming back." His face is grim. We all know there aren't a ton of executive chefs hanging around Mint Springs, and now that we're in trouble we won't necessarily get to be choosy.

Cade and Cooper get me back on the couch and leave me there to stew. I can hear them brainstorming at the dining room table, Lily and Hadley offering their advice now too. But no one asks me a damn thing, not even Sadie and Mae, and I eventually pass out there, dreaming of Jenna's mouth and the way her skin felt under my palms.

48

Jenna

I guess I should have expected one of the Allens to eventually show up at my door. I know I need to stop by the farm before I leave town for good. I owe them all at least that much. But I've been putting it off all day today, knowing I'm going to have to say goodbye to a family I've grown attached to. I'm leaving them with a mess, and no new opportunity is going to take away that guilt.

I'm putting the last of my things in my suitcase when Chance knocks. I look through the peephole, almost hoping it's Charlie. Of course it isn't him. He's sent one of his brothers to do whatever they've decided should be done. Begging me to stay or telling me to go to hell are both going to feel the same right about now.

"You're still here." There's relief in Chance's voice.

"I was just getting ready to call you. I'm guessing Charlie told you what happened."

"In a manner of speaking. He's a little drunk. Can I come in?" Chance peers around the doorframe and into my empty room. "Looks like you're all packed up."

"Yeah, I didn't have much to pack, really." I never bothered sending for more of my stuff and now I'm relieved to only have one bag to haul out of here. My heart and my pride might have taken a beating, but at least I'm traveling light.

"I really wish you'd stay. I don't have all the details, and I know Charlie can be a pain in the ass, but I'm hoping we can work something out. We need you at Sadie Mae's."

"I wish I could, Chance, but I think it's best if I cut my losses now. I had wanted to give you more time to find someone else, but then this new job fell into my lap. And Charlie fired me, so there's no real reason to stay." I give him a sad smile. This isn't how I had hoped to be leaving Mint Springs. Part of me was starting to think about never leaving.

"I know things with Charlie have been..." Chance tapers off. I don't know how much he knows, and I'm not about to tell him.

"It isn't all Charlie's fault. I knew better than to get involved with him. I should apologize to all of you for not staying professional. Frankly, I'm a little embarrassed." I don't regret my relationship with Charlie, but it'll follow me wherever I go. It's a cautionary tale for sure, but also a reminder that my divorce wasn't the end of the world. There are people out there who would want to be with me. Walking away from Charlie will leave me wounded for a bit, but I'll find a way to get over it. I have to.

"There's no need for that. Y'all are two strong personalities and, if I'm being honest, I had hoped I was wrong about how things would work out. We all want Charlie to be happy. You too. I'm sorry things are ending like this. Are you sure there's nothing we can do to convince you to stay?"

Chance is so sincere I almost wish it was possible to tell him yes.

"I'm on a flight out early tomorrow, and I'm starting in the new restaurant on Monday. I'll go ahead and drive to Atlanta tonight. No use staying all the way out here. I was planning on coming out to the farm to say goodbye before I left. It really is the best thing for everyone. I'm sure you'll find someone great to take my place." It's hard to imagine someone else running the kitchen at Sadie Mae's, even harder to imagine not seeing Charlie and that cocky smile every day, but eventually those feelings will fade.

Chance looks down at his feet for a bit. "Well, you're welcome back any time. I mean that. And I know Sadie and Mae would love the chance to tell you that in person."

"I'll be right behind you. I promise."

It's harder to say goodbye to Charlie's aunts than I thought it would be. When I pull up to their farmhouse, the porch light's on and dinner's obviously in progress. I get invited in and fussed over like I'm moving to Siberia and not simply going back to Boston.

Sadie packs me a bag of food for the plane that I'm pretty sure isn't going to make it through security. I doubt they allow passengers to bring tubs of mashed potatoes and gravy, but maybe airport security in Atlanta is used to that kind of thing.

"And don't forget that if you make biscuits you're going to need to be prepared for them to taste a little different. The flour's not the same. Do you have room in your bag for a five pound bag of White Lily? I think we've got an extra." Mae's making sure I've got all the essentials.

"I'm sure I'll be able to order it. No need to have me emptying your kitchen." I try to keep smiling even though the tears are threatening. "Thank you again for putting up with me and for everything you've taught me."

"Thank you for putting up with *us*." Sadie looks over at Charlie, snoring on the sofa. "He's a bit thick-headed, but he has a good heart. He's going to be full of regret in the morning for the way he's handled this."

"He doesn't need to be." I look at Charlie's face pressed tight against a pillow. "We both made mistakes."

"That's sweet of you to say, dear, but we're hoping he has one hell of a hangover tomorrow." Mae gives me a pat. "You visit when you get the chance. We know you'll be busy."

"I will." I hope it isn't a lie. I can't imagine coming back here to see the restaurant without me, or, even worse, Charlie moved on and happy, probably adding to the next generation of Allens. After one last round of hugs and another fleeting glance at Charlie, I'm back in the car. Charlie's family lines the porch, waving like I'm some sort of celebrity—like I'm someone important. And I wish I was any of those things right now instead of just a woman driving away from something she didn't even know she wanted.

49

Charlie

"Did you put in the order? Charlie? Did you put in the extra order with Faith? It isn't in here." Miguel's bent over a cardboard box, sifting through the things Faith dropped off this morning.

"What extra order?"

"The one we need for tonight. We've got that rehearsal dinner, remember? The one that insisted on squash blossoms? There aren't any in here. And we're short on tomatoes if anyone else orders a tart." Miguel's disappointment is written all over his face. "Maybe I should take over the orders. This is the third time, Charlie."

"I know. I'm sorry." There's no excuse. I should be able to keep on top of things like that. It should be easy to order what we need and make the schedule. By now it should be second nature. But, to be honest, I'm having trouble getting myself out of bed these days, much less making sure Sadie Mae's runs smoothly. "Maybe you should be in charge of that. You know better what we need in the kitchen." I can barely stand to be in there at all.

"Can you call over to Happy Trails and see if Faith can find some of the stuff we need? If she can't, we're going to have to call the mother of the groom and let her know we have to change the menu." We both know who's going to be in charge of that. I made the mistake, so I need to try to fix it.

"I'll call Faith, and if it's not doable, I'll call the family." I dread both those calls, but I'll make them. "Miguel, I'm sorry."

"You seem to be saying that a lot lately. Any leads on a new chef? That would help take some of the pressure off."

"Nothing yet. I'm still looking." The truth is no one can live up to Jenna. The bar's set pretty high now when it comes to executive chefs. Unfortunately, while I look around for the ultimate Jenna replacement, my ability to run both parts of Sadie Mae's is diminishing. Miguel is busting his ass, but he's not quite ready to take things to the next level. I need someone with experience and vision, drive and culinary chops.

I need Jenna.

But she's not coming back. She's probably happy as a clam up in Boston, enjoying her old life and all the perks that come with the new part. Most certainly not missing me and this backwater town. So I'm stuck here thinking about how I nearly had everything I wanted but was then too stubborn to accept it. I had to go and blow everything up. I've got what I thought was my dream all to myself now, and I realize it was so much better when I had someone to share it with. *Too late now, dumb ass.*

"Charlie! Charlie Allen, you get your worthless ass out here right now!"

I seldom hear Faith Baker yell, and it's been a while since I've heard her cuss. She tries to save her swear words for occasions that warrant them. Apparently, whatever I've done has been enough to get one of her coveted bad words combined with a little screaming. I'm almost afraid to walk out of the office.

"What are you yelling about?" I yell right back from the doorway. "There's no need to involve everybody else in all this." I gesture to the rest of my staff, all now frozen in place like statues. They've been witnesses to plenty of unprofessional behavior in the past few weeks.

"I'm sure this isn't the worst thing they've seen here in this restaurant." Faith puts her hands on her hips. "I'm coming in there. You'd better be ready to explain yourself." Her determined walk tells me she's not joking. "Miguel, I brought you your squash blossoms!" His thank you gets the door closed on it. Another very un-Faith-like maneuver.

"To what do I owe this unexpected visit?" I ask before she turns her angry eyes on me.

"*Unexpected*? Seriously? You called me begging for vegetables. Coveted, hard to find vegetables. Do you know how many squash I just sacrificed for your blossom order? I'm going to be short in a few weeks because I helped you out. You have to quit doing this, Charlie. You're affecting my bottom line now too. I love you, but I can't keep rescuing your ass." That's two cuss words I've gotten in the span of five minutes.

"I'm not asking you to. If you didn't have the produce, you should have said so." It's a rude thing to say, especially to my best friend, but I say it anyway. *Yes, universe, I'm still a dick. Thanks for those life lessons.*

"What the hell is wrong with you? I just told you I did you a favor and that I love you, and that's what I get? You really are trying to push everyone away, aren't you?" Faith looks me directly in the eyes, not blinking. If I want a fight, she's going to give it to me.

But I don't want a fight, not really, and she's the only one who'll call me out on my behavior. Miguel will skirt around it, and my brothers have been trying to give me as much tough love as they can stomach, but only Faith can say it to my face.

"I don't want to push everyone away." It comes out like a whine.

"Then quit doing it. It works, Charlie. You already proved that with Jenna."

"I don't want to talk about Jenna." The reaction's immediate and protective. Not even Faith gets to poke that soft spot.

"You don't have to talk about her. We can all see exactly how you're feeling. It has to stop, Charlie." Faith means business. "There's more at stake here than just your broken heart. You have a business to run, one that plenty of people are relying on now. You've contracted too many local businesses to throw in the towel. What are those people supposed to do if you run Sadie Mae's into the ground? What about your brothers? You need to get your head out of your ass."

I am racking up the swear words today from Faith. Wait... "Who said my heart was broken?"

"Good Lord, Charlie." Faith rolls her eyes. "You were gone for that woman from the moment you met her. Don't try to pretend all of this isn't about her. She left you, and you deserved it, but that isn't a reason to ruin your business."

"But I miss her." It's the first time I've said it out loud, the first time I've told anyone else.

"Duh. We all know that, but you're going to have to start compartmentalizing some of this shit."

"Shit?" That's a big deal for Faith. Hell, sure. Damn? Occasionally. But literal poop? I'm in trouble now.

"This restaurant and the way it runs needs to be separate from your plan to win Jenna back. If you don't do that, you'll end up with nothing for her to come back to." Faith puts her hands out, frustrated, and gives me another eye roll.

"You think she'll come back?" I'm desperate for Faith to tell me she thinks I have a chance.

"She'd be a fool to, but it's possible. You do have a few strong points even if you are terrible at handling rejection."

"Tell me what to do, Faith." I need coaching, obviously.

"You already know what to do, but don't run this restaurant into the ground in the meantime. Jenna's going to be extremely disappointed if you trash this place before she can realize this is where she belongs."

"I thought you didn't like her." Faith's made no secret of her dislike of Jenna.

"I don't, but *you* do. In fact, I think you might even love her if you let yourself think about it for a minute. I don't have to like her to see how much you need her."

I think about that for a minute.

"So what you're saying is I might have a chance."

"A slim one. But maybe I can help you improve your odds a little."

Thank God for best friends.

50

Jenna

I should be happy. More than happy. I should be thrilled. Ecstatic, even.

This job is more than I could ever have imagined. My new boss is extremely hands-off and extremely rich. He wants this restaurant to be successful for bragging rights, and he's given me carte blanche to make that happen. From staff to ingredients, all I'm hearing is yes. I should be smiling all day long and sleeping like a baby. Instead I'm frowning like I've been given some truly bitter medicine and staying up half the night wishing I had deleted Charlie's number in my phone. I spend a good chunk of time writing texts I never send, pouring my heart out and then deleting them.

"Kevin, have you ever been on a float trip?"

"Is that a new kind of LSD? I've only really ever used the regular one." My sous chef looks at me, not a hint of humor in his voice.

"Um, no. It's when you get in one of those inflatable inner tubes and float down the river."

"The river here? I'd never get in that. It's completely

polluted, you know that, right?" He looks at me like I've got two heads. "Even if people row on it, I don't think you can swim in it."

"No, not here... Never mind." Kevin is a genius in the kitchen, but he's not likely to love my stories of country living. A few months ago I would have felt the same way.

"Do you want me to take a look at the ice cream? I think we might have gotten it right this time." Kevin's excited. He's determined to make arroz con dulce in frozen form. No matter how many times I tell him there's no reason to try to improve on the original, he doesn't listen. He likes using all the bells and whistles, and there was a time I would have been interested in following him. Now, however, I want the classics. Don't give me a deconstructed chicken dinner. Who needs that? I'll take a vat of Sadie and Mae's mashed potatoes and gravy over any of that any day.

"Jenna? Where are you, lady?" Addison calls from the front of the restaurant. She's in her usual leggings and a T-shirt so she can throw a chef's coat over them in an hour or so. Addy's been wearing that uniform for years now. It goes well in the kitchen and on a ride home from work on the T. Not that she needs to take the subway now, since she lives walking distance from her perfect little restaurant space. We've both ended up with exactly what we wanted.

Except I've got this Charlie-sized hole in my heart that keeps making it impossible for me to appreciate it.

"They claimed not to have any *culantro* but I told them it was for you and some magically appeared." She does a little *poof* motion with her hand. "You're going to have to start going to that market yourself. Those ladies are cutthroat."

"Those little grandmas?" I pretend to be shocked. "They're harmless."

"I'm not so sure. They seem to think I'm up to something

nefarious." Addison shrugs. She's the least suspicious looking person I know. If I wanted to try to pull off something, she'd be the person I'd use. Right now I mainly need her for stopping by the Latin grocery on her way over. And moral support. Lots of that.

"Just don't touch the baby," I warn. Eventually that kid will be in kindergarten and Addison won't be freaked out by him following her around the tight aisles in his rolling baby walker.

"They didn't have guava paste either, for some reason." She shrugs. Somehow even the Latin market can get me missing Mint Springs. Who would have thought that tiny town would have every ingredient a Puerto Rican cook could ever want?

"What's Master Chef got going on back there?" She leans around to try to see what Kevin's up to.

"He's trying to make rice pudding into ice cream."

"Still?" Addison asks.

"If it's possible, Kevin will figure it out."

"You don't sound thrilled."

"It's so...unnecessary. I can see why he wants to do it, but it doesn't improve on the original, I don't think." I remember the way Charlie devoured my arroz con dulce, the way his family had swooned over it like it was something you'd serve royalty. They didn't seem to think it needed to be "elevated."

"I hear you, sometimes the original is the best. But I don't think it's Kevin who's bringing you down." Addison reaches for my hand. "Still hurts?"

"Of course it does."

Addison understands how attached I'd gotten, how easy it had become to picture myself staying. But that wasn't meant to be, and my time with Charlie ended, just like I predicted all along. He'll find someone else eventually and start the life he's been putting off. I'll be another one of the flings he had before he decided to settle down.

"It's okay to admit you might have made a mistake. This place is great, but it might not be what you really want." Addison's eyes sweep the room. When we started cooking school, my own restaurant was my dream, a place like this would have been a close second. But now, this grind isn't energizing me the way it used to.

"I don't think it was a question of want," I offer.

"Of course it is. Unless you want to go ahead and admit it's more of a need. Jenna, I'm going to give you what I think is the cold, hard truth. Georgia had started to grow on you and you liked the slower pace down there. You started to see yourself with Charlie long term and you got scared. All the other stuff was just an excuse." Addison's eyes lock with mine. "Try and deny it. You needed someone to remind you there's more to life than sweating in a kitchen. He isn't Frank, Jenna. You don't want to let yourself believe he might be a good choice."

I don't doubt that Charlie would make a good partner. In plenty of ways he's a great one. He's got no problem with a strong woman at home. At work? That's another story. It was when he decided to flex his muscles there that things fell apart.

"I think I've nearly got it," Kevin yells from the back of the kitchen. He comes running with a bowl of pure white ice cream and a hand full of spoons. "Taste it and tell me what you think."

I dip my spoon into the frosty concoction and slide a small bit into my mouth. It's creamy and smooth, undeniably delicious. But it lacks the bit of resistance you expect from rice pudding. The flavor's there, but the experience isn't.

"It's good," Addison says, rolling the bite she's taken around in her mouth. "What are you thinking of pairing it with?"

It's a conversation I would normally love having. I'm passionate about food and relish talking about it. But this feels a long way from Sadie and Mae's kitchen and even farther from my abuelita's. There's something real in that kind of cooking that I'm never going to be able to recreate here—and I'm not sure anyone wants me to. I can't imagine Kevin and Addison weeding a garden or milking a goat. The secrets they've learned about feeding people come from culinary school, not years of trying to show people how much you love and care for them. Maybe it isn't any less important, but it feels less immediate, less necessary.

"What if we deconstructed one of those cookies you make, Jenna? The ones with the guava paste?" Kevin's getting excited, ready to take one of my simple recipes and change it into something complicated.

"They didn't have guava paste at the market." I shrug. The cookies get to live to see another day.

"I'm sure one of the big distributors carries guava paste. We probably need it for other things, too, right? I'll make some calls." Kevin doesn't wait for me to agree or give him permission, he takes off to the office at a run. He's excited, and I can't blame him. He's doing what he loves. That's what I'm supposed to be doing, too, although right now it doesn't feel that way.

"You can still change your mind," Addison says.

I'm not so sure.

51

Charlie

I'm sweating through my suit jacket. I can't blame that on the weather, because even though there's a heat wave in Boston right now, the inside of this restaurant is a cool sixty-five degrees. I don't have to ask anyone to know. If Jenna's running this place, then that's what the thermostat says. I've been sitting at the end of the bar for hours now, waiting for things to slow down enough for me to catch Jenna's eye. I may have made a miscalculation with that part of the plan, because not only is the kitchen in this place closed off from the dining room, it's packed in here and has been all night.

"Can I get you another?" The bartender's probably ready for me to move on.

"Sure." I slide my empty glass toward him. I should slow my roll with these drinks, but I know I'm taking up valuable real estate. "What time does the kitchen close?"

"Midnight. You want to look at the menu again?"

I've already ordered more food than I could have ever eaten. I wanted to try everything, to try to find Jenna's influence. Some of it was easy to identify. She's kept some of her signature dishes. Others I struggled with. They didn't seem to fit with what Jenna would make, and even though they were delicious, I couldn't find her anywhere.

"I'll take a look." I'm sure I can make room for rice pudding, but it's not on the small menu he hands me. I run my fingers over the embossed letters. "You don't have arroz con dulce?"

"No, we've got this though." He points to the bottom of the menu. "It's ice cream, but I think you'll like it. Everyone raves about it."

I read the description, shaking my head. Rice pudding ice cream? Of all things. "I'll try it."

The bartender seems content with that decision and he's quick with my whiskey. I can't help but admire the staff here. They're efficient and helpful, all in perfectly pressed black shirts. The decor doesn't scream Jenna, but it's warm and inviting. I know she didn't have a hand in decorating this restaurant, but I look for hints that she's here none-theless. I'm sure if I could see inside the kitchen, I'd imme-diately see her stamp. It's the thing I can't manage to maintain at Sadie Mae's no matter how hard I try.

The ice cream comes out quickly, and I stare at the tiny bowl in front of me. It's one of Jenna's recipes, but completely inside out. The ice cream gives me only a hint of what I love. The bits of what would have been a cookie make me long for the ones Jenna made in my kitchen the night she wowed my family with her grandmother's recipes. It's like seeing a ghost. I want the real thing, but I'm getting smoke and mirrors.

I'm pondering this as the real thing walks out from behind the saloon doors of the kitchen. Jenna looks good, smiling and happy, as she checks on the patrons. I've seen her do this over and over again in my own restaurant, accepting compliments and making people feel like they're the only ones in the room. She excels at this the same way she does at so many things and I'd taken it for granted.

When she sees me, her smile disappears. I wave, but her brow only furrows. Surprising her at work might not have been the smartest move, but I needed to make sure she couldn't avoid me. I'm starting to think even here she might be able to keep me at arm's length. She motions for the bartender and they have a conversation that includes far too many glances down at my end of the bar to be about anything but me. When she comes my way it's with a large fake smile plastered on her face.

"What are you doing here?" She doesn't bother with pleasantries and doesn't touch me.

"I came to see your new place. I like it. The food's delicious." I try to relax, pretend we're just two old friends having a chat, but that doesn't work as well as I'd hoped. I've bet everything on this visit, and if she decides to, she can put an end to all my plans.

Jenna looks at my dish of melting ice cream. "You didn't seem to enjoy your dessert."

"It lacks the things I love about the original." I should probably keep that to myself, but Jenna doesn't look offended.

"That it does," she says, and finally lets that toothpaste advertisement she's got on her face relax a little. "What do you want, Charlie?"

"To talk to you. I didn't get to say goodbye, and I regret the way we left things." I want to reach out and touch her, to pull her close to me, but I resist. She's far enough away that doing so would look desperate and possibly get me thrown out.

"I don't know what there is to say." Jenna shakes her head. "You could have called."

"I figured you wouldn't answer, and there are some things I really need to tell you. Can we talk once you're done here? I can wait." I send up a silent prayer. *Please let her say yes.*

Jenna frowns. "You'll be waiting a while."

"I'd wait forever."

My speech starts to sound more and more ridiculous as I wait for Jenna to finish up and come out from the bowels of the kitchen. I'm sure she's taking her time—the place is nearly empty before I see her come through the swinging doors, looking like the city girl she was when I first saw her. She sits down in the stool next to me, and I get a hit of the coconut and spice that can only be Jenna. It's enough to remind me why I came here and why I can't leave empty-handed.

"You look good." Again I resist the urge to touch her.

"You look exhausted."

I laugh. "Realizing you've made a huge mistake will do that to you."

Jenna blinks. "Charlie…"

"I'm not looking for your sympathy, Jenna. I know what went wrong and most of it's on me. I deserve a little suffering for the pain I put you through—for the pain I put everyone though. I'm willing to accept that. But I can't accept the way we left things." I take a breath. This next part is the hard sell, and I have to get it just right.

"If this is an apology, you can stop. I'm not angry

anymore. What's done is done. Things worked out for the best, I think."

No, no, no. I'm not letting her steer us down that path. Jenna might be stubborn, but so am I, and I came here to convince her of one thing and one thing only. Accepting my apology ain't it.

"Let me stop you right there. I appreciate you being so forgiving, really I do, but I'm here to offer you an invitation. I've made some changes, and I'd like for you to come to the farm to see them for yourself. Plus, it's Mae's birthday—a big one—and she wants all the family there to celebrate."

"I'm not family, Charlie."

"The hell you aren't. Now, you aren't going to disappoint a little old lady on her birthday, are you? I bought you a ticket. At least say you'll think about it." My palms are sweaty, and I feel like my expensive dinner might be about to reappear all over this polished wood floor. I'm pretty sure I'm going to hell for using my great aunt's birthday as an excuse to lure Jenna to Mint Springs.

"I do miss Mae," Jenna confesses.

"She misses you too. Everybody does." *I do. God, I miss you.* "Say you'll be there."

"I'll think about it."

"That's enough for me."

For now.

52

Jenna

Mint Springs hasn't changed much in the two months I've been gone. Everything's still right where I left it when I decided to return to Boston, but I've never been so excited for a place to be frozen in time as I am today. I drive past Southern Comforts and know Lily's mother and grandmother are inside. I nearly wave at the cars already in the Bootlegger parking lot. I consider going out of my way to stop by Hot House Flowers, but I'm impatient to get to the farm and don't want to end up with the perm Hadley's mother keeps insisting I'll love. Even the clerk at the hotel acts like I never left, hardly looking up to give me my key.

My heart is beating a million miles an hour as I drive up the gravel road toward the distillery. I've changed into my party dress, and my gift for Mae sits next to me in the passenger seat. Hopefully she loves the recipe card holder I had made for her. It can keep all the loose index cards they have organized. I even added a few of my own to get them started, making sure not to leave out any of the steps to make pasteles.

Cooper and Chance are outside, and they wave me into the parking lot. They look suspiciously underdressed for what I've been told is a very special party.

Chance leans in once I roll down my window. "Hey. Long time no see." He gives me an awkward hug by threading his arms and upper body into the car. "Come and have a drink with us."

"Shouldn't we be going to Sadie Mae's? It's almost five."

"We've got time. Come in for a second. I've got something for you to try," Cooper calls out. "It'll only take a minute."

I put the car in park. I'm happy to see these two, but also anxious to get over the thing I fear the most: seeing Charlie.

I'd been able to keep it together when he surprised me in Boston. That was on my turf, and I could hide behind the armor my job gives me. I was steel, and nothing was going to change that. But sitting with him and seeing how awful he looked—still handsome, of course, but sad in a way I hadn't known was possible—it had been difficult to keep my heart hardened. That's part of the reason I agreed to come back, Charlie's hold over me is still strong.

I accept Cooper's hand as he leads me into the distillery. I've worn a pair of heels that would be fine in Boston, but aren't loving the gravel of this parking lot. I'd planned on only one trip from the car and back, so Cooper's help is appreciated.

"We added a new drink. Well, a new drink and a fancy cassis." Cooper points toward the giant chalkboard menu hanging behind the bar. I squint at the new special printed in bold letters.

"A blueberry margarita?"

"Yep. Your recipe. There's a blue balls joke in there

somewhere, but I promised Charlie I wouldn't tell it." Chance gives me a sly grin.

"I think you sort of just did." I tilt my head. I've missed Charlie's brothers.

"And check this out." Cooper hands me a curvy bottle of deep blue liqueur. "That's for you."

"For me? I don't understand."

"Not for you, exactly. We're going to sell it, of course, but it's the one named after you. The blueberries are from Miller's. It's called Blueberry Boss. Charlie picked out the bottle. You'll have to ask him about that." He clears his throat.

I hold the bottle up to the light and tilt it a bit. The dark liquid inside sparkles.

"It's got hints of ginger. Sweet with a little bite." Chance slides a fresh margarita in front of me. "Taste this and let me know if we got it right."

I blink back tears. "The liquor is supposed to be named after family members."

"Exactly," Chance says. "And that one's yours, Jenna, because you're family. Now drink your margarita so we can get moving."

I'm positive we're late for Mae's party, even though I drink my margarita as fast as possible. I'm not here to ruin anyone's birthday.

"Don't you two need to go home to change?" We're in one of the golf carts, driving down the hill to Sadie Mae's. "I thought this birthday party was going to be dressy."

"That's tomorrow," Cooper shouts over the hum of the engine. "Tonight we're celebrating something else."

"What?" The wind swallows my question and whips my hair around. By the time we get to the restaurant, I'm sure I look like I've been riding a rollercoaster.

"We're celebrating our new organizational structure. Look." Cooper points to the Sadie Mae's sign. It's draped with a banner that reads: *Under New Management*. Underneath the original sign there's now a new addition: *Jenna Bard: Executive Chef.*

I turn to look at the two of them, my mouth hanging open. "I don't understand."

"Go on in and Cade'll explain everything." Chance shoos me toward the front door with his hand. "Can you make it in those shoes? I swear between you and Hadley we're going to have a broken ankle out here."

"I can make it," I assure him as I pick my way to the front door, still stealing glances at my name there on the sign. *What the hell is going on here?*

Walking back into the restaurant is like getting hit with a wave of nostalgia. It looks the same, and I can still smell the lingering scents of all the dishes Mae, Sadie, and I spent so much time testing and perfecting. It's like coming back to your childhood home, and I get a twinge of sadness. Cade and Charlie are seated at one of the round tables near the center of the room. They both stand and beckon me to come closer.

Charlie looks impossibly handsome but oh so nervous. His hand shakes as he comes over to pull out a chair for me. I sit wordlessly and wait for them to explain what's happening.

"Thanks for coming," Charlie starts.

"You told me this was for Mae's birthday."

"Yes, and that's not entirely untrue. We're having a big party for her tomorrow, but I needed to get you here for this, and I didn't think you'd come any other way." Charlie looks contrite. "I'm hoping you'll stay for tomorrow, but if you don't want to, I'll understand."

"Let's get the business out of the way." Cade slides a piece of paper in front of me. "I realize you might not be in the market for a new position, but we'd like to make you an offer."

"Hi, Cade." It feels off to not at least tell him hello.

"Hi, Jenna. We missed you. I'll hug your neck once we get done with this." He smiles. "That's a diagram of our new org structure. As you can see, Charlie's not running the restaurant anymore. He's still working here, and he's managing the front of the house. Front manager and executive chef are equal positions and both report to me."

I look at Charlie. "You can't let them take the restaurant from you. This is your dream." A fierce bout of protectiveness surges through me and I get ready to give Cade a piece of my mind.

"No one's taking anything from me, Jenna. I'm giving it." Charlie gives Cade a nod. "Explain the rest."

"We'd like for you to come back as executive chef. We've got a new offer of compensation." He slides another piece of paper toward me and I scan it quickly, my eyes snagging on something that's too good to be true.

"This gives me a portion of the company." I look from Charlie to Cade and back again. "You don't want to do that."

"We actually do. It starts as a small percentage but then increases over time. It would make you not only an employee but a part owner. Hopefully that makes you more comfortable reporting to me. You and Charlie would be equals." Cade shrugs. "I'll leave you two to talk about it. There's no rush. Take your time thinking about it. But I do need that hug."

I stand unsteadily and wrap my arms around Cade. "Thank you."

"Don't thank me. It was Charlie's idea. We'd be thrilled for you to accept the offer, but we'll love you no matter what you decide. Hopefully I'll see you tomorrow. Mae's party should be a good time." He releases me and gives Charlie a pat on the back as he walks away.

I sit back down and stare at the papers in front of me. It's a great opportunity, one that rivals anything I've ever been offered before. There's just one problem.

"Why would you do this?" I stare at Charlie across the table. "It's crazy. You're giving up the thing you wanted most in this world."

"I have always wanted to run my own restaurant, you're right. And at one time I did think it was the thing I wanted most in this world, but it turns out I was wrong about that. I've been here trying to do this without you, and it isn't the same. I have the restaurant, but it doesn't mean anything if I'm here by myself. I need you, Jenna. You're what I want most in this world."

I look at Charlie, so full of hope and so willing to make this sacrifice for me. "I don't know what to say."

"Say yes, Jenna. Just say yes."

53

Charlie

She's going to say no.

Holy shit, not only am I not going to get the girl, Sadie Mae's is about to lose the best damn executive chef I'm ever going to find. I've put my heart on the line, and she's about to hand it right back to me.

"But you making this commitment to me doesn't make sense."

"Why not?" Confusion floods through me.

"What will you do when you decide to start a family? Or get married? How will you explain giving all this to me?" Jenna holds up the papers. "It's too much."

I've offered her the world when it comes to a job, but I haven't told her how I feel. Of course she's got reservations. And there's only one way to fix that.

"I haven't been good about saying things outright. This isn't my strong suit for sure, and I want you to know this upfront. But Jenna, the way I feel about you... It's more than I can probably put into words." I look into Jenna's eyes, searching for some understanding there. "I'm hoping you want to come back for the job, but I'm hoping you also want to come back for me."

Jenna blinks. "No, Charlie. That's a terrible idea. Eventually you're going to want more than fun; you're going to want to do what Chance and Cooper have done. You'll find some local girl and make use of that giant house of yours. And I'll be what? Your ex who's never leaving?"

"I *hope* you're never leaving. I don't want to make promises I can't keep, Jenna, but all those things you think I want? You're wrong. I'm excited for Chance and Cooper. I love that they wanted to become husbands and that Cooper's becoming a dad, but that doesn't mean that's the life I want for myself." I reach for Jenna's hand across the table and she lets me take it. "I'm not saying this because it's what I think you want to hear. I'm never going to want the exact lives my brothers have chosen. I want one of my own. I want one with you."

"It's asking you to give up so much." Jenna's bottom lip trembles.

"What am I giving up? I get the job of my dreams, the smartest, sexiest, most beautiful woman in the universe, and I get to live here with the people I love the most. This is what I want. You'd be giving me something, Jenna, not taking something away. Give me the chance to prove that to you."

"But how can you be sure?" There's that inkling of mistrust, the one Jenna's got from being hurt before. She looks up at the ceiling. "You could change your mind."

"And so could you. You could get tired of my bubble baths, and foot rubs, and my undying affection for you. There's no guarantee. I love you, Jenna. I love everything about you. Give this a shot. We can make it last."

"And you'd be what? My boyfriend?" Jenna looks dubious.

"You can call me whatever you want. Move in with me or get your own place. You want to get married? We can do that. What matters to me is that we do it together." I'm hopeful, but ready to be shot down all the same. I'm asking Jenna to trust me in a way I know she doesn't like.

"And we'd be equals here at work."

"Yes."

"But I'd be the boss at home?" The way she's looking at me has my heart nearly beating out of my chest.

"Most of the time."

"Then we might have a deal." She looks at me and cocks her head to one side.

"I have something that might convince you." I go to the back of the restaurant and open the rear door, fishing around until I find the leash. "Come on, buddy," I mutter under my breath.

Jenna's eyes widen. "You didn't."

"I did, and it is a huge pain in the ass to get a baby goat into a pair of pajamas." I look into the large eyes of the world's tiniest goat and feel the sensation of warm pee on my forearm.

"Are you sure we should let them do that?" Jenna yells in my ear. The band we hired for Mae's party is really throwing down. She'd wanted a horn section so, by God, we found her one.

"Probably not, but you only turn twenty-one once, right?" In truth, Mae's done it several times now, but that isn't stopping her and Maggie Gentry from doing vodka shots off the ice sculpture. That had been another request I'd had to scour North Georgia for. But the way Mae's eye lit up when she saw it in the middle of the restaurant made all that effort worthwhile.

Chance and Cooper are dancing with their wives, and Sadie's out on the dance floor too, cutting a rug with Mr. Sims from the liquor store. Hadley's not as limber as she used to be now that she's getting bigger, but Cooper makes sure none of her dance moves are too complicated. I'm still technically on duty, but I trust everything's running smoothly, and it's going to be even better once Jenna gets down here for good. That'll take a minute, but I can be patient. Now that she's agreed to give us a try, there's nothing standing in the way of me getting what I want.

I offer her my hand. "Do you want to dance?"

"Do you know how?" Jenna looks ready to laugh.

"You've seen my moves and you doubt I'm a professional on the dance floor?" I pretend to be wounded. "You are a mean, evil woman."

"I've seen your *moves*," Jenna jokes, giving some pretty serious air quotes. "Those don't always translate the way you think they do."

"That's not what you said last night," I remind her, and then lead her out on the floor with the rest of my family.

"Where's Cade?" Chance yells as he swings Lily out and pulls her back in.

"No idea. He was here a little while ago." I search the crowd for my missing brother.

"I saw him duck out a little while ago with Faith," Jenna tells me right before I dip her. "Impressive," she whispers in my ear.

"With Faith? That makes no sense." I get us both upright and scan the crowd again. "Why would he be with Faith?"

Jenna's smirk is hard to miss. "For the obvious reasons." She smiles. "Never mind. Dip me again."

And I do, until we're all so tired of dancing and laughing that we have to call it a night.

"That was an epic party," Jenna mumbles into my ear as she's drifting off to sleep. "I love you, Country."

And I got the best gift of them all.

EPILOGUE

Three Years Later

Jenna

"What do you say we cancel our party and just stay in bed all day?"

I don't bother lifting my head from my pillow. "You love this party." Our annual start of summer party is all Charlie has been talking about for months.

"I do love this party, but I love this—" He slides a hand around to pull me flush against him. "More."

I wiggle my ass against him, taking advantage of being the little spoon. "If we're quick..."

"I don't want to be quick." Charlie's mouth latches onto my neck. "I want to take my time."

I groan. It's hard to resist an offer like that, especially with Charlie's hands starting to wander. "We'll have plenty of time once we get to Puerto Rico."

It'll be the second time Charlie's been to the island. The

majority of my extended family's there, and I wanted him to get a better idea of what he was getting himself into. Not just my crazy family—I wanted him to see everything, taste everything. That requires more than a long weekend. After that first trip, I realized I wanted more of that connection, and Charlie agreed. He promised we'd make it a priority, and he's followed through. His brothers have agreed to divide up the time we're away to make sure the restaurant never skips a beat, and I've got Miguel in the kitchen to keep things on track. But I know it's a big ask, so we wine and dine everyone before we leave.

"But that's nearly a day away," Charlie whispers in my ear. I can feel his erection against my ass and know I'll give in eventually. Everything for the party's ready; staying in bed a little later this morning is doable, I just need to make sure Charlie doesn't think he's getting his way too easily.

"And you think I'm going to give in?" I try to keep any teasing out of my voice, but Charlie obviously doesn't buy that. He keeps one hand on my breast, letting his fingers pluck the nipple a little, while his other hand makes the slow journey down my body. He traces the outline of my navel.

"Is there anything I could do to convince you?" They're magic words and the heat of his breath on my neck has my skin tingling.

"I have a few suggestions."

"I have the perfect plan to kick this party up to ten." Charlie gives me all his fingers in the air.

"I'm not sure this is the kind of get together that really needs to be anywhere near ten, Charlie." I try to give him a little side eye, but he doesn't seem to notice. "And things will probably get rowdy enough just by having your brothers all in the same place at the same time."

"You don't even want to hear my idea?"

"Does it involve the large sheet of plastic you've stretched out across the lawn?" I tilt my head toward the view of our front yard through the kitchen window.

"Awe, that's cheating." Charlie shakes his head. "Bet you don't know what it's for." He gives me a cocky grin.

"Other than killing the grass, you mean?" I keep arranging the cookies I've made on the platter in front of me.

"It might do a little of that," Charlie confesses. "But only if we leave it too long. I promise to roll it up as soon as we're done with it."

I want to roll my eyes, but I'm not sure if that will deter Charlie or encourage him.

"You see, we put water on it from the hose—"

"And then people slide down it? I know how it works."

Charlie looks impressed. "Then you know how fun it's going to be. I thought a city girl wouldn't know anything about a slip and slide."

"There are plenty of things you don't know about me, Charlie Allen." I lean forward and give him a smacking kiss.

"Intriguing." Charlie wraps his arms around me and pulls me close. "But have you ever used a tarp to make a swimming pool out of a truck bed?" He pulls back to get a good look at my face.

"What? Now that I know nothing about." Every day's an adventure with Charlie. "Not to rain on your parade, but do you think a baby shower is really the best place for one of those?" I gesture toward the lawn and the accident waiting to happen.

"Technically this is our celebration of summer party. We're only letting Faith and Lily use it as a baby shower because everyone's already going to be here."

"Pregnant ladies do not need to use a slip and slide."

"But think of the rest of us," Charlie argues.

"The rest of you don't need to break any arms, least of all you. Puerto Rico won't be nearly as fun with your arm in a cast."

This seems to sway Charlie a little bit, but not enough to abandon the idea entirely. "I think the kids will love it."

"There are really only two kids, Charlie. Caleb might love it, but we need to check with Mindy first. And Annie is barely two years old. There's no way Hadley and Cooper will let her slide on that thing." Although, I've been proven wrong before. I can almost imagine Cooper taking his daughter down the contraption in the yard.

"What about Cecil? He'd love it."

"Cecil is a goat. Don't you dare try to put my goat on that thing." I give him a stern face.

"You're always trying to ruin his good time."

"Cecil has plenty of fun, trust me. He's lucky Sadie and Mae have forgiven him for all the laundry he's pulled off their line." My goat is a menace on this farm. Despite being the most pampered animal around, he cannot stop himself from getting into trouble. I might love him unconditionally, but he tries the patience of the rest of the family.

Charlie's hand snakes lower, palming my ass. "When is everyone else supposed to get here?" I know exactly what that question means, even without the eyebrow waggle.

"Too soon for that, unfortunately." That doesn't keep me from kissing Charlie again, moving closer until I'm pressed up against him. "Later." It's a whispered promise and one I won't have any trouble keeping once we say goodbye to our guests tonight.

"Hey, hey, the party's here!" Cooper's voice booms through the house.

Charlie gives me one more squeeze before letting me go. "Where's my girl?"

I pretend to pout, but I know who has Charlie's heart. I've got a lock on it, sure, but his niece is a close second. Charlie takes her from his brother as soon as they come into the room, and Annie snuggles up against his chest.

"Y'all getting ready for this next group of babies? How's Charlie going to do his patented uncle hold with two?" Hadley gives him a kiss on the cheek.

I give Annie's head a stroke, letting my fingers enjoy the silkiness of her blonde curls. Charlie's the baby whisperer around here. Luckily, we live close enough to have him offering his services at a moment's notice. His commitment to being the fun uncle is easier when we're only walking distance away.

Annie reaches for me, and I take her in my arms. "Hi, pretty girl. I made some cookies special for you." She gives me one of her big smiles, showing me her newest teeth. I had never thought I'd like kids, let alone babies, but I think Charlie's got the right idea. I'm looking forward to having more kids around here, especially since I can give them back to their parents when I need a break.

The rest of the family comes through the door in a giant wave of hugging arms and chattering voices. Sadie and Mae have brought their latest round of pickles. Lily and Faith immediately open the jars for a taste test after comparing bellies. There's more love and laughter over the course of the afternoon than I probably enjoyed in an entire year in my old life. When we gather around the fire pit at the end of the day, I can't think of a more perfect way to welcome summer. Charlie's eyes meet mine over the glow of the fire, his handsome face beaming at me as he holds his sleeping niece in his lap. It's more than just this day that's perfection. And I get to do it all again next year. And the year after that.

Forever, if I'm lucky.

ACKNOWLEDGMENTS

Thank you all for reading *Make It Last*. Another Allen brother finds his happily ever after! I hope you loved reading Charlie and Jenna's story as much as I loved writing it. Those two were difficult to wrangle sometimes—characters rarely do what they're supposed to all of the time—but in the end they decided to cooperate. I always enjoy getting to go back to Mint Springs and I hope you do, too.

As always, there are some people to thank...

Thank you to my editor, Kiezha Ferrell. Despite some bumps along the way, we managed to get this book ready for publication.

Thank you to Austin Ryan for her proofreading work and for helping me to iron out the details of the epilogue when the words wouldn't come.

Thank you to Kate Farlow for another beautiful cover. The Mint Springs series looks good because of you.

And, finally, thanks to my kids. This book took some long days and y'all made sure there weren't reasons to quit. Writing is solitary work, but I get plenty of visits in my office with "helpful" advice, ridiculous memes, and terrible music. There's never a dull day around here and I wouldn't have it any other way.

ABOUT THE AUTHOR

Jessie Harper writes steamy, contemporary romance with a slightly Southern flavor. Originally from Nashville, Tennessee, she has lived all over the world—from Europe to Asia. She currently resides in Park City, Utah with her husband, three children, and more rescue animals than she ever intended. She appreciates a nice glass of whiskey, homegrown tomatoes, and well-delivered sarcasm. She hopes to never have to "bless your heart."

For updates and more visit www.jessieharper.com. Or sign up for Jessie's newsletter so you never miss a thing.

facebook.com/JessieHarperAuthor

twitter.com/jessiehromance

instagram.com/jessieharperromance

bookbub.com/authors/jessie-harper

amazon.com/Jessie-Harper/e/B089PV285Y